# BLACK DAWN

A TITAN NOVEL

CRISTIN
HARBER

ISBN-10: 1-942236-17-4
ISBN-13: 978-1-942236-17-7

www.CristinHarber.com

Cover Design and Interior format by The Killion Group
http://thekilliongroupinc.com

# DEDICATION

To my sister, mom, and dad.
That which does not kill us makes us stronger.
~Friedrich Nietzsche

# PROLOGUE

Matt Pindon threw back another shot. Only live once. Yup. That was his motto for the weekend. Hell, for his life. He and his boys were kicked back, shouting at the ladies and throwing a party for one of their buddies' farewell to bachelor-dom. It was all good.

He stood and swayed, trying to remember if he'd eaten the meal he'd ordered at the bar earlier or if somewhere in this place sat a lonely burger and fries. He faltered when leaning to look for the food, thought better of it, then slid back on his barstool. Screw food anyway. It'd just kill his buzz.

"Matt, man, you gotta make it through tonight." Parker shook his head, drinking a beer. "Enough, maybe?"

Matt slapped him on the back. Parker Black was a solid dude, one of his best buds. They had nothing in common anymore but could still sit around, share some war stories—though Parker's were often *classified*, the asshole—and drink a good drink to have a good time. It worked out.

"Enough? Nope. Matter of fact"—he ran his numb tongue over the roof of his mouth, his gauge for just how plastered he was—"I need another beer." Life was too good to him. He knew it. Owned. Played it. Another drink, another broad. It was all a game, and he lived to win. The odds were in his favor almost every time, so who was he to complain? He threw his arm up, flagging down the bartender. "Hey, another round."

Parker shook his head again as he'd done so many times before. That shit grated on Matt's nerves, but they were boys from the beginning. They came from nothing and nowhere together. Parker more than Matt, so as much as Matt needed Parker, he thought that Parker needed him too. *He* was Parker's family. And that meant Matt wouldn't tell Parker to quit the responsible guy routine.

The bartender arrived with a beer and a rag, wiping up and switching out the old for new. Matt grabbed the longneck and slugged half of it back.

"Seriously, man, you doing okay?" Parker asked.

"Always." No way would Matt 'fess that he'd been fired—again—from another security job. If he didn't watch his ass, he'd be slinging a Taser at the mall to catch shoplifters. Then again, if his fuckin' douchebag bosses ever opened their damn eyes and saw that he had other shit going on, they might not make the mistake of firing him.

"Right." Parker chuckled as though he didn't believe him. "I'm out. Got a work thing I have to hit up sometime tonight."

"See ya." They bumped fists, and his buddy walked away.

That was Parker. Always working. The guy could've done half the crazy shit Matt had in high school, but he'd worked on breaking the mold for geeky nerd guys by clocking gym time. Then he could've done the real world alongside Matt, but nope, Parker chose a paid ride to a fancy college. And shit, now the dude was at a bachelor party and dipping out of a bar to *work*. What the hell?

Matt didn't get it. Didn't want to get it. What he wanted was a motherfuckin' blow job from a pretty girl, to do another shot with his boys—where were they anyway?—then he wanted to pass out in his hotel room.

"Hey, is anyone sitting here?"

Matt shifted on his barstool and saw gorgeous. She was the kind of cool that rocked his world. Beautiful with a style that screamed sexy and confident, and *that* kind of scream he wanted in his bed tonight. Blond hair that was a shade darker than platinum and blue eyes that shone so light and bright in a bar of fussed-up, boozed-up women. This woman was out of his league, and that kind of challenge was a rarity. *Hell, challenge accepted.*

"Seat just freed up." He could throw down a line. Could try for something she hadn't heard before, but she was the best of what New York City had to offer. Maybe she was a model. An actress? "How's the night treating you?"

She smiled, took the seat, and paid no attention to him. Still, he didn't feel a hard-to-get vibe. Nor did he get the too-good-for-you attitude. He got… nothing. She was just there, waiting to order a drink. How about that?

"I'm Matt."

She tilted her head, letting strands of hair sweep over pale skin. "Lexi."

"Here by yourself?"

"Nope. A work thing. A contest, I guess. I won. Yay me. So I'm here to celebrate." She signaled the bartender then looked back over. "Hundreds of people are in town for my… work thing, so if you're some creepy serial killer dude, look elsewhere. People would notice me missing."

He laughed. "Let me celebrate with you."

Her lips quirked at the corners. "Think you've celebrated enough already."

"Nah, bachelor party. Night's still young. It's my job to get hammered."

"And end up by yourself? Where are your buddies?"

"Honey, I couldn't care less where they were, sitting next to the likes of you."

She smiled primly and shut him down with a bat of her eyes. That was the problem. Couldn't throw lines at a girl with class.

He laughed, drew back. "Too cheesy. I get it. You're not that kind of girl, even if every man in this bar is praying that you are."

Lexi pivoted on her barstool. "And what kind of girl is that?"

He worked his jaw back and forth, knowing he was too damn buzzed to keep her attention if he didn't nail whatever was about to slip from his mouth. "A woman like you walks into a bar, and this man—hell, any man—prays for a look. Maybe a kiss. He wants a green light to get your number as much as he wants to take you to his room. There's a whole lot going on in a lot of men's heads right now, seeing as you appear to be a free agent walking into a bar that's sausage city in the middle of NYC."

She looked over his shoulder, her eyes drifting across the

room. “Doubt that.”

“You aren’t even playing coy with me, are you?” He stole a glance over her curves. “That’s about one in a million.”

“I’ll make it easy for you, Matt.”

He leaned in. “You remembered my name.”

A gentle laugh fell from her lips. “I remember a lot.”

“Make it easy for me, peaches.”

She made a face. “Don’t expect a kiss. No crazy hotel room romp just because I sat next to you. I didn’t ride here—”

“You took the train from where?” Because he would offer to take her back. Damn.

A less-than-sweet smile curved her dangerously deceptive lips. “More like a Gixxer.”

“Like a GSX-R?”

Her eyebrows lifted. “Know something else that goes by Gixxer?”

That leather-clad, smoky-eyed beauty with all that power between her legs… “Fair warning, peaches. I might’ve just fallen in love.”

She laughed, downplaying what might have been the sexiest thing he could imagine. “I didn’t head three hours north to give my number to some man I’ll never see again—”

“I drove three hours. It’s meant to be.”

She gave him another disinterested smile. “I’m not trying to be rude—”

He blinked. “Where do you live?”

“Not here.”

“But *where*, peaches?”

“That’s not a cute name for me, thanks.”

“God, you seem like a sweet one.”

She tossed her head back and laughed. “Does that crap ever actually work?”

“You tell me.”

“You’re persistent,” she lobbed back.

“I’m who you were supposed to meet tonight. Trust me.”

Now it was her turn to blink slowly. “Maybe.”

The bartender finally showed up. “Need something?”

She stole her eyes away from Matt and ordered a beer.

A beer. *Longneck, domestic. In the bottle.* were her exact

words. The motorcycle-riding princess was his wet dream incarnate. He'd joked about it before, but after her drink order, he was, without a doubt, in love. Or at least staking claim. Everything about her stole his heart. Or made him want to get her out the door, away from every other asshole there, and see what she would do next. This was the type of woman he'd never let go.

The bartender arrived with her beer. "Starting a tab?"

She shook her head. "No, just this one."

"You and me, peaches." Matt bounced his almost-empty beer bottle between his hands. "We're going to start over."

She shifted those baby-blue eyes up. "Didn't realize we'd started anything to begin with."

"Let me take you out to dinner. In DC. Where we both live."

"I live in DC?"

"Three hours away."

She assessed him. "I could've come from any direction."

"Fate wouldn't let you sit next to me if we weren't supposed to meet."

She studied him then sipped her beer. "Another line, Matt."

He laughed. "Give me an answer, Lexi."

"No, but I appreciate the invitation."

He clutched a hand to his chest. "Oh, woman. You just killed me. Give me one reason to say no."

"I don't have to."

"But you want to."

She turned on her stool. "I don't trust you. I don't trust a single guy in this room."

"Not even a little?" Everything about her made her more interesting. "Fine, fuck it. New approach."

"Are you going to narrate every way you ask me out?" She laughed.

"Here's the deal to prove my point. Give me your number. I'll stop hitting on you and go find my buddies. We'll do our thing, you head off to do yours. And within the week, I'll give you a call. Dinner. In DC. Deal?"

She didn't say yes.

He leaned closer. "If you don't give me an answer on the date, I'm going to make a play to get you in bed right this damn second. You'll love it. So win-win either way for you."

"You're kind of an ass."

A guy tapped her shoulder.

*What the motherfuck?* A territorial growl began in Matt's chest.

The guy who could've been the poster boy for Geeks Without a Chance stepped closer. "Excuse me, are you—"

"No," she answered before the guy finished the question.

"Back away, dick." Matt threw a protective arm around her.

The shoulder-tapper backed up, tucking his tail like the little nerd boy he was. "Shit, man. Easy."

Matt stared down the skinny little fucker. Scrawny. Brainy. Straight out of a computer lab somewhere. And dude thought he could interrupt Matt? In what world did that guy stand a chance? Shit.

His eyes shot to her. "Thought I recognized her—"

Matt's gaze narrowed. "You didn't."

Computer boy backed away. A few seconds ticked by, then she peered up at Matt. Clearly she was unnerved, and for every line he'd thrown at her, it turned out all he had to do was act as if he were her man already. Easy enough.

"Thanks," she said, wary of the world.

He raised an eyebrow. "Sure you're not some famous model?"

At the joke, she relaxed, and he leaned into her. "Not even close."

Though she could be by the looks of her. "So my offer…"

"Your offer." She glanced at his arm possessively around her and almost looked relieved to have someone caring for her in a bar full of nameless faces.

"Yes or no, Lexi?"

"Yes."

He leaned forward, brushed the hair back from her ear, and whispered, "Three hundred miles to meet a girl from my backyard. I'll take it."

She scrawled her number on a napkin. "I have to go deal with work stuff. But it was nice to meet you."

As she left, he pocketed the cocktail napkin with her digits and finished his beer. Alright. Nicely done. But that didn't take care of him for the rest of the night. He turned toward the crowd and went in search of someone who'd be interested in him right now.

# CHAPTER ONE

*Two years later...*

Bass thumped hard. The lights were low and dark with flashes of red. The warehouse vibe was chill, and the party raged. Lexi Dare was in her element, with her people, and no one was the wiser that it was, yet again, a party celebrating her. SilverChaos. Whenever there was a big corporate hacker challenge during the day, one of the top dogs in the cyber world threw a rager that night.

Tonight was all her doing, though few knew who she was. Anonymity was comfortable. It had been her one constant over the years, even if some hackers had tried to connect her name and handle. To most, she was just a regular party girl who worked the underground scene. Friendly enough, she vibed out with the crowd and knew with photographic precision ninety-nine percent of the room's occupants, even if they didn't know her. They were a tight-knit community that functioned fine without real names, hidden in their cloaks of anonymity. Only a couple nosey ones made her nervous. She'd been in the mix since she wandered in so many years ago as an abandoned teenage prodigy with no one but a foster sister and a notebook full of code that no one but her understood. Until she'd met these people.

They made her feel accepted, as if she had a shot at what having a family would feel like. At those parties, she felt as though she were returning home for a reunion. Really, that just showed how little about family she knew and how much of it she craved.

Now she was back to where she'd started years ago: lonely and abandoned. These events were the only social activity she had anymore, the only ones that let her feel normal, and she clung to them, hoping to retain some of herself even as she knew that with every day in the real world, the real her faded.

Her leather pants and smoky eyes? She'd hide them when she went back home. Either her foster sister would keep her clothes or Lexi would stash them deep in the closet where Matt would never find them. It was just too… hard to find the right balance between living the expected, suburban, almost-a-housewife life and being the real her.

"Blondie!"

She turned toward the voice she'd heard before. It was the second time that night he'd made an approach. He was a nice-looking Asian guy who went by Phiber, and he wasn't half bad at corporate hacks. What he'd put forth during today's corporate-sponsored competition was solid. But his wardrobe, what looked like dozens of layered shades of black, did him no favors, and his ego was the size of Silicon Valley. He *really* thought himself the excellent hack.

"Blondie's not my name."

His head jutted awkwardly with each bump of bass. "Drink?"

"No, I'm good."

She was one of the few women there that night, or in general. It wasn't lost on her that she was attractive. Men did double takes when she rode up on the back of her sporty racing bike or when she pulled off her helmet and her fuck-yeah braids were tousled. She didn't mean to look like that—it was just how she could breathe. According to her fiancé, it was also how she attracted attention, which was why he had a problem with everything these days.

How she dressed.

When she worked.

Her bike was too dangerous.

Her makeup was too loud.

Even now, Lexi ground her molars together, briefly weighing the idea of being without Matt—which meant without anyone who called her family—against the idea of being alone in this filled world of loners.

Things weren't great at home. Matt pushed the line from being a jerk to just being an asshole. But loyalty was important. Trust was too. Family forgave—that was what he reminded her of constantly. Family filled that void she'd always had. Matt was her family. *Right?*

She pushed out a breath, not wanting to deal with reality. Matt thought she had a security clearance, that she worked a freelance techy "geek" job—God forbid the guy rub two brain cells together—and she had to travel to clients. It was one of the few things he let her do without him anymore, but that was primarily because they needed the steady income from her work.

She'd lied to him from the get-go about exactly what she did to earn a living. Maybe that made her a bad person. Maybe she'd known without realizing it that she was headed down a road that looked perfect but was rocky and dangerous. When he'd dangled a permanent, protective connection in front of her, she jumped at it. Too hard.

Well, this *was* her work, and the deep, dark hacker underground wasn't a security-clearance type of job. Without even asking, she knew there was no way Matt would allow her in this world. *Her* world. Where she was literally the best of the best.

But seriously, when did she have to ask to have a job? To do what she'd done for years? Simple answer—the second he'd slipped a rock on her ring finger.

Phiber tried again with his dance moves and a smile that highlighted a scar above his lip. "If not a drink, then just want to party?"

She held up her left hand and wiggled her fingers to highlight the engagement ring. "Thanks, but I'm good, Phiber."

The guy smiled, probably because she knew his handle. "Tonight's really a rager."

Apparently her subtle "no thanks" hadn't indicated that she wasn't in the mood for conversation. Though truth was, she could use a chat. Not that she was lonely. She had friends. Maybe. Just online now, it seemed. She was falling further away from the girls she'd once been close to. All except for her foster sister, but even Meredith hadn't seen Lexi in weeks.

"Yeah." She bit her lip and nodded at Phiber instead of focusing on her troubles. "It's crazy tonight."

"You hear SilverChaos did all this?" Phiber slugged back his drink. "Mad props to that guy."

She stepped back. "Yeah."

"Think he's here?" He laughed. "Could be me. Could be you."

"Except you're Phiber."

He shrugged. "But who are you?"

She needed an exit *now*. There was no way the guy would pin the elite handle on her, but why risk it? She clapped her hand on his back, patting him like a dude. "See ya, buddy."

Lexi tugged on her leather string bracelet, fidgeting, and moved away. She felt Phiber's eyes still on her, and even though he couldn't know she was Silver, she had the heebie-jeebies. She melted through the crowd, chatting with others who didn't creep her out. One weird guy wouldn't ruin her fun as she hid from home, avoiding her jerk of a fiancé. Though he was so much more than that lately. Her fingers brushed her tender eye.

*Stop thinking about him.* Shaking her head clear, she tried to focus on the music, dancing to the beat from the sidelines of the makeshift floor, but her heart wasn't in it. Why did she lie to herself? It wasn't Matt's attitude anymore, nor was his drinking just a random occurrence since losing *another* job. Matt had crossed the line. More than once. A push. A slap. All came with an apology and excuse. He shouldn't have been drinking. He'd never do it again. She *made* it happen, and God, she knew better.

But it happened more and more often. Not every day. Not even every week. That would be, like, *abuse*. This was more like… abuse. Shit. She couldn't even admit it out loud, couldn't even tell Meredith. Nope, like a little wimp—like nothing who she was—Lexi could only hmm and hum when anyone asked questions. All she did was bury her face in her computer. Well, that wasn't entirely true—she'd also rescued Bacon Byte, her cute, slightly morbidly obese pug. But even

Bacon's sweet sneezes and snores didn't turn Matt into a civilized human being.

Who threatened to hurt a dog? Whether it was off-handed jokes about letting the poor thing gorge herself or jumping at Bacon to scare her, Matt made Lexi's heart race. Awful people were mean to puppies. Now when she went out of town for her "web security" meetings, she asked Meredith to puppy-sit. So much for Operation Melt-Matt's-Blackened-Heart.

How did she have a man's ring on her finger when she didn't trust him alone with her dog?

"Easy," she murmured to herself.

She was the queen of abandonment issues. Bouncing from one foster home to the next had really done her in, which was why she showed up to these absurd competitions and kept next to no winnings, donating as much as she could afford. If she could make one little girl's world happy with stupid money, then yeah, she didn't need to bring home major dough. But all of that charity still didn't make her comfortable with the idea of walking away from the only man who claimed he'd never leave her or let her go. *Ever.*

Lexi wandered through the crowd. A few high fives and a couple hellos later, she was posted in another corner, eyes peeled for Shadow. Her broker dealt with the upper echelon of the hacker world. As a rogue independent contractor, he knew every important corporation and government contact interested in buying her high-tech projects: patches, programs, codes, and exploits. Over the years, he'd made himself her father figure as well as her business adviser.

*Lose the douche.* Those were Shadow's only words of wisdom when she mentioned the engagement.

As if it were that simple. Shadow had been by her side since she was seventeen. Last year, for their ten-year working relationship anniversary, he took her to Paris, where they disabled the security and paid off the guards for a private tour of the Louvre. Shadow had a lot of friends in dark places.

"Silver." His familiar voice caught her from behind.

"Hey." She smiled then watched him nod hello as he handed her a fresh drink, switching out the one in her hand. "Good times, right?"

"Not bad. How's life?" He always asked the same question, recently with undertones about concern over the wedding she hadn't started to plan yet.

For how close she was to Shadow, it was peculiar that he hadn't met Matt—that she knew about. Actually, now that she thought about it, given how confident his dislike of her fiancé was, Lexi was sure that Shadow had met Matt.

"Same as it always is." She stared at her new cup.

Carefully, he touched her chin, turning her face, and pushed away one messy curtain of platinum hair. There was a fading bruise on her eye that she'd caked makeup over. In the dark strobe lights, it'd be hard to see, especially given the smoky smudges of black and gray she'd painted over it, but nothing ever got past Shadow. He prided himself on it. Steal from him, he'd steal back. Lie to him, he'd force the words back in your mouth. Ignore the truth—even if it was a black eye that was impossible to avoid—he'd make sure that it was most certainly not ignored.

"Care to explain?" he asked simply.

"No." She toyed with the leather strings on her wrist.

Shadow would read into that and would be right. Nothing had changed, at least not for the better.

The lines around his eyes tightened. "You ready for Monarch?"

"Absolutely." The website hack that exploited the social media site was her best work to date. Flawless maybe, definitely untraceable. Program had been absurdly complicated to put together, but it was a beautiful work of code.

Monarch's social media site had a security hole. Lexi had mapped out and rewritten the code to access and/or fix that hole. It would go to auction if the company didn't want to purchase the program. Shadow had made the offer privately, but they'd declined, as expected.

That was how those things worked. When Shadow put the code—which she generally just referred to by the site's name, Monarch—on the auction block, it would likely sell in a hotly bid contest. Her cyber creation would give its new owner access to all of the data the social media site housed: names, ages, credit cards, family, locations, and more.

Everywhere she went, Lexi wondered how many people around her plugged their information in Monarch. It was just as popular as Facebook, Twitter, and Instagram, but offered a slightly more niche focus for military families. Every time she caught a glance of someone in the real world using Monarch, she wanted to tell them not to post that picture, not to notify the world of where their significant others were stationed, details on their kids, or when they left on vacations. Just stop with the oversharing.

She almost wished Monarch bought the program just to be safe. But even had she given it to them, they might not have touched it. So typical of a mega-corporation. Most of those companies didn't buy the fixes to their website problem on the *zero day* market. It was cheaper to let a malicious, black-hat hacker steal consumer data than it was to fix mistakes. A public apology and a year's worth of credit monitoring, and they were out of trouble in the public eye.

Lexi wasn't malicious, but she did earn a living in that shadowy area between right and wrong. Exploit sales were huge business. Governments bought various hacker programs like they were equipping an army—because they were. She was a manufacturer of cyber bullets. Every country with an intelligence agency bought them to spy on *everyone*. Their own people. Foreigners. Governments. Allies. Enemies. Whoever.

The auctions were as legal as buying a can of mace, and Lexi happened to be *really* good at creating products for Shadow to sell.

He bent to her ear to fight off the loud music. "I put out some whispers. Everyone's curious. Uncle Sam is salivating. They want Monarch in a bad way."

No surprise. That was almost the clichéd response. Even though she'd known it was a good patch, hearing potential bidders respond was a boost to her confidence. And here Matt thought she played on her computer for shits and giggles. Nope. She was aiding in cyber spy craft. Too bad sometimes she wasn't strong enough to protect herself.

She sighed, fidgeting with the long, skinny, metal-and-leather necklaces draped over her chest. "I have a couple more weeks of work. But yeah, let's start looking at the calendar for

Monarch's auction." She released the jewelry and took a sip of her drink, noting that Shadow had had the bartender go heavy on the ginger ale in her bourbon soda mix.

"I'll want you there in person, Silver."

She nodded. She loved any excuse to get out of the house, but he would expect her to sit on a hard chair all day, bored, just in case there were questions. "Sure."

"Sure? How about a hell yeah. A sale this big? It'll move fast, lots of intel flying. It'll be exciting."

Placating him, she nodded. "I love in-person, but I love even more that *you* love handling the business side."

Shadow stepped even closer and dropped his chin to give her a fatherly stare. "I'm telling you, this one will be off the charts."

"Off the chart. Got it." She nodded, giving his stare right back. "I said I'd be there."

"But you're not appreciating it, Silver. Fast and furious. Split-second decisions, immediate approval and counters. Exciting stuff."

Lexi groaned. "Got it. Super exciting. Where are you thinking?"

"Probably DC this time."

"So close to home." She chewed the inside of her mouth, wishing she had another excuse to get away. "Couldn't we do Maui? I heard there are tons of tourists to steal cell signals from."

He smirked. "Looking for a reason to get out of the house?"

Her stomach jumped as he called her out. "No."

"You and Bacon could always come stay with me for a while."

"Where's home these days? Canada?" She and Bacon Byte didn't handle the cold well in Virginia, even with all of Bacon's padding. "Think we'll pass."

"That little roll of pudge would keep you warm. I'll throw in a couple T-bones, and the pooch would be sitting pretty."

She tried to hide her grin in her drink. "Aw, leave Bacon alone."

"Alright." His face sobered. "If you want to talk…." He shook his head as though he couldn't believe this conversation was still required. "I get where your head is."

The base dropped on a new beat, and Lexi embraced the living, breathing energy that pulsed around her. "Ha. You have no idea where my head is, Shadow."

"I know where you're from. I know *you*. But—"

"Enough." The strobe spun, and she tried to let a streaming jet of red lights blind her. A headache from that would be preferable to making eye contact with Shadow. "Please don't give me the I'm-worried-about-you conversation."

"I am." His voice rose over the beat then dropped along with the bass. "And I'm also worried about this sale."

"Why?"

"It's going to be epic. Third-world dictators and freakin' who knows who else will want it. It's getting a lot of attention."

"They always do."

He sipped his drink slowly and sighed. "Not like Monarch."

"So… what do we do differently?" Shadow was at her level: elite. There were very few salesmen out there like him, so she trusted his suggestions.

"I might see if we can get eyes and ears on the deal, just as an added layer of security. Someone to watch all the modes of communication for anything sketch."

"Have anyone in mind?" she asked. She could think of a few contacts he'd use. A couple of them were in the room, and she'd heard one of them once claim SilverChaos's accomplishments. So not out of ego but more annoyance, she wanted to be part of the decision-making process.

Shadow tilted his head. "Maybe your partner-in-crime?"

Wait… no. Shadow couldn't mean…? "I don't know if we're thinking about the same guy."

BlackDawn wasn't even on her short list, though he was actually more talented than anyone she had initially thought about. *Combined.* The request seemed a little novice to ask of him, but who else would be considered her partner-in-crime?

She'd never met him in person but chatted with him almost every week. Years ago, they'd formed an alliance because sometimes hacks needed more than one set of hands. Sometimes code needed another mind mulling it over.

BlackDawn was one of the very few hackers who could hold their own at the highest echelons. But she and he were also slightly competitive.

He wasn't one for these parties, never came to the hacker events—not that people knew who she was when she showed. So maybe he was in the room. Her eyes skimmed the crowd.

"Silver?" Shadow asked. "Scowling at a party?"

"Just thinking…"

His eyes narrowed. "About?"

"No. Not him."

"Have a reason?" he asked, leaning in for whatever she would divulge.

Which wouldn't be much. Black was a talented hacker somewhere in the world—US-based, she presumed, because they'd worked on what she could only assume were American military cyber offenses. That was his specialty. But still, he was her competition, and while they might play allies in the field—occasionally butting heads in heated discussions over who was right and wrong on things that had no right and wrong—business was a whole other world. She didn't want him helping when it came to securing her sales.

Lexi shook her head, wrapping the long string of necklaces around her fingers again. "Not particularly."

Shadow chuckled as if he could read her mind. "Alright, Silver, get out there and enjoy your party."

With a nod, he melted into the night, leaving her to survey the scene. The place rocked out—lights bouncing, bass dropping, and bodies dancing and drinking. Phreaks, gamers, hackers, and groupies. Matt would hate it. The people—the geeks, the nerds—he'd blame for ruining his night out. Didn't he see she was one of them? Didn't he see *anything* about her? She looked at her engagement ring. It wasn't even a style that she ever would have chosen. But she wasn't the girl who pined over the perfect ring or the perfect dress. She wanted a perfect *love* who held her tight, promised security, cherished her, appreciated who she wanted to be more than who he could put on display.

Shifting her gaze from the ring to her drink, she wondered if maybe there was more alcohol in that glass than she realized.

Growing up the way she had, she knew just how lucky she was to have a man who'd promised to never ever leave… right?

Still, surrounded by hundreds of people who didn't know her given name, she was more comfortable there than at home. They accepted her. Respected what she did. *They didn't hurt her.*

Not that most times she'd even admit that to herself.

Phiber kept his eyes on the waif of a woman. She was blond, confident, and watched the crowd of dancing bodies under the makeshift strobe lights as if they were her people. His gut said they were—she was in the know, dropping his handle and chatting with the likes of Shadow, who was almost infamous for the amount of deals he'd brokered and connections he had.

After weeks of crawling into every dark corner, trying to pin down SilverChaos through all of the hacks attributed to that handle, Phiber had wormed his way into enough intel that said the woman who'd declined his drink offer was Silver. How about that? Silver was a woman. Not that he was sexist. He didn't care who Silver actually was as long as the bank transfers from his mysterious Taskmaster continued to arrive, along with the codex message for his new tasks.

Each request from the unknown sender had grown in difficulty, almost as though the first ones were tests. As he completed each challenge, Phiber became more interested in what the end goal was. Though by now, he had a guess. Whoever had contracted him wanted the Monarch exploit. They wanted to worm into Monarch's website and siphon data about its users. Their intent had malicious undertones, and their means were obviously sketchy. No way was his employer legit—otherwise they would just bid in the upcoming auction. SilverChaos was one of those hack snobs who cared who bought their—*her*—product. She wanted good people, which wasn't Phiber or Taskmaster.

At this point, he guessed Taskmaster was positioning him to steal Monarch's zero day patch, either online or in person. Lifting a laptop or hacking her system? Both would be simple. He was elite enough, even if his peers hadn't yet given his handle that designation. The most concerning thing would be if she kept her creation in pieces until the auction was complete.

He watched Silver continue her conversation with Shadow. That guy had some secrets and a vat of industry knowledge.

Rubbing his hands together, Phiber itched for the opportunity to find all the parts of Silver's program, in both hard copy and hidden in the crevices of the cyber world. A physical file extraction wouldn't be problem; breaking and entering was almost a hobby for him, as his rap sheet showed.

He pulled out his phone and tapped out a quick message. *Silver identified. Send bank transfer and next job.*

# CHAPTER TWO

The unmanned aerial vehicle—the UAV—bore down on the blip on the screen, chasing what Parker knew was the team he worked with, and he couldn't disarm the damn thing. He couldn't hack it, couldn't do shit with it, and if he didn't crash it in the next five minutes, three of his favorite people would be smears on a mountainside.

"Parker, what the fuck." Jared Westin slapped the wall of the shit-motel room they'd bunkered down in.

They were working off a crappy signal in eastern Europe with a few laptops networked together. Not his normal equipment and *not* what he needed to keep the boys alive. They'd lost all their hardware in an explosion, and this relatively simple job would have been so much easier had he been in Titan's nerve center. Hell, even in a satellite office. But there'd been no time for that.

"Parker," Boss Man snapped again.

"Give me a second. Fuck." Sweat beaded on the back of his neck while his hands flew on the keyboard. Every screen, every angle he tried, and nothing. He couldn't hack the operating system, and his boys were about to die. "Damn it."

Jared paced the room. The tension was enough to kill them both. Had Parker known this was what the guys were walking into, he'd have been prepared. But no. They'd gone rogue, adding on to the mission objective on their way back to their rendezvous point. Now Parker was trying to keep them alive with no resources on an operation that should have been fast, furious, and simple. Fuck.

"Swear to Christ…" Jared cracked one knuckle at the time.

"Give me a minute."

They didn't have that. The monitors showed that they were clearly being outplayed by someone and needed another set of hands and better technology—exactly. More computing power and another set of hands.

He switched laptops, dialing into a network, and sent out an SOS to one of a very few elite hacks that he'd worked with on the regular. Crucial seconds ticked by, then Silver lit up the screen. Parker's breathing calmed because now he could get back to work. A few keystrokes later, providing Silver all the info needed, Parker switched back to the other laptop. They had worked enough jobs that they knew how to play off one another. Code raced across the screen. His fingers banged the keyboard as he glanced at what Silver was throwing up too. All good stuff. This could be enough to save the guys.

"Damn it, Parker," Jared growled, staring at the screen with the footage of the team failing to outmaneuver the UAV that Parker had only managed to slow down. "What's the problem?"

The guys had next to no cover, and even though their vehicle was armored, they couldn't withstand a direct hit from above. Jared cursed from across the room. Time was slipping away, along with the possibility of success.

A new code sequence ran across his screen. He read it, fed off it, and manipulated the lines to further attack their enemy. His fingers flew on the keyboard, their coding seamlessly integrated on an offensive attack. Screen after screen showed that partnering with Silver had given him the needed speed and data. The anticipation of their impending accomplishment gave him a burst of energy, like Red Bull for the soul. There was no doubt they'd found the right sequence.

"There! That'll do it." Parker froze over the keyboard, and his head lifted to watch the screen. The live feed showed their men as hunted prey. Nothing changed. "Dive, fucker, dive."

He glared at the UAV. His eyes dropped to the screen, confirming that they had done what was needed to take out the drone. The pressure in the room intensified. Whoever was on the other side of the remote's navigation system was top-notch, but he was better—partnered with Silver, he couldn't be stopped. So what was the problem? It should be game over.

*Come... the fuck... on...*

"Gimme an update." Jared paced.

"Wait a second." Because Parker couldn't doubt what was on screen. Black and white intel. Straight fact. They'd disarmed and disorganized the drone. Time would send it to its death.

"Parker..." Boss Man crossed his arms as though he needed to restrain himself. If the guy could rip the drone out of the sky and crush it in his fist, he would. "End this. Now."

Parker knew that, but he didn't have time to tell Jared all the hows and whys it would work, because then he'd also have to go into the reasons it might not, and no one wanted a risk analysis of the team's survival likelihood. His chest cranked tight. If the men in that vehicle—Winters, Roman, and Cash—died, Parker might as well join them. Titan for life. He gnawed his bottom lip, holding an uncertain breath.

Another second clocked by.

The UAV suddenly nosedived, exploding behind their vehicle. Jared punched his arms into the air. Parker's head dropped down, and he let out a ragged gasp. Even if he'd known it would happen, waiting was still the worst.

Pacing again, Jared looked on the upswing of that adrenaline rush as he dialed the satellite phone. "You fuckers stay on course next time." Then he threw it onto the motel room bed. "Too fuckin' close."

"Agreed," Parker mumbled, aware that his nervous system was coming down from his own adrenaline high. He loved the rush. Every time. Whoever said computer shit was boring certainly hadn't seen what Titan could do with a few laptops and a piss-poor foreign internet connection in some pay-by-the-hour motel room.

Boss Man rubbed the back of his neck. "If I smoked, I'd fucking need a light. Shit."

Parker leaned back in the chair, wanting to shut down the operation, inventory their loss from the explosion earlier, and get back to the States. A flash on one screen caught his attention, and he swiveled his head.

Silver: *Almost got your ass burned on that one, buddy.*

No kidding, asshole. He smiled, but before he could agree, another message popped up.

Silver: *But I needed the distraction. Shitty day.*
Black: *Almost just had one of those.*

Shitty was relative. Laying buddies in the ground, almost losing a team to a rogue UAV, that was what defined a shitty day. Either way, he now owed SilverChaos in their ongoing back and forth.

Parker wondered if Silver knew his broker, Shadow, had asked Parker to scout and check out all of the interested buyers for the guy's Monarch deal. This was business, and not their norm. If he and Silver kept track of who'd helped out who more over the years, whose favor would it come out on top for? Probably a draw. Either way, Silver was as good as Parker was, and today, he'd been a great resource to have. Ooh rah to that.

# CHAPTER THREE

God, that was such a rush. Chills still skated up and down her spine. Lexi never asked questions when she worked with BlackDawn. The objectives always blew her mind, as if they were playing high-stakes games that were real life. But, damn, tonight had made her feel alive, as though she wasn't hiding in her own home.

Forget the fact that she was sure they'd just saved the occupants of that vehicle. Given the coordinates of that UAV, she'd helped with something bigger, something patriotic. Protecting soldiers overseas? Maybe so. Hacks like that one gave her purpose, unlike developing things like Monarch. That just earned her money, even if she donated a solid portion.

Lexi shifted in the chair in the corner of her bedroom. She was ducked under a blanket with her screen's brightness turned down to two percent so as not to disturb Matt. Bacon was curled up and snoring on her feet. She thought about staying put—maybe she and her pup could go to sleep right there on the floor. Hopefully Matt was still asleep—or passed out. He'd barely mumbled when her cell phone chirped that BlackDawn was looking for her.

She wondered if Black was already scouting her auction buyers. Over the years, he'd impressed her so much that she'd even thought about breaking hacker protocol and digging into who he really was. Her fingers twitched over the keyboard. It would be so easy to dig and find out more about him—well, maybe not, since he was so much like her. It'd be almost impossible to learn details that she didn't want shared. But it'd be fun to try—

"Would you get your stupid ass off the computer already?" Matt's drunken, sleep-scored voice broke her thoughts.

Her blanket-covered head dropped, her curious smile washing away. Still, she didn't pull the blanket off. She set her laptop to the side and scooped Bacon's deadweight up to her chest. "I thought you were asleep. Sorry."

Her fiancé grumbled, thrashing the pillows and sheets noisily. "How am I supposed to sleep when you're over there clacking on that damn thing? Shit."

Slowly, she peeled the blanket from her head and squeezed Bacon, who licked her neck. "It was important."

"Stupid computer games in the middle of the night are not important."

"It wasn't a game. It was work."

Matt rolled over in bed and propped himself up. "Baby, no one's working you tonight. I'm the only one who gets that privilege, so unless you want to *work* right now, turn the computer off so I can either get some sleep or a blow job. Your choice."

*Asshole.* How in the world was this where she was in life? "Don't talk to me like that. You're drunk."

"You blowing me or what?"

Tears pricked her eyes, and even though her sight had adjusted to the dark room, everything went blurry. But she wouldn't let him see that. "You're being a dick."

"Peaches, dick's the name of the game. If you keep running your mouth, dick's what you're about to choke on."

"You're disgusting when you're like this. I'll sleep on the couch."

"Oh, come on, Lex. I'm playing."

She shook her head. "I'm going to go watch TV."

"I wish you wouldn't make me so mad. Why do you do that to me?" he grumbled. "Why do you push me? It's like you want to be all alone in the world with no one to love you like I do."

Those words… always her fault. She didn't believe it. But she couldn't help her lonely reaction. "Matt, stop."

"How's a pretty little nerd girl like you going to find—"

"Stop." She dropped her head to Bacon's and wished she

could walk away. She could. She would. It would happen. Soon. She just needed to… not be scared.

"Come on, peaches. You know I'm just playing. Get in bed."

Against her better judgment, she moved to the far corner of the bed, put Bacon at the foot of the bed, then perched on the edge before finally lying down.

His grabby hands ran over her back, pulling at her hips. "Come here."

"No."

"Baby, you know I just say those things to make you pay attention to what you want."

What a high opinion he had of himself. *She wanted him? She needed him?* But hell, she hadn't left him, so who was she to call him wrong? She squeezed her eyes shut as she lay straight as a stick on the edge of the bed. "I'm sleepy. Tomorrow. I promise."

Matt leaned over and cackled in her ear. "Stupid computer cunt. If you didn't have me, you'd be all alone. No one to love my girl. Just remember that. You belong to me, peaches. We're meant to be together."

His slurred speech apparently over, he turned over and plopped against his pillow with a drunken snore. She listened for his breathing to signify that he had passed back out. Finally he did, and she stared at the black ceiling. How did she live these two lives? How was she so confident and successful in one arena, but when it came to real life, she became weaker?

If she could get him to stop drinking, everything would be normal again. She could do that. Then she'd have the security that she craved, and he'd stop with his tirades, punches, and pushes. Just sober him up. Or she could leave…

In the middle of the night, it all felt hopeless. Instead of replaying the constant battle of leave-versus-one-day-it-will-be-better, Lexi focused on their weekend plans. They were meeting up with a few of his friends, so even if he did drink, he wouldn't be a complete jerk to her. At least while they were in public. Plus there was a good chance that Parker Black, the crush that she'd never admit to, would be there too.

Her heart picked up its pace. She was excited to get out, but really, she was ecstatic to see him. She quickly turned her head to see if Matt would somehow react to her thoughts.

No. Nothing but a drunken snore.

Lexi pinched her eyes closed in the dark, trying to ignore her thoughts of Parker, and focused on the weekend. Matt had plans to go to the range with the same group of guys, who he behaved in a semi-decent manner around. Those guys weren't impressed with day drinking. They didn't laugh and joke about dickhead bosses when Matt lost yet another job.

Maybe this weekend could be the start of turning everything around with Matt. Except she wasn't in love with him. There had been too much damage done. Her insides were broken, and she felt no happiness for him when she smiled. Each night she prayed that morning would come, that dawn would break and a fresh day would show a different life.

Her fingers twirled the engagement ring in the dark. Matt wouldn't allow her to just walk away. Their lives were so entwined that she didn't see how it was possible to extract herself. Her GSX-R was at Meredith's after he had banished it from their home, and Matt never let go of his truck keys. Her friends avoided their place due to Matt's snide remarks and comments. Not even Meredith came over. Whenever Lexi wanted to go out, he always had a reason why she shouldn't. Couple that with working from home, and Lexi was alone in a way she couldn't escape.

But the weekend was coming fast, and soon she'd be face to face with Parker, who never said a misspoken word but somehow always looked as though he believed she could do anything. Like she could walk away from Matt. Her stomach soared again, and she wasn't sure if it was because of Parker or the idea of leaving. Maybe both.

God. Her reaction to Parker was dangerous. She turned quickly, burying her head in her pillow. Parker wasn't always around. He often traveled for work. Matt and Parker had grown up together, and that was the only thing she saw as tying the two men together. Except maybe their jobs and military-camaraderie stuff. Parker did something similar to Matt—well, when Matt could keep a job. Which wasn't often anymore. Parker worked in security, maybe? He never talked about it, but wow, he was built for it.

Shit.

She cringed harder into her pillow and tried in vain to ignore the pop of excitement she felt about Parker being there. First, because that'd be horrible for her to think. She was engaged. To an asshole, but engaged nonetheless. Second, Parker was such a nice guy. Not super quiet, always with a few ball-busting lines, but he seemed extraordinarily intelligent. She didn't know why she thought that. Maybe his word choices? Maybe how others in their circle deferred to him on questions?

The guy was into numbers, which she totally got. When they talked sports, Parker talked statistics. When they talked news, his answers were based on risk and analysis. All of which magnified his smoldering blue eyes and tousled near-black hair. Intelligence made a man crazy attractive. His broad chest and sculpted butt were pretty amazing too.

Holy shit. Her cheeks heated, her core clenched, and she tugged the covers over her face, smiling like a girl crushing on a daydream. If Matt *ever* thought she'd even checked Parker out… sadness bloomed in her chest. Thinking about Parker proved that she wasn't broken. She wasn't incapable of feeling something intense for a man. She might not have had a spark for Matt, but it was possible for it to happen. Maybe that made her even more broken than she thought. Oh, hell.

Under the covers and in the cloak of the night, Lexi slipped off the ring and wiggled it around. The weight that fell off her without that little diamond on her finger was scary. She had to leave.

Then she'd be alone again. Just as she'd grown up. Which really shouldn't be as off-putting as it seemed. Once a loner, always a loner. Except being forced away from her friends now was different than growing up in a dozen foster homes, and it seemed like an eternity until the next hacker convention.

Wiggling her free finger against the mattress, Lexi made the risky-but-powerful decision to sleep without the ring on. She tucked it under her pillow—and her recent constant insomnia suddenly faded. Crazy how much easier breathing felt after just taking that thing off.

Matt woke with a hangover that he could only blame on the woman next to him. Had she cooked him a meal when he'd gotten home, a little food in his stomach would have stopped this headache.

"Peaches," he grumbled, rubbing his hands over his face, "wake up."

She murmured in her sleep, and her stupid-ass dog snored at the foot of the bed.

Matt kicked at the dog, but he was too tangled to find purchase on the mutt. "Fat ass."

Lexi stirred. "Hm?"

"I love you, peaches. Wake up."

Slowly her eyes opened. She stayed with her head against the pillow, but her eyes met his. She didn't crawl over to him, didn't offer breakfast, a blow job, or anything worthwhile. "Morning, Matt."

"What, no love for your man?"

She blinked slowly then dropped her gaze away. "You can't really ask that, right? I mean, come on. Why are we even doing this?"

"You're still pissed about last night? Forget it. I had a couple too many." He reached to pull her close, and she flinched. "Don't be like that. It was nothing. Besides, you were working on your computer, right? Why do you leave me alone in bed like that?" He leaned over and kissed her shoulder. "If you didn't obsess over work, I wouldn't have to fight to make everything okay for us."

"You were awful to me."

"Come on, don't be mean to me." He kissed her shoulder again, and she didn't relax. "Time to make up, c'mere."

"I don't want to."

Anger thumped in his chest. "What is it with you saying no? It's like you're trying to hurt me, you know that? Like you want to throw away what I've given you."

"You're turning this around on me," she sniped at him like a bitch with her thong crawled up her cooch.

"Damn, you're a bitch this morning." He crawled over her, morning wood jutting in his boxers. "You make me into an asshole. I'm not that guy. Why are you always pushing me?"

He flexed his dick against her.

She didn't move. Didn't react.

He rolled his hips against her. "Make up with me."

"You want breakfast?" she asked. "French toast sounds awesome, right?"

"Nope." He pressed his mouth to her unmoving lips. "I want you."

"I don't want to."

His hand ran roughly over her stomach and grabbed at her breast. "Since when did you start sleeping with a bra on?"

She shrugged timidly. "Fell asleep like that after working."

"Peaches. Seriously. I keep saying it. It's like you want to hurt me," he growled against her ear. "Like you want to be some rejected lonely girl no one would ever understand. I understand you. I take care of you. If you didn't push me, none of this would happen."

She snagged the covers and tried to tuck them in between them as his hands jammed down her pants. He scraped his fingers between her legs—she was dry as the Sahara on a summer day.

"What the fuck is wrong with you?" he asked.

"I don't want to!" She pushed at him, and her hand caught his attention.

His eyes narrowed. He grabbed her bare left fist then the other, just to make sure he wasn't wrong. "Where's your ring?"

Color faded from her face. "Must've fallen off." She scurried underneath him, digging her hands under the pillow. "See? Here?" She slipped it on.

"What are you now? A dry-pussied whore, sliding her ring off," he yelled in her face.

"Matt, stop. You haven't even been drinking."

"You think I need to drink to show my woman what the rules are?"

"Stop!"

Rage poured into his blood. He sat up then kicked her dumb-ass dog off the bed. "You. Do *not* tell me what to do. Do you understand me?"

"I'm leaving."

He grabbed her, not letting her up from the bed. "Why the

fuck do you make this happen?"

"I haven't," she whimpered, bending to submit to his pull. "I—"

He yanked her pants down to her knees, and she squirmed, rolling hard as if she would run out of bed. "Stay."

Bacon growled, jumping back on the bed. He yipped at Matt's back and bit the back of his legs.

"I'm going to kill this dog. You know that? Fucking slice it's throat."

"No. Please." Her voice shook.

A round of pleasure ran through him because she knew he'd really do it. "Behave, and I won't. Simple. If that's how this has to be, peaches, then so be it."

He got up, grabbed the biting, barking mutt, and threw the dog out the bedroom. He relished its squeal, then he slammed the door.

"You're not drunk," she whined.

He shook his head and dropped his pants. Then he descended on the bed, ready to take what he needed by any means necessary. With each kick and thrash, confidence bled into his veins. Every lost job, every moron boss, every jealous inclination calmed in his thoughts when she finally gave up and took what he had to give.

"Such a good girl. I love you so much."

She lay there, not looking at him until he turned her head to make her eyes meet his.

"I said I love you, peaches. I wish you wouldn't make us fight." He pressed his kiss to her mouth, but she didn't kiss back. "So stupid. It's like you want me to kill your stupid fat puppy just to get your attention."

"No!"

"Then I said I love you."

"Love you too," she mumbled.

"I won't ever do that again. I'm sorry if I hurt you."

She sniffled. "Please don't hurt Bacon."

"Don't make me, and it'll be okay. Okay? Deal? Are we good now? We both understand what we need to?"

"I want you to stop drinking."

He laughed. "That's not the problem here."

She shook her head, still pinned under his weight. "I'm going to go stay with Meredith."

*Smack.* Her head snapped to the side.

"If you leave me, I'll bring you home. Remember that. Without the fleabag."

"Please get off me."

"When you understand."

She nodded violently. "I understand."

"Please don't make me do this again."

"Okay."

"Good." He kissed her, and she opened her mouth. "All is as it should be."

# CHAPTER FOUR

Phiber spent hours on the computer in a Virginia coffee shop, diving through the underworld channels of all things SilverChaos. There weren't many crumbs to find. Most of his information was based off of whispers and guesses about who Silver was, almost never with any kind of consistency. He had told the Taskmaster that Silver was someone he'd approached at the last con party, but they wanted proof. More than what he had provided with his guesstimation and gut instinct.

So he moved down to where she lived, following her when he could, and went about his confirmation plan. It was the equivalent of manual labor. He was, by hand, pulling every scrap of discarded security footage he could find from the locations where SilverChaos had won or played a part in a hacking event, and every major highway, airport, and parking garage in a five-mile radius to those events. He ran facial recognition programs, vehicle identifying programs.

For as elite as Silver was, she didn't know that she was being hunted by him. By whoever his employer was, which even he couldn't figure out.

"Perfect." He leaned back in his chair and took a bite of his scone. He clicked send, and the file with all of his compiled proof that showed he was correct in his research, still keeping himself relevant by not sharing who she was—even that she was a she—went to the Taskmaster.

He spent the next hour waiting for a reply. Then the next two hours drawing out a lunch of coffee shop muffins and granola bars. Phiber tapped his fingers, bounced his toes, and hit refresh on his computer a dozen times an hour. He wanted an acknowledgment that he had pulled off a feat. That he had all the proof that would earn another task and a bank deposit from the Taskmaster.

His cell phone beeped, and Phiber jumped for it.

*Confirmation accepted. Bring Silver to a secure location. Bank transfer incoming.*

What? Like kidnap her? His stomach tightened, uneasy at where this was going. Abduction pricked at his morals. She didn't look like much. He could probably carry her under his arm even if she kicked and screamed. But there was a difference between stealing a program and information, and stealing a woman.

Phiber hit refresh of out habit, and a bank notification email popped onto the screen. He clicked it. He wasn't a greedy fuck, but damn, that was a lot of money. Running his tongue over his teeth, he leaned back and nodded, accepting that he was willing to be bought, that upping his rap sheet from breaking and entering to kidnapping wouldn't be that bad if he didn't get caught. Which he wouldn't. He was cocky enough to know he was good.

Grabbing his cell phone, he tapped out a message.

*Not a problem.*

Then he prayed the woman got out of her house more often than she had in the last few weeks. It'd be easy enough. He'd just grab her. Right? Or trick her? Coerce her? Shit. Dealing with people was his weakness. He wasn't suave, and she'd probably recognize him. Maybe he should just knock on the door and put chloroform over her mouth. Kind of cliché, but it wouldn't always be in the movies if it didn't work.

He rubbed his face, uncomfortable with how the assignment had devolved but encouraged by his bank account. If he could stalk a person online, real life should be easier. He popped a piece of stale scone in his mouth then took off to go research secure locations.

Lexi wandered the grocery store aisle, wasting as much time as she could. Matt had dropped her off out front and watched her go in. She was certain he was waiting at the curb, ready to take her bags with a smile and a hug. The world thought he was such a good guy. On the surface, he was attractive with a fun personality. But the guy was rotting from the inside out.

The more she thought about it, the more she was sure that he would hurt her if she tried to leave. Like *really* hurt her. Not just force her to bed and violate her or hit her. God, for how smart she was, this was confusing. Especially the sex. It wasn't sex—it was rape. Or assault? How did it work if the guy was her fiancé? If she eventually gave up and just let it happen to get it over with? The process wasn't as painful when she opened her legs, so what did that mean?

A cold chill ran down her spine, and she spun, certain Matt could see her shopping and read her thoughts. But he wasn't there.

God, now she was going crazy. But she couldn't shake the feeling he had eyes on her. She squared her shoulders and pushed down the aisle, not wanting to get caught lollygagging. She sped down the rows, occasionally seeing the same guy with his face covered, hunkered over a shopping list, also filling his cart. Other than that, no Matt.

She turned the corner again, and the other man was gone. Maybe not on the same speed. This was crazy. Paranoia was getting the best of her, yet her senses tingled as though something wasn't right.

Um, yeah. Her fiancé had forced her to have sex that morning then threatened to kill her dog…

She pushed through the checkout line and briefly considered asking about a back door. She could run away to Meredith's. But a cold panic rushed over her at the thought of Bacon being used to punish her. The second she could get that dog alone, she was gone. Decision made.

Lexi took her change, ditched her cart, and took the bags on her arms. She rounded the corner and saw Matt waiting at the curb, as expected, right as she slammed into another person.

"Oh, God. Sorry." Her bags fell, the apples escaping. "Shoot."

She bent to grab them, and as she gathered them up, she looked at the man hovering over her. It was the hat guy from the aisles. But as soon she zeroed in on his Asian features and the tiny scar above his lip, her mind registered him hitting on her weeks ago, states away, asking if she knew SilverChaos.

"Phiber?" she asked.

He handed her an apple. "Hi. Nice surprise." His eyes looked predatory, as though he knew who she was and wanted something.

"You live around here?"

"Visiting." He smiled as he had at the last con party. "I was just heading for an early lunch. Be cool to talk shop if you want—" His eyes flew up.

An urge to run away hit her hard, and she backed into a solid wall of muscle. A hard arm snaked around her.

"And who the fuck are you?" Matt growled, clinging her tight to his side.

She didn't want him to be her white knight, but something was off in a big way.

"Just a co-worker." The guy threw up his hands, standing down to Matt's brutish nature and physical size.

"You know this guy?" His hand clasped to her shoulder.

"We've met once."

Matt's jealous rage glared off of his face. "Get in the truck, peaches."

She scurried away, unnerved that Phiber had been in her real-life world, though perhaps that was bound to happen eventually. Matt joined her in the truck, slammed the gear into drive, and sped off.

"You know that guy?" he asked again, distrust in his voice.

"I think we've worked on a project before. Or something. He recognized me, I guess. I didn't at first."

"Why'd you rush away from him?"

"I didn't."

"He the kind of guy you *like* to put out for? That nerd screamed computer boy."

She winced. "No, it's not like that."

"So you didn't want me to see him with you."

"Matt, really, it's not like that. I promise." But what was it like? Her eyes closed, and she recalled that scary, hungry look in Phiber's eyes.

"I'm not a jealous guy, peaches. But I swear to shit, you push me."

"I know you're not," she lied. Damn it. She could barely run from one guy, and now another had unnerved her? "I'll put a roast on, and everything will be fine. I was just caught off guard."

Her stomach turned, but the more she thought about running into Phiber, the more she didn't trust her reaction. It had been completely over the top. Matt was making her paranoid. Really, the people she worked with were loners who did *not* do well with normal interactions. Couple Matt rushing up behind her when she backed away, and the guy was probably scared to death. The whole thing was harmless.

"A roast sounds great."

"Great."

His eyes roamed over her body, making her feel more like a trophy than a person. "You know, Lexi, you're the only girl who's ever going to be in my world."

The words were sweet, but the tone was a threat. "Of course."

"You and that damn dog. Safe as long as we're together."

# CHAPTER FIVE

The day had come and gone. Matt had headed out with some guys from the neighborhood, leaving her alone to stare at the empty backpack that she could easily pack and leave with. Two days had passed since she'd run into Phiber, and for those two days, Matt had treated her like a queen. His distrust had melted away the second they arrived at home. He didn't make any moves on her and told her everything she cooked was delicious. The guy even threw a load of laundry in the wash. He apologized over and over for being a dick, saying that he couldn't imagine a life without her in it and sometimes his temper and jealousy got the best of him.

It was all bullshit.

Right?

Why did she even doubt?

*I'm so sorry. I hurt you. I shouldn't have. I love you, peaches.*

Her stomach turned—she hated the nickname peaches—yet, staring at the empty bag, she couldn't begin to decide what to pack or where to go. She exhaled, hating and doubting herself. She rubbed her head and wondered what her breaking point was if it hadn't been passed already?

Enough. Lexi tried to concentrate on Monarch. If she sold it for what Shadow was banking on, then they could quietly put that money into her savings account, and maybe she could just disappear. By the time she came back from wherever she'd hidden, Matt would have moved on. Maybe.

Bacon jumped into her lap, and she rubbed her sweet head. "I won't let anything happen to you, sweet little Bacon Byte."

Bacon sneezed and wheezed—wow, Lexi needed to help her rescued little pug lose some poundage. Somehow the dog had become her best friend. She chatted with Bacon, cuddled her as if the dog was the cure to Matt. As if she didn't need to fear being alone when she had the pup in her arms.

"You and me, Bacon." Then she kissed Bacon's furry head and went back to work.

Screen after screen, Monarch was beautiful. The program she'd designed was just like its namesake, starting as something fragile and maybe even ugly. But this was a work of technological art. Strong. Gorgeous. Smart. It was—

A crash rattled in the backyard. Her heart sank. Matt was back, and that was his truck backing into the recycling bin. A dead giveaway of how much he'd had to drink. The truck door opened and slammed, then Lexi heard him curse the trash can for being there. Where it always was. Guess Mister Nice Doting Fiancé was gone. Big surprise.

Maybe he'd come in and rant over a game of pool lost. Maybe he'd come in and demand dinner at—she checked her phone—one in the morning. Whatever he did, she prayed he'd pass out sooner rather than later, ideally on the couch so she wouldn't have to hear his drunk snores.

Their back door crashed open, and he spilled himself inside. Her body went rigid. Even though she knew she should go meet him, she didn't move. Maybe she could pretend to be asleep.

Lexi jumped up when she heard him kick the kitchen trash can. It scattered across the floor as she dove into bed. Just another trash can she'd replace without comment. They seemed to always break. Often.

"We gotta go to bed, Bacon." She snagged the covers and buried them both in deep. Her pup licked her face, and she tried to shush her. "Sleep."

"Lexi!"

She held her breath and squeezed her eyes shut. *I'm asleep, I'm asleep, I'm asleep...*

"Peaches, where the fuck you at?"

*Go to sleep—*

Her bedroom door swung open and bounced off the wall.

Bile simmered in her stomach, inched into her throat. *Don't be an asshole tonight...*

Matt wandered into their bathroom, leaving a trail of clothes. The stench of the bar permeated the room. Cigarette smoke gave her migraines, and even on his clothes, his hair, his breath, it made her sick. The bathroom toilet flushed, and Matt staggered in the darkness. She couldn't see him but knew the haphazard, staggering steps he took toward their bed. Thank God he was passing out.

The covers tore off her. "You sleepin'?"

The sound in his voice made her want to vomit. There was something mixed in with the drunkenness and lust. He'd promised never again to take her like before. Said it was a mistake, that she had caused it but that he shouldn't have done it. Most certainly tonight, she had caused nothing.

"Sleeping, Matt."

"Roll over." He grabbed Bacon and threw her.

"Matt!"

"I'm gonna kill that dog if you love it more than me. Stuff its fat ass and put it in the living room to remind you."

Tears burned her eyes as she remembered when he'd forced her to have sex days ago. She had two options. One was over faster than the other. One left bruises on her hips and the insides of her thighs and came with a day's worth of him explaining why he'd had to do what he did. If push came to it, the lesser of two evils—sex with her fiancé—would happen. She'd been so stupid, stupid, stupid not to leave earlier.

"I was sleeping, baby," she mumbled, praying that it mattered this time. Her arms mentally reached for Bacon to make sure she was okay. "Tomorrow? Please?"

It didn't matter.

His hands ran over her shirt, pulling it over her head even as she tried to glue her ear to the pillow. "Love that body. All mine. Don't make me take what I need."

"No, Matt."

Bacon jumped on the bed, snarling, and Matt grabbed her. He threw her again, but this time out the door, which he closed with a slam.

"Said I was sleeping, baby."

"Are you trying to make me mad?" He crawled into bed. "Let's go."

Lexi swallowed her dread. It would hurt. God, it was disgusting. Him panting, breathing, sweating. But it was so much faster. *I'm done. This is the last time.* She'd make it through the night then figure things out. How would she leave when she had been wormed away from family and friends?

She tried to redirect him. "Did you have fun tonight?"

His fingers pinched her side, making her yelp. "Sound like I want to talk?"

Tears seeped silently down her cheeks as he yanked down her underwear. With her T-shirt shoved up, her fiancé crawled on top of her, breathing smoky-liquor stank into her face.

"I really don't—"

His hand covered her mouth, and his other hand jammed between her legs. She couldn't hide her tears as she sobbed. Matt never even slowed a beat.

# CHAPTER SIX

The sun poured into Lexi's bedroom, failing to shine away the darkness that hung over her. But it was a new day, and she would be gone by the end of it. But she needed to clear her head and couldn't stand to be around Matt while he got ready to go to the gun range.

He sat at the breakfast table, striking matches and blowing them out.

"Any more coffee?" he asked.

"Nope."

He struck a match and dropped it where Bacon lay on the floor, and he cackled. "Dumb dog doesn't know to move."

"Don't do that!"

"Put another pot on. Maybe I won't have to." He lit a match and dropped it. It fizzled out before it hit Bacon's fur. "Think she'd eat a lit match? Eats everything else."

Lexi's pulse pounded in her neck. "Don't hurt her."

He closed the matches and tossed them on the table. "I'd never hurt that dog." But his tone said he'd hurt Bacon just to stick it to her.

For the next two hours, she kept an eye on her dog and fiancé. Her anxiety built, and she needed to blow off steam. Bacon was asleep, hidden in a pile of clothes in the closet, and could only be found if one was listening for fat doggy snores. Matt was zoned out on the couch before he went out around lunch. She had just enough time to get outside, stretch her legs, and think through her day's plans. For as much Matt lorded over her, he never cared when she ran—her assumption being that he thought she was staying fit and attractive for him. It was one of the few times his narcissism worked in her favor.

"I'm going to go for a run," she said.

He eyed her as if he didn't trust her, which was smart because she was done. But her runs were nothing new. "Go burn off your breakfast, peaches. I think I'll keep Bacon by my side until you return."

They stared at each other until she nodded. He wouldn't hurt Bacon for no reason. She'd done nothing to encourage him to hurt the puppy, and she wouldn't be gone long. The chances that Bacon woke up and came downstairs or that Matt stopped watching sports long enough to do something to her dog were next to nil.

Lexi tied her running shoes and took off. As the *slap, slap, slap* of her soles picked up its pace, her mind numbed. Her limbs stretched, and she ate ground, pushing herself in the cool winter's morning. For a brief moment, she forgot about planning, about forced sex and threats against her dog. But it all came back when she eased out of a hard sprint and into a jog.

What if Matt did do something to Bacon while she was out—just because he was mean? Doubting her decision to leave, Lexi turned back toward hell to check on Bacon. She rounded the sidewalk, running, pushing herself until she couldn't remember last night. Or the last year. Or any of her decisions that had gotten her to this point. She used to be strong, confident… but now? The sound of her running shoes pounding was her only companion, the only one that knew how deep she was in.

The always-present stomachache tightened as she neared their street. As soon as she hit the driveway, her quiet self would take over. She was a thousand times more distant, more lost, and just… smaller today than she was last night.

She rounded the last bend in the road and saw Matt's truck—and *Parker's* Range Rover. Relief bloomed in her lungs, followed by something that made her a little dizzy. She'd hoped to see him tomorrow, but this was almost too much. It was as if her savior had shown up, even though he had no idea she'd cast him in the role. How and why she'd mentally latched onto him made no sense. Looks and smarts were something to appreciate, but hoping that he would somehow help her… that didn't matter because Parker was there.

It had to be a sign. Or something. She needed to leave. Or keep running. Never stop and turn back. Except she was drawn to Parker—and couldn't leave Bacon with Matt. God. Parker had never shown an inkling of a flirtation toward her. Lord knew she didn't dare look at another man for too long, and certainly not Parker, who was all mysterious cool guy. Big and handsome, almost like out of a movie.

How were those two even friends? Even if it was a friendship that stemmed from back in the day. Then again, no one knew who Matt had become. No one would believe her. Matt had said that once, but he was right. He was brassy and ballsy, a guy's guy, not an abuser. No way would he hit his woman. *No way…*

Except he did.

She bounced on the toes of her running shoes. Why couldn't she run away? Right now. Leave everything behind. Shadow would get her money and help her get a new life. She didn't need to pack a bag, but all of her notebooks—a diary of every time she should've left written in detail—her journals with her work, what she didn't keep online was still inside, and obviously, she wouldn't leave her dog. Matt would kill the poor girl. He said so all the time.

Lexi rubbed her temples and gulped a breath before turning up her driveway. She could smile at her fiancé, be cordial to Parker, and not give Matt anything to be jealous or crazy over. But if he knew what was in her head… then she'd be dead.

A couple yards away, the door opened, and she looked up. Parker. Oh… he wore a form-fitting Henley painted across his defined chest. It highlighted the thickness of his biceps and taper of his waist, and he wore jeans that, even from a distance, curved over his backside—and his front side—in a manner that was sinful. Every part of that man looked muscled. Even his strong neck and stout jaw shouted that he was utter male perfection.

Her mouth watered and her breath froze, a spellbinding contradiction that only served to remind her that he might have been the sexiest man she'd ever seen.

"Hey, Lex," he said in that bottom-of-the-canyon voice that made her shiver. The door closed behind him, separating him from all that she hated inside that house.

Her cheeks felt flushed, but that was okay since she'd been running in forty degree weather. As he casually downed the stairs, his powerful thighs stole the show, and her lungs boycotted normal breaths. Again, she could blame that on exercising in the cold. But what she could say and what was the truth… those were two very different things.

"Hey." She waved, averting her eyes in case Matt saw her.

Parker walked toward her from the landing. "Didn't know you were around."

Warily, she cast her gaze up. "Out running."

He stepped closer. If they both extended their arms, their fingertips might touch. A round of shivers ran down her back.

His eyes narrowed almost immediately, as though he could sense her concern. "You doing okay, sweetheart?"

Panic set in, and she took one enormous, probably obvious, step back. "Yeah. Of course."

He stepped forward, his blue eyes studying her in a way that made her want to cry for help. "Haven't seen you in a while."

"I, um—"

Matt pushed the door open behind Parker. "Hey, peaches, get inside. You're going to freeze that sweet ass off."

She cringed and cast her eyes down, embarrassed that Matt had spoken like that in front of Parker. "Okay."

Matt jumbled down the stairs and smacked her butt harder than he needed to, not that he needed to at all, as he passed. "We're headed out. Be back later."

He was leaving her alone? Now? She was getting out! But she didn't react when she heard Matt open his truck and turn over the engine. When she finally glanced up, Parker still stood there, his jaw tight, the tendons in his neck prevalent.

Oh, heaven help her. A woman could fall in love with that kind of intense focus. But instead, she fought the pull of his navy eyes and glanced over his shoulder at Matt, whose distrustful gaze was on her.

Matt got out of his truck. "There are a couple dogs that hang down at GUNS. Think I'll take your mutt with me."

"What?" She spun, terrified of what that meant.

He smiled as if he knew her afternoon plans. "Think she'd get some exercise running around. It'll be good for her."

Lexi watched Matt hustle inside and come back with a squirming, snapping Bacon. "Please be careful with her."

"'Course." Then he tossed her in the second row of the dual cab.

Her throat stung, worry alarming her.

"You sure you're good, Lex?" Parker pushed again, taking another step closer.

Her eyes flicked from him to the window where Bacon pressed her snout, then went back to Parker.

He tilted her head. "Dog'll be fine at the range. Don't worry about that."

"Okay," she whispered.

"I promise, sweetheart."

His trustworthy voice was like a hug. She liked that he called her sweetheart, that he called her Lex. But Parker had no idea. Or did he? He watched her for seconds too long, and without a doubt, Lexi knew Matt would be pissed even if she hadn't done anything to warrant the reaction.

Resigned to the fact that when she left, she might not see Parker again, she ignored the concern on his face and faked a smile that was sad-but-practiced. "Always."

Just another lie. Even as her heart reached out to Parker, Lexi walked into her house without so much as a good-bye so she could grab her laptop, wait for Bacon to return, and disappear.

# CHAPTER SEVEN

Five hours with the same thing on his brain: Lexi Dare. Shit. Parker had spent hours at GUNS with Matt, hitting targets and checking on new spec ops weapons that were for retail sale. The dog that Matt insisted was called Fatso stuck close to Parker the whole time. Even now, the poor thing sawed logs in the backseat.

None of his afternoon had cleared his mind, and as they pulled out of GUNS's parking lot, Parker rubbed his jaw, unable to ignore the unspoken plea on Lexi's face. His gut instinct screamed that something had been wrong this morning, and it wasn't the first time his sixth sense had been on fire when it came to Lex. But earlier, without saying a word, she'd confirmed it.

He drummed his fingers on the steering wheel as he drove Matt's truck back. Matt getting loaded on beer he'd snuck in and running through rounds wasn't on the approved activities list at GUNS, and Parker had ended things before Matt got them thrown out. It wasn't news that Matt was an asshole, but he was an asshole that everyone got on with. More or less. His drinking thing was getting out of control, and if Parker wasn't concerned before today, he was now, after Matt had turned a day at the range into a BYOB activity. Was that what had caused the look on Lexi's face? The less-than-subtle changes Parker had noticed for months?

The hollow look on her face, when she hadn't always looked like that, ate at him. That, and there was the distance in her icy blue eyes, almost as if their shine had dulled. Except today when he'd walked up to her, shoving his hands into his pockets to keep them off her. At *that* moment, those icy blues shined.

The girl was gorgeous. He'd thought about her more than he should, her delicate face always hanging in the periphery of his mind. Her blond hair always looked sexy-tousled, as if she'd been up to no good, and it framed her fair skin and pink lips like a not-so-innocent frame. She was sweet and sexy, quiet but funny. Everything about her was incredible—also off-limits.

Parker clung to the wheel as though he were wringing her fiancé's neck. She was too good for Matt. Really, too good for anyone Parker knew. But how would he know that? They just had an innate connection he couldn't shake. He tried to concentrate on the road, on relaxing and blowing off steam after coming home from a Titan op that had almost gone bad.

"Ha." Matt threw his drunk head back. "Did you hear Sugar's pregnant?"

Parker didn't like Matt's condescending tone. "Yup."

"Jared Westin as a father. Fuck me."

Parker shrugged, wondering if he still felt needled because of Lexi or because of Matt questioning Sugar and Jared as parents. "The man already has a daughter. I'm not sure what you're getting at."

"Adopted," Matt scoffed.

"Same thing." But what he wanted to say was so the fuck what. Parker had wanted to be adopted when he was a kid. That lost feeling ate at him while growing up with guys like Matt, who had the same folks picking him up from school every day, same people to go home to every night. But nope, not Parker. He'd been stuck in the system, bouncing all over their damn county until he finally took control of his future—education and the Marines. He'd been smart, smarter than any single person he'd ever met. He'd made a plan, worked it, and it had paid off, though he couldn't seem to let go of Matt. Old friends, like habits, died hard?

"Jared with kids? Shit, I can't see it."

"Jesus, man, you don't even know the guy that well." Bashing anyone in Titan should be an instant sayonara—except he wasn't quite ready to lose the glimpses of Lexi. "What's it to you if they have kids or not?"

His irritation intensified. Maybe Parker needed to unload a few more magazines if for no other reason than to have something in his hands that wouldn't get him in trouble. He ignored Matt's jackass ramblings, thankful when they finally pulled into the driveway.

Parker's eyes tracked to the spot where Lexi had stood, looking so gone, then he twisted to see the sleeping dog named Fatso. "Everything all good with you and Lex?"

Matt's hands bunched. "Yeah. Of course."

Almost word for word what Lexi had said. Parker tapped his thigh. What the hell was his problem? Butting in when nothing needed saying. Addressing something he could sense but couldn't see—that wasn't his thing. Parker dealt with black-and-white facts, not this ache of the unknown ricocheting in his chest.

Matt pushed open the passenger door, grabbing Fatso roughly, as Parker slid the truck into park.

"You coming in?" Matt slurred, dropping the pug, who ran toward the door.

"Yeah." Because Parker still couldn't get rid of the sense that something was off with Lexi. "I told Sugar I'd pass something along to Lex."

Matt's eyes narrowed. "She's out."

"Oh, right. Just tell her it's something about a fundraiser." *For adopted kids, asshole.* "Sugar said Lex might be interested."

He nodded. "I'll tell her."

"Catch you and Lex at Winters's tomorrow? Sugar can just tell her herself." Parker grabbed his gear bag from the back of the truck.

Matt stood, frozen and staring at the street. A car parked two driveways down pulled out onto the road.

"Everything okay?" Parker's eyes narrowed as he tried to ascertain what the problem was.

Matt continued to stare down the road. "Did that guy look like some nerd boy to you?"

"That car?"

Matt nodded.

"Didn't see him. Looked like a neighbor driving off. Why?"

"Thought I'd seen him before." Matt bristled. "Never mind. Nothing." He gave Parker a chin lift and hustled inside, letting the door slam shut.

"Jesus, dude." Paranoia much?

All day long, all Parker had heard was excuses. Why Matt's bosses were crappy, why the jobs he'd left were shitty. The whole world was up on his ass and concurrently trying to take him down. Listening to all of that bullshit was draining, though the day was still young. Parker needed to get a burger and make a quick run by Titan HQ to see what was going on. Work didn't stop because he was off site. His hands slid over the back pockets of his jeans and came up empty. No keys. He'd left them and his wallet in Matt's truck when he'd opted to take his buddy's keys and drive them back.

He dropped his head back then let go of his gear bag and made his way back to Matt's truck. Locked. Great. This was getting better and better. Parker headed to the front door. He was too tired to deal with another round of Matt Pindon bullshit.

Bounding up the stairs, he knocked and pushed the familiar door open as the dog yapped from inside. "Hey, man. Need your keys to open—"

Lexi was against the wall with Matt's hand wrapped around her throat. He was inches away from her face, and she was crying, shaking her head, and kicking as if she was treading water but losing the battle.

"Matt! Fuck, man." Parker ran in and grabbed his shoulder, dragging him back.

Matt spun, sputtering with beer on his breath from earlier. "Not your business. Out."

She dropped to the floor, her hands covering her neck, and gasped as though she were a fish out of water, desperately trying to find stasis again.

Matt stomped, swinging at the dog. The dog looked at Parker as if Fatso was turning over the keys to Lexi's safety then scampered up the stairs.

"Man, my keys are in your truck, asshole." Parker lasered in on her. "Lex, you—"

"Get out!" Matt pushed Parker with both hands.

"Enough of this shit." Parker wrapped an arm around Matt's neck and pushed him into a chokehold. He counted down and gave Matt's neck a hard squeeze before tossing him to the floor. "Lex, go outside."

Matt gasped on the ground. "The fuck"—cough—"you will."

Parker's eyes popped in disbelief. "Are you fuckin' kidding me?"

Matt reared up and lunged, but Parker caught him by the shirt as if he was pulling off a K-9. Lexi didn't move from her spot on the carpet.

"Out of my house, man," Matt snarled, acting like nothing Parker would leave alone with Lexi.

Parker angled toward her, holding back her fiancé. "Lex—"

"Don't talk to that whore." Matt's hands clapped down on Parker's biceps. "She's mine to deal with."

"What are you even talking about? God," she whispered hoarsely. Tears ran down her cheeks.

He struggled toward her. "*I saw that guy again. Slut!*"

Parker had a code, same as most men, and there was no way Matt, acting like a 'roided-up motherfucker, was getting out of his hold. "You've got three goddamn seconds to power your ass down."

Matt twisted toward Lexi. "Walk out the door, peaches, and I will kill you."

Parker narrowed his eyes at the sharpness of the words. He pushed Matt back, hard, then pushed him again and put himself between the couple. Matt rolled his shoulders and paced two feet either way, prowling and ready to attack. Lexi didn't move. Clearly tonight wasn't the first time she'd heard him like this.

"Lex, sweetheart." He kept Matt an arm's length away. "Speak up. What do you need?"

Silence.

"You want me to go?" Parker tried again. But no matter her response, he wasn't leaving. Not like this.

"This is between me and her." Matt stepped closer. The ice in his voice sent chills down Parker's spine. "Stupid, smart-ass motherfucker, think you're so goddamn clever. Think you know everything. Not everything is about computers and shit, Parker. Get out of my damn house."

It wasn't the first time Parker had heard the smart-guy lines. When Matt was drunk, he got his shit in a tailspin and hated on everyone. That was Matt. A first-class asshole. But this, what Parker just saw, was past the line.

"God, man, shut up. You move an inch toward her, we're going to blows." Parker had height and weight on Matt, and his senses were in hyper-overdrive, ready to protect her, to care for her… carefully, he crouched without turning his back on Matt. "Lexi…" He put two fingers under her chin and lifted her face to his. "Tell me what you want."

Her eyes locked on his, and he could've sworn her lips formed to say *you*. But she flinched as her gaze jumped. Parker spun up, countering the attack he saw coming in his peripheral, and he slammed Matt to the floor with a swift right hook. He enjoyed the impact that knocked out the guy.

"Fuck," Parker growled and jumped up. He turned to her. The woman before him, lips rolled together, eyes squeezed shut, broke his heart. "Lex?"

Seconds ticked by until she gave him the most honest look he'd ever seen. The most scared one too.

"There was no one here. I don't know what he's talking about. Please don't leave me with him," she whispered.

Those last words were all Parker needed. He slipped his arms around her slender frame and carried her out the door. Right before they crossed the threshold, Parker snagged Matt's keys to gain access to his own. Behind them, Matt rolled on the floor, waking and moaning. It took practiced restraint to keep from kicking Matt's ass again.

"Don't"—Matt pushed up to hands and knees—"you dare leave."

Parker held her to his chest and glared with the open front door at his back. "I don't know what's been happening here, but fuck you." Then he walked out the door with Lexi in his arms.

# CHAPTER EIGHT

Parker held Lexi against his chest. The ease with which he lofted her against him and the moment when her tense body relaxed against his was trouble. Her hair tickled his neck, and there was something too intimate about the hold. She smelled like sweet citrus. Like sugar and lemons. His mouth watered. Couple his visceral reactions with the plain fact that he did *not* want to let go, and the situation was complicated. That was problematic because he wasn't familiar with complicated.

Keeping her soft curves against him, Parker opened Matt's truck, got his own keys, then opened his Range Rover.

As soon as he set her down, he regretted the loss of her weight in his arms. Instead of backing away, he leaned across her body and shoved his keys into the ignition. She needed a warm place to sit, but mostly he wanted to feel her close again. As he pulled back, blocking the door to keep out the cold, he studied her red neck and sad eyes that wouldn't look at him.

Parker ground his molars, trying to contain the explosive energy that pooled in his fists. "Tell me not to go back in there and kill him." Despite the growl in his words, he shook loose one fist and touched her chin, angling her face for a better look at her neck.

But her hands batted him away. "It's nothing."

"God, Lex." He took his hand back, wanting to put it on her thigh but instead shoving it into his pocket. "We've got problems if you believe that."

One slender shoulder shrugged. "I'm fine."

The hell she was. She wouldn't look up, wouldn't say more than two hoarse words at a time, and his guess was her throat was bruised. Fuck that dude. "Don't move. Lock the door. Just stay here."

She didn't respond.

"Lexi?"

Her near-vacant stare jumped to his, and surrounding her icy blue irises were tiny exploded blood vessels in the whites of her eye.

"Stay, sweetheart." He locked then shut the door and charged back inside.

Parker knocked the door open, ready to go to blows with the asshole he'd known for years in the house that he'd been to a number of times. Matt was leaned back on the couch, beer in one hand, remote in the other hand, surfing the television as though what had just happened hadn't. He didn't look up as Parker crossed the room.

"What the motherfuck?" Parker's fists were balled, his muscles ready.

Matt leaned back, not a care on his face. "It was nothing. Forget it."

"Are you out of your damn—"

Matt raised his beer. "Have a drink or get out."

"Dude, you had your hands around her neck."

"It wasn't what it looked like."

"Are you fuckin' on crack?"

His head tilted. "You got a thing for my fiancée?"

"Jesus fuckin' Christ. I've got a thing for common decency."

"I'm not gonna fight you over her. She'll come back. Tell her one simple word: Bacon."

"What?"

"Tell her I've got Bacon."

Screw it. Parker didn't care. He slammed out the front door and headed back for Lexi. His muscles shook from wanting to crush Matt. Parker's mind ping-ponged over a million memories. What had he seen before, what had he missed, why had Matt changed—really changed—for the worse? Growling, Parker jumped into his seat after Lexi unlocked the doors then he threw the SUV into reverse and peeled out of the driveway without looking at her. He couldn't, because shit, if he did, there was no telling what would come out of his mouth.

They slowed through stop signs. He didn't know where he was going, but they were working through the maze of suburbia hell.

"Sorry," she whispered. "He's your friend. I didn't mean to put you in the middle of that."

"No friend of mine would ever hurt a woman." Parker's grip strangled the steering wheel as though he was trying to force himself not to turn back. His knuckles went pinkish white, and he still hadn't stopped jamming his molars together.

"Just sorry," she said again, even quieter than a whisper. Her voice broke his goddamn heart.

"Tell me that hasn't happened before, Lex."

Again with the silence.

He heard her sniffle, then he looked over. Fuck him—fresh tears. He was so far out of his league with the last fifteen minutes that he didn't know the right move. "Has that happened before?"

Silence.

"Jesus. Fuck." He slapped the steering wheel. "Are you kidding me?"

"Snapping at me won't make a difference," she mumbled.

He'd never felt his heart before, but at that second, he did, and it was shredding. Matt had laid hands on her more than once, and Parker hated coming to terms with knowledge he should've already had.

Finally, she shrugged. "I'm not me with him anymore. Maybe I never was. I shouldn't have put up with it. It's on me."

Parker yanked the steering wheel over and shifted to park. Everything he did with Titan, everything he'd done in his life hadn't prepared him for the anger and helplessness churning deep inside. "I don't know what to say."

"There's nothing to say." She shifted her gaze out the window.

"Why not?"

She looked back, obviously believing whatever she was about to say. "What's the point?"

"So—"

"Can we stop this?" Lexi's face pinched. "It's humiliating,

and I just want to—I wish you hadn't seen that."

"Why?"

Her head hung lower, her eyes closed. "Doesn't matter."

"Does to me."

"It's done. I'm not going back, and he doesn't want me back. End of story. Nothing left to talk about."

The air around them felt thick. The winter sunlight shone through the window, highlighting her softness, making her vulnerabilities stand out. He put the SUV back into drive and maneuvered onto the road. Tension hung between them, and his chest ached. Parker cracked the window, letting a slip of cold air rush against him.

He still had no idea where they were headed, and he wasn't ready to admit that out loud. The thing about Lexi was she was always the one he liked to be around. Yeah, Matt had been his boy since they were kids, but Lex was the fun one. The one with the smile, the one who made him laugh, even if it had been a while.

"Hungry?"

"Kinda." She picked at her nails when he made a turn.

His mind ran the gamut of options. His place wasn't too far. "I'll swing by somewhere, grab some takeout, then you can figure out whatever you want to do along the way."

Parker let off the brake and headed down the street. For being in suburbia, there wasn't a single drive-through. What the hell?

A pizza place's sign caught his attention, and he pulled in. "Pizza?"

"Sure."

He shifted into park. "What do you like on it?"

"Whatever." She studied her fingers knotting and re-knotting.

"Lexi, toppings. What do you want on your pizza?"

She looked up. Her innocent, blood-speckled eyes seemed so surprised that he cared. "I'm not the girl this happens to."

Except she was… and he wanted to rain hell. "But you are hungry, sweetheart."

Her forgotten smile came out for a second then disappeared. "Sausage and banana peppers." Then her cheeks heated, and her eyes dropped. "But cheese is totally fine."

"Sausage and banana peppers?" It was a sliver of the girl he had known before, full of personality and unexpected answers. "Alright then."

"Thanks."

"Hey, does 'bacon' mean anything to you?"

Her color faded. "Oh, crap."

"What?" Maybe he should've kept that to himself. What was it, a code for him finding her, hurting her? "Never mind. Just ignore that."

"I shouldn't have dragged you into this, Parker. I'm really sorry."

Parker cupped a hand over her fidgeting, nervous fingers. The simple touch made electricity shoot up his arms. "If you recall, *I* carried *you* out." She blushed, bringing some of her color back, and that surprised him, adding warmth in his chest to go with the shock of electricity. "Be back in a minute. Okay?"

"Okay." She nodded, and her shoulders shivered before she tried to hide it.

"Warm up." He'd been so fired up from wanting to pummel Matt. It had to be forty degrees outside, and he had the window cracked open. Parker pulled a jacket from the backseat for her, cranked the heat to full blast, then jumped out into the cold.

Sausage and banana peppers. As though she was too lost to realize it was okay to order what she wanted. Maybe he should call Matt and tell him to get his ass off the couch, whether he wanted a fight or not. Parker pushed into the pizza place and bounced on the balls of his shoes as he waited in line to order and pay. *Bacon, bacon, bacon. What the fuck did bacon mean?*

"Ten minutes." The cashier handed him the receipt and change. "They'll call your number when it's ready."

"Thanks." Parker dropped the change into a jar then headed to his Rover to wait.

It was empty. No Lexi.

Concern hit him hard in the gut. Matt? No… right? He pivoted, looking for her. Nothing. Just the sprawl of a shopping center on both sides of the street. Maybe she needed something from the grocery store? Had to hit the bathroom? But she didn't have a purse and would've gone into the pizza place. This didn't make sense.

He walked by a few storefronts. Nothing she would likely go into. A blinds store, a pet food store. Where was she? Parker circled back to his vehicle, and still she was nowhere to be seen. He saw his jacket abandoned on the passenger seat. Finally succumbing to the dread that prickled at him, Parker pulled out his phone and dialed Matt.

"Hey," Matt answered.

"Where is she?"

"Lexi?"

Rage made Parker's muscles bunch. "Yeah, you dickhead."

Matt chuckled. "You told her about Bacon. Nice job. She called from a convenience store. I'm on my way to pick her up."

"Pick her up?" What the fuck had just happened? Parker hustled to his still-running SUV and gunned the engine, pulling out and leaving tracks. "Where?"

"Good looking out for my girl. Thanks, buddy." The call ended.

*His girl*? Parker stared at the blinking screen then looked up and saw the sign for a convenience store. Matt's truck was ahead with Lexi, head down, shoulders slumped, making her way toward it from the wall full of lotto and phone card advertisements.

Parker honked, and her head snapped up. She saw him, *had to have*, but she didn't give him any more acknowledgment as she dragged herself toward Matt's truck and got in the passenger seat. Matt had to have heard him too. The asshole barely waited for her door to shut before he took off. As he passed Parker, Matt stayed facing forward, but his left hand went up, shooting him the bird.

"Fuck you too." Then Parker slammed his fists onto the steering wheel because he didn't know what to do as they drove away.

# CHAPTER NINE

All the threats Lexi had ever heard about Bacon played through her head until she was dizzy with the certainty that her poor pup would be dead on the couch when they arrived home. Matt was mean and growing meaner by the day. He'd even tried to burn Bacon that morning. Where had her mind been when she'd left without the dog? Well, she hadn't been thinking. Breathing had been her problem. Her throat felt as if it had been crushed, and her mind hadn't gone to her dog. What it had gone to was the protection Parker had offered. His arms had surrounded her with a manly scent tinged with the smell of outdoors and gunpowder, like some superhero aphrodisiac.

Yet there she was, without Parker and back with Matt. But she really hadn't *been with* Parker. He had been a ride. A good man who wouldn't stand by when she was crumbled on herself. Parker likely thought she was stupid, and maybe she was. But the idea of leaving her dog alone with her fiancé, when Matt had clearly issued that last warning, was too much. Plus if she really was going to leave, she couldn't just have her savior carry her out the door. She needed her computer and notebooks. They were her livelihood and her evidence—selfies after a rough night or her notes jotted down about what he did and said—if she did ever confront Matt.

Lexi bit her tongue when Matt jumped the curb. They headed home at breakneck speed. She needed to survive until she could get her dog, her stuff, and leave. Her mind slammed into overdrive. What should she do? Say? Matt needed to think she'd been stupid or scared. Something. It was best to start simple. It also needed to start now, in the truck, where they were semi in public. If his hands were on the steering wheel, they wouldn't be on her.

"I'm sorry, Matt."

"Bet you are." Lines furrowed across his forehead and anger tinged his skin red.

"I really am. That got out of control. It was all my fault. I'm sorry."

He glared at her. "I saw your co-worker outside the house, driving away."

What? That was what had started it? She'd had no idea. He had simply had stormed the house and thrown her against the wall. "I promise you, I don't know what you're talking about."

"He was there."

A cold chill ran up her spine. "I never saw him."

"Then I'm pissed you begged Parker to pick you up. Fuckin' slut."

"No." She swallowed her disgust and put her palm on his thigh. "It all happened so fast. I never want to fight with you again."

His hand slapped down on hers, his fingers crushing her bones.

She winced, leaning forward. "Ow, Matt—"

He smashed her fingers together. "You comin' home for me or that mutt?"

"You!"

"You're really sorry?"

Wincing into his hold, she nodded. "Yes, that—ow—that hurts."

"You know how bad it can really hurt. Don't pull that shit again." Then he flung her hand back. "I forgive you, peaches. But your ass will make it up to me."

Her head dropped. "I know."

"Be thinking how."

She ducked her head further, not wanting to think of how he'd expect that kind of repayment. "Okay."

"And, peaches?"

"Yes, baby?" she mumbled.

"You leave me again, no warnings about the mutt. I'll find you and drag your ass home."

# CHAPTER TEN

If there was one thing Parker enjoyed about walking into the Winters's house, it was the food. Mia Winters loved to cook, and Parker loved to eat. So did everyone else on the team. But they had wives and kids and babies on the way, so more often than not, the rest of Titan was well fed when they were home. Parker relied more than he should on Muscle Milk and Power Bars in place of meals. Mia knew that and fed him well. She mama-beared the shit out of him sometimes, and that was a perk of being best buds with Winters.

Judging by the lack of other vehicles outside, he was first there, and that was planned. He needed Mia's opinion on yesterday because he was furious—and worried. After Lexi had gone back with Matt, Parker had headed back to GUNS, then hit his gym and worked out to the point of delirium. Neither activity cleared his mind. So his next step was to talk to Mia, the woman who knew how everything emo worked, because he was choking on a ton of it.

He pushed through the front door that had been left open for the incoming crowd. "Hello? Anyone home?"

"Kitchen," Mia called.

"We're in the kitchen," squeaked a high-pitched, girly voice.

Parker smiled at Clara's repeated words. He rounded the hall and saw the kids before Mia. "Hey, short stack. How's it going?"

"The baby's not listening." Clara's little nose crinkled in annoyance. "He's stealing all my snacks."

Mia popped up from behind the island counter with a pile of platters and set them down. "Don't let Ace have *any* of those cookies."

The evidence was all over Ace's face. He'd had at least one cookie, by evidence of the chocolate smeared from his chin to forehead, and his smile was huge as he reached for more. Parker scooped up the boy before they all got into trouble and headed for the kitchen table.

Mia scowled, grabbing a wet cloth. "Clara. Do not feed your brother any more sugar."

"Sorry, Mama." She set the cookies down and abandoned the adults and her brother in the kitchen.

"Mama Mia, smells good in here." He gave Mia a kiss on her cheek. "You're too good to us."

"I know it." With expert finesse, she wiped all of the smudges off Ace before the kid could think to scream, then she headed to what smelled like a giant vat of chili and a couple other pots. "Speaking of which, you want a beer?"

"Sounds good." He popped up and headed to the fridge to get it before Mia could move. "Where's Winters?"

"Out in the garage. You're here earlier than I expected—" She stopped stirring whatever. "Nothing you do is ever accidental."

His muscles went tight as he thought about yesterday's shit storm. "Nope."

She put her hands on her hips. The woman was petite, but she didn't mess around. "And you're not heading to the garage."

He shook his head. "Nope."

"Alright. Spit it out before the troops storm the spread."

Still holding Ace, Parker walked over to eye the food. "You know Matt Pindon?"

"You've brought him around before. Isn't he going to be here today?"

"I doubt it."

"Why?"

"I saw him wrap his hands around his woman's throat."

Mia turned off the burner. "Sit down."

He smiled because when Mia got all bossy-therapist, good usually came of it. "Yes, ma'am."

She wiped her hands and sat across from him before taking

Ace into her lap. "Start over. What are you talking about?"

"I walked in on them fighting yesterday. No joke, he was choking her. I pulled them apart. She left with me but went back home to him."

"She went back to him?"

He nodded. His fury at Lexi for pulling that stunt just killed him. He'd had every intention of bringing her and a sausage-and-banana-pepper pizza home with *him*. Then what, who knew. But damn it, he liked her being in his arms, amplifying how much he'd liked her from afar.

"Is she safe?" Mia asked.

"I don't know." The doubt made him sick. Not knowing the answer to a question wasn't something Parker was familiar with. He always knew what he wanted to know or knew a way to determine it. He could assign a value to a situation, do a risk assessment. But this Lexi situation—he didn't know what she thought or if she was safe. It made him feel as though he were bursting out of his skin. He wanted to call her, yell at her for being stupid and question her so it made sense.

Mia's eyes focused on him, and Parker swore she could read his soul. "Who is she to you?"

"Matt's fiancée."

"*To you*, Parker. A friend?" Her eyebrows raised.

"I don't think I know her well enough that I'd say friend." But somehow he'd had eyes on her since she first walked into Matt's life.

"But?"

His thoughts had been semi-easy to ignore until yesterday, and now he couldn't stop replaying every stolen look, every questionable action, the way she'd gone from the wild woman Matt brought out on occasion to a toned-down version of a Stepford wife. Parker jumped out of his chair. "I don't get this."

"Get what?"

"It's—" His chest twisted. "Personal."

"I can see that. So why?"

"She's a good person and doesn't deserve that shit."

"No one deserves that, Parker."

"I know. It's—I just like her." He shrugged. "She deserves

better than that."

"You have feelings for her."

"Come on, Mia. I'm not here to talk about what *I* feel or whatever. I'm worried about a girl who—" A girl he'd been feeling deeply, who always made him curious, who even made him feel guilty. He dropped back into the chair. "I care about what happens to her. What do I do?"

"You have a conversation with her. You make sure she gets to a safe place, and you ask her if she values her safety. If she knows her self-worth. Then you hold her hand—"

His eyes shot open. "Whoa now." Even though he vividly remembered placing his hands over hers in his car and the sense of calm that had washed over her sweet face.

"*Figuratively*, and help her realize that she is worth more than that."

Parker leaned his elbows on the table and buried his head in his hands. Behind him, Winters's boots came down the hall.

His hand slapped Parker's back. "What's up, boy genius?"

Parker rubbed his eyes and pushed back. "Matt's *persona non grata* for anything Titan."

Winters held his eye. "Alright. Won't be allowed in this house."

"Alright."

"Want to let me in on what's going on?"

Parker was closer to Winters than anyone else in or out of Titan. Winters had spent his share of time with Matt and never liked the guy, but he didn't say much. Old friends were old friends. That was the way things went. Winters and Parker had a much different relationship. They saw eye to eye on most jobs and were a tactical yin and yang. Winters would blow things up and could escape almost any situation, given enough brute force. Parker preferred the analytical, strategic planning side of operations. Either way, they trained together, tested together, stayed in shape and sharp on weapons together. But letting anyone besides Mia the psychologist in on Lexi's issues was too personal.

"Later," Parker said.

Winters looked at Mia then back at Parker before picking up Ace. "Alright, later."

Clara ran back into the kitchen. "Cash is here."

Which meant a very pregnant Nicola would be inside in a minute. Soon she would be followed by Roman and a pregnant Beth, then Jared and a pregnant Sugar. So many pregnant women, it was almost scary. Parker had never had anything like that—babies, uncles, aunts, all that family stuff. They were like a living, breathing security blanket.

Mia, maybe thinking the same thing, moved back to the stove. "We'll talk more later. Okay?"

"Yup. Appreciate it."

She nodded. "Not sure you know this, honey, but you're allowed to color outside the lines if you want."

He chuckled because that was something he'd never do, and the statement, much like every Lexi-focused thought, didn't make sense. "I don't know what that means, Mia."

"One day, it might make sense."

"Maybe." Parker sat back in his chair and watched everyone come in.

So much had changed since Mia Winters started having big meals after Titan came home from jobs. The guys used to all get together, have a bonfire, and barbecue whatever was around. They still did that, though maybe not in forty-degree rainy weather. But now serious love was put into the food. That was a difference.

Another knock sounded on the door before it opened down the hall. "We're here."

Rocco walked in with Caterina tucked under his arm. Squeezed between them was a bundle of blankets. Parker watched the room ooh and ahh over the new baby. None of the Delta guys were there yet—no guests outside of Titan had arrived—so he was literally the only single guy in the room. It was just their core group, and while he wanted to be there, he suddenly couldn't stop wondering what in the world Lexi Dare was up to and if she was okay.

# CHAPTER ELEVEN

Lexi trembled as Matt guided her into the house with his hand on the small of her back. She didn't know what to expect, but whatever his punishment for her was, it would be the worst yet. But as soon as her feet hit the carpet, nothing.

She wanted to run and find Bacon, but she also didn't want to remind Matt how much she loved her dog. So she sat on the couch and watched him go about normal everyday life. Still nothing in terms of her punishment happened.

Bacon ran over to Lexi. She scooped the dog up and cuddled all the pug's squirmy rolls, but Lexi kept her eyes on Matt. Maybe it was a mind game. He'd told her to think of her own punishment. Maybe this was part of that.

She squeezed Bacon tighter and whispered, "I'll never let him hurt you."

Matt reappeared with a beer and threw himself on the couch with her. "Sorry, peaches."

Her heart stilled. She didn't know if this was a test. She clung to her dog, uncertain how to respond. "You don't have to say that."

He took a swig off his beer. "Serious. I fucked up. Shouldn't have done that—though you shouldn't have put me in a place where I lost control. Maybe that car I saw wasn't what I thought. But…" He shrugged and slugged back more beer. "But I didn't mean for that to happen."

"Okay," she whispered.

"C'mere."

Terrified, she inched across the couch and had to put Bacon down when the pup growled. Lexi perched against his chest like she knew he liked, and Matt tossed his arm over her shoulder and settled in to channel surf as if he hadn't choked her earlier and she hadn't run away with his friend. They watched TV until her stomach growled. Her mind went back to the pizza place, where Parker had ordered what she wanted without comment or question.

"You hungry, peaches?"

Lexi bit her lip. "I'll start something. Sorry—"

"No, I got it. Just relax. You've had a hard day."

She'd had a hard day? Because he'd choked her the day after he'd had sex with her when she hadn't been a willing participant. "Matt, it's not—"

"Sit," he growled. "See, there. Why do you have to bring out the worst in me sometimes?"

"I'm sorry."

He kissed the top of her head. "How's spaghetti sound?"

"Really great." She nodded enthusiastically, hoping to cover her confusion.

"Good answer." Matt pushed off the couch and headed toward the kitchen. It was a semi-open floor plan, and she saw him putter around the pantry.

Over the next three nights, he made dinner, not letting her out of his eyesight except for very quick errands. It was confusing, and his condescending jabs were sandwiched between compliments. None of it made sense. He bought her flowers. He said he loved her. He did things that should've been sweet, but all they did was muddy the waters. She wanted to leave. She wasn't in love, but every time she blinked at his words or responded too slow, Matt gave her lines that tied her down.

*"I'd never leave you, peaches. Just like you'd never dare leave me."*

*"Lexi, if you tried harder, last weekend would never have happened like that."*

*"I know you better than you know yourself, peaches."*

And she couldn't forget… *"It would be awful if something happened to Bacon, wouldn't it?"*

Everything he said reeked of manipulation, but she couldn't entirely disregard the attention, the promises of love and to never be abandoned. She seriously needed a break. Just a breather, a few hours where Matt wasn't watching her work or commenting about everything.

Facts of life dictated that Matt would have to leave her alone eventually. He had a new job lined up. She was counting down the days until he started. But while he had her on his hyper-vigilant crackdown, she was able to work through the last details that Shadow needed for Monarch. It also let her map out ways she could disappear so that if Matt hunted her down, she and Bacon would be far off the grid and unfindable. Interesting how she could find or hide anything on screen, but when it came to *her*, she didn't know what to do. She didn't even have her own transportation. Well, until she got her Gixxer back—how would that work with a dog? If it came to running, she'd figure it out. All part of the recover-Lexi plan.

Finally, it was the day. Matt had a new job, and it was still too early for him to get himself fired.

She sent Shadow some of what he needed and nervously putted around the house, psyching herself up to leave. Despite the days of Matt being semi-nice, she knew deep in her heart that even his nice words were caked with lies. Her bag was packed with a change of clothes, cash he didn't know about, a roll of crackers, a jar of peanut butter, and dog food. She planned to take the bus to her sister's, camp out there for the night, and disappear until she had to meet up with Shadow in about two weeks for the auction.

So far, Operation Get the Fuck Out was going well, despite the churning, guilty-excited nausea rolling in her belly. Even Bacon knew it was go-day. The pup never left her side.

She called Meredith, but there was no answer. The voicemail beeped, and she sighed. "Hey, Mere, sorry to leave this as a message. We need to catch up soon. I'm changing things for the better. Call me. I love you. And, Mere, I really miss you."

Ending the call, she checked the screen. The clock flashed two o'clock. Matt would be at work for another couple of hours. If Lexi was on her normal schedule, she would've worked at the dining room table until she had to start dinner. Just like the perfect soon-to-be Mrs. Pindon.

She looked at her trembling hands. "Just walk out the door."

Bacon yapped in agreement.

It was so close. Just feet away. Her escape that could change everything. Freedom tickled her tongue, making her blood rush with the excitement and anxiousness of the unknown. Lexi swallowed the last of her self-doubt and squared her shoulders. Of all days, today was the anniversary of their first date. How ironic and appropriate. She grabbed her bag and laptop and headed to the door with Bacon on a leash.

But it opened when she was still feet away.

*Matt.*

Her stomach dropped. Panic rushed through her veins.

"Happy anniversary." He smiled at her, then his gaze drifted. "What's going on, peaches?"

"Hey." She tried for a smile but knew it didn't ring true. Faking it when so much uncertainty ran in her blood was near impossible. "Happy—" Her throat knotted. "Anniversary, baby."

"I wanted to surprise you. I left work *for you*."

"Awesome." Bullshit. He'd been fired again. And on day one? God. What now? Please don't let it be drinking…

His gaze locked on her bag. "What's in there?"

"Nothing." She took a step back as he took one forward. The scent of beer finally hit her. "I was headed to the grocery store."

"With Bacon and your laptop?"

"We needed some air. I was going to work outside." Waiting until the afternoon seemed like the stupidest move she'd ever made. "It's nothing."

She tossed aside her bag and casually dropped her laptop's bag. She needed to distract him. An anniversary hug. Or a blow job. Something. Anything. That was her new, quickly made plan.

She stepped forward. "Glad you're home." She put as much sexiness into her voice as possible. "We can celebrate."

"Open the bag, peaches."

Lexi stepped toward him. "That thing? Why don't I show you—"

*Smack.* The back of his hand hit across her face. Blood

seeped into her mouth as Bacon growled and attacked Matt's leg. He kicked her dog, making the poor thing squeal. If Lexi hadn't been numbly shocked, she would have screamed. Matt reached for the dog and hooked Lexi as she tried to run for the door.

"You're on the couch—" He threw her down then stormed to the front door. "And you're gone." He tossed her dog, leash still on, out the front door, and slammed it. "Why do you make me do this?"

All she could think about was the bag. If he looked in it, she really would be dead this time. Lexi closed her eyes and waited for him to beat her until she blacked out.

# CHAPTER TWELVE

Parker rubbed his eyes as he stared at the screens. The past few days, he'd run through his normal schedule but felt like a shell. Nothing much was happening, but he still liked to keep an eye on the Titan teams around the globe. Tossing a pen and ignoring his nearly all-consuming concern over Lexi, he flipped from screen to screen, doing absolutely nothing.

His cell phone rang, stealing his attention from the uninteresting screens, and he didn't recognize the number. His thumb hovered over the button. For a brief second, he hoped it was either Lexi calling to explain or Jared with something to take Parker's mind off everything. He accepted the call. "Hello?"

Nothing.

He checked the screen. The number wasn't ringing a bell, and he remembered almost every phone number he'd ever seen. The line was still live. He tried again. "Hello?"

"Can you help me?"

The familiar voice was a sucker punch to his stomach. Lexi's barely audible, tear-soaked whisper nearly leveled him.

"Lex?" He never should have let her get in that truck. He should've gone back to their house and done something. Anything. All his fury and anger was gone, his protective thoughts making his muscles twitch to get to her. "Lexi, where are you?"

"Please." She sniffled. "There's no one else I could ask." Her voice shook. "Please."

"Where are you?" But his fingers were already flying across the keyboard, calling up a program that would triangulate then pinpoint her exact location. The coordinates flashed on screen, and his heart jumped. She was calling from *his* home address.

Her phone cut off before she could respond. Parker ran out of Titan HQ and jumped in his Range Rover, bypassing anyone who asked what the hell was going on. When he pulled out of the parking garage, sleeting rain hit his windshield, and wind whipped his SUV. His mind processed a thousand questions that spider-webbed from a few basics. Why was she at his house, and where was Matt? He punched redial on his cell, but it went to voicemail.

*Hey, it's Lexi. Leave a message.*

"I'll be there in ten." He coasted through lights, blew past the speed limit, used the shoulders, and when he finally hit his street, he floored it. Parker yanked the steering wheel, sliding into the driveway. In the whipping sleet, Lexi, without a jacket, sat on the front stoop of his house. Her dripping hair hung over her face, and she hunched over a package while cradling Fatso the dog. It took him a micro-second to snap out of his terror-fueled trance, and he moved fast.

"You okay?" No. Fuck. No, she wasn't. "Goddamn it."

The little dog growled and yapped and squirmed to kill him. Parker worked fast to open his door. He twisted the key, punched in the code, and disarmed the anti-asshole sensors as the biting rain slapped down. The rain howled as he quickly crouched in her line of sight. Lexi was doubled over, and her face was swollen. He grabbed her and the dog, dragging them, dripping, over the threshold. Her frozen body shook and trembled against him. There wasn't time to ask how she'd gotten his phone number or if Matt had dropped her there like that.

A quick assessment said she'd been knocked around, and that was just what he could see on her face. The blue tinge of her lips didn't help the bruises he saw on her cheeks. "Do you need to go to the hospital?"

She shifted her head slightly, barely signaling no. He went to touch her, and Fatso went berserk.

"Easy, Bacon," she whispered.

Fatso was Bacon? Made more sense but still… water poured off of her, and her hair stuck to her face. She clung desperately to whatever that was in her arms.

"We need to warm you up. Get you guys dried off. Let's go."

She nodded. Her gaze finally shifted up, and he saw that her eyes were sob-and-slap swollen. There was blood on her shirt, as if her nose or mouth had been bleeding. The rain must've washed the evidence off her skin. He couldn't tell what was blue from cold and what was just bruised.

Without thinking, he took the heavy, flat, plastic-wrapped bag from her hand, set it on the floor, and wrapped her in his arms, holding her so that he could breathe. The dog whimpered, and Lexi stiffened before she relaxed into his hug.

He apologized in murmurs but didn't let go, running his hands over her soaked back. "I shouldn't have let you go with him."

Her frail shoulders bunched, but she didn't speak.

"Come on, Lex."

"Wait." The faintness in her voice sounded like she looked. Weak, water-soaked, and wary.

"Yeah?"

"I need to—that's my computer." Her teeth chattered so hard, the words were barely intelligible. "I need—to make sure—it didn't get wet."

He blinked. If there was anyone who would get that, it was him, but that she'd said it caught him off guard. "Okay."

Lexi peeled the plastic away with bluish, shivering hands and displayed a computer bag. She popped it open and smoothed her hand over a nice piece of equipment. He got why she didn't want rain to touch it, but what he didn't get was why she had something so high-functioning. It wasn't for normal use. But that didn't matter at the moment.

"It's the most important thing I own," she said as though reading his mind.

Interesting and curious. "You're both still freezing. Let's go."

Parker tucked her against him, his eyes staying on the computer for a half second before her cold, tense body brought his focus back to her. She leaned against him, and he moved them toward the hall bathroom then thought of the one in his bedroom. A steam shower. Heated floor. The water could rain down, and he could make that room cook like a sauna.

"Just a little farther." He pushed through his bedroom and into the bathroom before setting her on the edge of a large soaking tub he'd never used. Bacon curled and shivered at her feet. "Shower or bath?"

Her mouth opened, but the chattering teeth seemed to be the only thing she could do.

"Shower's faster." He twisted the water on, turned it for steam, and hit every switch in the room to make the bathroom as warm as quickly as he could. He turned to her, suddenly unsure of the next move. "Can you... are you okay? To do this?"

"Yes." But her hands covered her face.

Shit. "Lex." He dropped in front of her again. Seemed as though he'd done that too many times recently, always trying to make sure she was okay. If he'd done the right thing the first time, none of these other times would have happened. "What's the matter?"

"This is so embarrassing," she whispered.

Her scratchy voice was broken, and it dug into his chest. Steam billowed around the room, but still, he couldn't move from her. He wanted desperately to make this right. Carefully, he touched her cheek. Well, almost. He didn't touch her, but he could practically feel her skin. "I'm sorry I let this happen to you."

"You didn't." She shook her head, letting her hair tangle with his fingers.

"Oh, sweetheart." Slowly, he rubbed a few wet strands between his thumb and forefinger then tucked it behind her ear. He pulled back, found some towels, and rubbed her dog dry while she watched. "I'll throw some clothes in here."

"You don't have to do that."

"Both of you are cold. Shower for you. Towels for him."

"Her," she corrected. "That's Bacon Byte."

Parker rolled his lips into his mouth to keep from smiling. Much cuter name than Fatso.

"No, it's okay. You can laugh." She shrugged. "She's pudgy."

"Alright, Bacon. Dry enough?" He tossed the wet dog towels into the corner as Bacon tentatively sniffed his knuckles then licked his hand. When Bacon had been with him and Matt at GUNS, the dog acted semi-uninterested in him though she had avoided Matt. But different environment, different dog. "I think she likes me."

"She's smart. I rescued her. She needed some looking out for—so I couldn't leave her with him. The going back thing… I know it sounds stupid, but she's helped me. I couldn't leave her."

Parker pushed off the ground and studied her. She had bruises on her cheeks and forehead, yet she was still the most beautiful thing he'd ever seen. "There were other ways to help your dog."

"I know." She bit her lip. "I panicked. Matt said if I ever left, he'd kill Bacon."

"What the fuck," Parker grumbled.

Bacon barked.

"Thanks, Parker." The warm room had faded the blueish tint on her skin. "I'm sorry I came here. I just…"

"I'm glad you did."

Her eyes locked on his. It was the absolute wrong time to feel his heartbeat, but when she cast those icy blue eyes at him, the ground fell away. He cleared his throat and turned, not allowing himself a glance back. Anger and guilt warred for prominence, along with a fierce need to hold her and physically warm her body. Shit. He rubbed his face as he slipped out the door.

Standing in his bedroom, listening to the shower run, he thought back to Mia's words. *Coloring outside the lines.* Everything he did had order, but the woman making his heart pound? She was messy and complicated. She was broken, and he didn't know the first thing about mending hurts. Work was the only thing he knew. But Lexi, who was likely stripping at that very moment, made him want something he was incapable of. Suddenly Mia's word made sense in a way that confused him. He wanted what he couldn't, shouldn't, and absolutely wouldn't have. A broken woman needed more love and attention than he knew how to give.

# CHAPTER THIRTEEN

That second Lexi was probably crawling under the hot spray of his shower. Emotionally, he didn't have that component that made him swoon and stutter over women. Maybe a blessing, not necessarily a curse, but Parker saw the world analytically. That equated to sex being sex and dates being something to do, but none of it had ever given him "the feels." If logic couldn't be applied to a situation, he likely wasn't interested. Relationships weren't logical, which was why, until that point, he'd been more than happy for simple and no-strings.

"Shit," he blew out as he paced at the foot of his bed.

Out of every person in the world, Lexi had reached to him, and now he needed to find her clothes to change into while she lathered in his soap and shampoo. Okay. Clothes first, then he needed a drink. Anything to calm his shit down. Quickly, he ran through his drawers and pulled out a T-shirt, sweatshirt, and sweatpants.

Those in hand, he knocked and called through the closed bathroom door, "Can I throw these in?"

"Sure. Thanks." Her quiet voice was muffled by the shower, as though she'd spoken through the streams of water.

"Incoming." He cracked opened the door and tossed the clothes.

For a split second, his mind questioned taking a glance, an accidental slip of the eye, just to see the water and suds pouring down the swell of her breasts, the slide of her flat stomach, and endless slope of her legs. Then his deviant mind made him feel like a pervert, and he cringed. He beelined for the kitchen, mumbling at himself to get it together. Sporting wood over a battered girl who'd asked for help was about as responsible as it was intelligent.

He pulled out a bottle of bourbon and a shot glass and made quick work of throwing down a drink. The burn in his throat alleviated some of the pressure, but Parker still let out a curse. He didn't need liquid courage. What he needed was an impenetrable shield.

His phone rang, and Parker glanced at the screen. Not Jared as he would've expected. Winters. Maybe he should've expected that more than Boss Man. Running out of the office as though he knew where the promised land was would likely raise some eyebrows.

He swiped the screen to answer. "Hey."

"What was all that earlier?" Winters asked. "Your ass ran out of the office like it was two-for-one day at Spy Depot."

Parker rubbed his hair. He couldn't put into words what he assumed had happened to Lexi—Matt had hurt her because Parker had interfered in their lives. Remorse for not fighting for her flooded his system. "I'm at home. I had to"—*protect, save, find*—"help Lexi with a couple things."

"Lexi Dare?"

"Yeah. She needed me."

"I bet." Winters laughed, but it quickly died down. "This have something to do with you spouting shit about Matt being *persona non grata* at my place?"

"Yeah—" The shower shut off. Despite the shot of bourbon and the call from Winters, Parker couldn't have been more aware that she was naked and nearby. "You calling for work?"

"No." Winters chuckled again.

"Alright. Get you back later then." He didn't wait for him to respond. Parker pocketed the phone and hung onto the counter. Literally, he clung to it as though he needed an anchor. His fingers flexed into the granite as he ordered himself to pull his shit together. He was furious. Wanted to find Matt and end him. Tear him apart limb by limb. God, he wanted to rant at Lexi for going back, then he was struck by a worry that she'd run home again. "Fuck."

Her footsteps, followed by the click of the dog collar, came toward him. He was no more ready to see her than he was five minutes earlier. Hell, he was worse off.

"Hi."

Parker pivoted to see Lex swallowed by his sweats, and that did something to him. All his anger at Matt paused as Parker's mind jumped to what was underneath his clothes. Or not underneath. Her clothing-covered breasts swayed as she came to a stop, their peaks making him dizzy with thoughts of sliding his hands over her just-dried stomach and roaming north. He gripped the edge of the counter even tighter as the pinch in his chest and the rush of blood to his cock made him equal parts asshole and aroused.

"You can't go back to him, Lex."

She nodded. "I know."

"You did before." And his mind wanted to explode over that.

"Yeah. That was a mistake."

"I'm going to kill him, you know that? It's taking everything I have just to stay here."

"Please don't. I want to forget all of that ever happened." Her towel-dried hair hung around her face, torturing his fingers. "I never wanted to make you mad. Apparently that's what I do really well though."

"What?"

"Make men mad." Her head turned down.

Shit. "No, sweetheart." He stepped toward her and instinctively pulled her to his chest, dying inside at how good it felt to hold her. "I'm not mad like that, like him. I… hated that you went back to a bad situation."

He gave her a light squeeze then released her, realizing that he couldn't cling to her for no reason. They were barely friends and whatever comforting excuse he had to hug her didn't give him permission to just hold her. His arms wanted to stay around her body though. Parker swallowed away that addictive feeling. He even tried to tamper his desire to obliterate her asshole ex, though he was curious why Matt would have left her on his door step or even given her Parker's number. Maybe it was Matt's way of saying Parker was to blame for the bruises? All over again, he wanted to avenge every mark on her beautiful body. Instead, he moved back to the counter and clamped his hands on that.

She tugged at a strand of damp hair. “Thanks for the clothes.” A quiet laugh spilled from her lips. “Hot, ugh. I’m such a mess.”

Hot in a way that made him hang tighter to the countertop. If he wasn’t careful, his bones would shatter from the force. “Nothing wrong with how you look, sweetheart.”

She blinked. He stared.

This was wrong. So very wrong.

She needed space and a therapist. She needed *Mia*. There shouldn’t have been any tension between them. But the thick air and the sparks pounding at his pulse points hit him strongly. He didn’t feel as though she needed counseling and a change of scenery. He felt as if she needed *him* in a way that was much more than a place to hide.

Which was why he had to go. He pushed back from the granite, heading to the fridge for no other reason than it was something to do.

“I know I owe you more of an explanation for showing up like I did, for dragging you into this twice.” She scrunched the hanging hem of his sweatshirt and nervously played with it. As she did, a line of creamy skin showed on her stomach, where his sweatpants hung, rolled on her slender hips, reminding him how bare she was underneath and how those pants were a touch away from sliding down.

Parker sucked down a breath. “I have questions.” That was putting it mildly. “I know people who can help you. I can help you. I… want…”—*you*—“to help you.” Bacon rolled over at his feet, and he realized how deep his voice had gone, how much he felt in those words. “Tell me anything you need. It’s yours.”

She licked her lips then looked down the hall. “Can I throw my clothes in your dryer?”

“As long as you don’t get redressed in them and leave without a word.”

“I won’t. Do you maybe have a hair brush or something? A girlfriend’s? Or…”

He shook his head. “No girlfriend. No brush. But there’s a comb in the top drawer by the sink.”

She bit her lip and ducked her head. "Thanks."

As she turned, he couldn't help himself. "Lex."

She stopped, raising her eyebrows. Her porcelain skin was marred by bruises and a pink hint on her cheeks.

"I'm glad you called me."

They stayed staring at each other as though there was so much more to say. "Glad you answered."

Lexi padded out of the room, leaving him to drink in a long breath and watch the clock on the microwave. One minute passed, and it felt like an eternity. Anxiety barreled through him. He paced then took out his phone and dialed Winters.

Winters answered on the first ring as though he'd been expecting the call. "Hey, buddy. Calling back so soon?"

Parker had no idea what to say or where to start. All he knew was that Winters, more or less, got shit like this and probably already knew Parker was neck-deep in Lex. "It's wrong, right, man?"

Winters chuckled. "That woman's good-looking. But she's also engaged, *right*?"

"I hope like fuck not."

"Then why are you calling me like I'm your AA sponsor?"

"I have no idea. She needs something I have no idea how to give."

More laughter. "Man, you are in over your head, aren't you?"

"I'm never in over my head, jackass," Parker snapped. "Except, maybe."

"You gonna enlighten me about all that *persona non grata* shit?"

"Not my place to share." He leaned against the wall, pressing his forehead against it and wanting to slam his head, but waited for Winters.

"Do you have a woman in your life that you'd hurt if you hung out with Lexi?"

"You already know that answer."

"Right," Winters grumbled. "I'm playing you right now, you get that? I'm running through your stupid-ass checklists and trying to figure out what your risks are."

Shit… he thumped his forehead against the wall. The

situation was literally driving him to beat his head against the wall.

"Your boy Matt?" Winters's voice dropped low and sounded angry. "From what I saw between them, I don't think she mattered to the guy. He was out for fun; she was his trophy. Like a possession. He never looked at her the way I've seen you—"

"I didn't—"

"Just shut up and listen, Parker. I don't have the details, but going by my few interactions with him and her, I'm guessing he crossed a line. He's a dick. He would."

"A line was definitely crossed."

"And if you're worried about some kind of code when he didn't respect his woman? That'd be enough for me to say you have nothing to worry about."

Parker mulled over all the truth that Winters had just thrown down. "Probably right. But that's not my hesitation. She's... been hurt."

"This is the thing. You have to get over your right-wrong, nothing-in-between mindset. Let that computer brain of yours take a vacation." Winters waited a two-count before continuing. "And no matter what situation you're in, *you* won't hurt her."

"I think she's in a bad place."

"Alright then. People get in bad spots. They also get out of them with the help of people they trust."

"Right." Maybe. Was he that guy? More than that, he *wanted* to be that guy for Lex.

"Matt wasn't a winner to begin with—though the asshole could put on a good show—and he has done nothing but gone downhill. But her? She's a good one."

"She is." Parker pulled his forehead off the wall a half inch then dropped it back.

"She is what?" whispered from behind him.

*Lexi.*

His eyes pinched tight. "Catch you later." He hung up on Winters without another word and pocketed the phone before slowly turning to take her in.

Her arms were crossed, and her hair was twisted into a

messy knot on top of her head. Strands of nearly dry blond hair framed her face. The woman looked like a broken angel.

"Hey," he said.

An angel who was pissed, hurt, and confused all at once. "She is what?"

He said nothing as he mapped out the words he wanted to say and weighed them against what she might want to hear. Not that he would make up a lie for her benefit, but maybe there was a filter he could use. Damn it, he had no idea which direction to go.

*She is... here. Sweet. Scared. Beaten and engaged?*

"Parker?"

*She is the single most distracting thing I've ever experienced.*

Her eyes flashed to frightened, and her pink lips pulled into a frown. "If you just told Matt I was here..."

"Are you kidding me?" But that was his confirmation that Matt hadn't dropped her there with Parker's number. So how did she end up on his steps? "I didn't call Matt. What kind of dick do you think I am?"

"I can leave. I didn't need to bother you, burden you—Bacon, where are you? We need to go." Her hands went over her face then she dropped them hard. "I shouldn't have—"

"Stop." The walls were closing in. He needed to shout that she was safe, make a case that she shouldn't leave. Damn, what he really needed was to crush her body to his and kiss her mouth to shut down the wild distrust. But instead, Parker crossed his arms, trying to get a hold of his reactions. "Lex—"

"She is *what?*" Lexi yelled, exasperated and distrusting.

And that was it. Her begging, pleading for something that she already should know.

"She is *fuckin' gorgeous.*"

# CHAPTER FOURTEEN

There it was. The God's honest truth, and the more Parker looked at her—those sweet lips parting and a blush hitting her fair skin—the more he wouldn't back away from the statement. But just because he'd said the words didn't change the circumstances. She was in a bad place, and he was consumed by the possessive need flaring in his chest.

Lexi didn't say a word.

She didn't step away.

Nothing that needed to happen was happening. Instead, her gaze locked on his, and a hunger he couldn't get a grip on beat in his blood. He worked his jaw, feeling the tendons flex in his neck.

"So there it is, sweetheart, and now I have to go… do something." Because saying he needed to back away from her was just rude, and he couldn't stay in this staring contest. The stakes were too high. If she ran from him, it'd be a gut-shot, hurting more than it should. If he stayed, every part of his body would want to press against hers, to walk her across the room and take her against the wall.

"You think I'm gorgeous?" Her icy blue eyes darkened, as though her body was silently begging for more.

He silently laughed, shaking his head in disbelief. "Lex, the whole world thinks you're gorgeous."

Her lips rounded into an unsure O.

Parker lifted his chin, a quiet gesture to say good-bye, and turned. Leaving was the right thing to do even if it was the only thing he didn't want to do. "You can have the whole run of the place. I'll be in—"

"Two years," she said to his back, "I spent with Matt."

He dropped his head and ran a hand over the back of his neck. He had no idea what she was going to say, and he wished to hell the sound of her voice wasn't quickly becoming an addiction.

"I didn't have a family, and I bounced from foster house to foster house. When we met, he just… took over, almost parenting me, telling me what to do… I thought he was assertive, but he really wasn't. He was weak and narcissistic. Matt was an asshole who didn't want me to be me, and I let that happen."

Parker turned, almost seeing himself for a moment. Except he'd let go of anything that could hurt him as he bounced between foster homes. He'd latched on to the methodical side of his brain, forgetting how it felt to feel lost and unwanted. Forgetting how to feel in general—except that was all he'd done with her recently.

Lexi rolled her lip before continuing. "I saw it coming, which just shows how stupid *I* am. I thought I was protecting myself. I thought it would change when really all I wanted was a person to lean on. To know he'd be there. Because I've never had that, and I was so hungry for it, I took the bad kind of being there rather than have nothing at all."

For all the things he wanted to do to her body, his arms ached to hug her. Hold her. "Sweetheart—"

"I moved through the stages, hoping things would magically change, but they just got worse. I clung to the idea that it was okay because he loved me."

Parker swallowed against the pain in his throat. "A guy touches you like that, he doesn't love you."

"I know. The thing is, *I* didn't love *him*."

Thank fuck for that. But an uncomfortable moment hung between them.

Her fingers fidgeted until she sighed. "So thanks for letting me get my head on straight. I'll be out of your hair after a couple of calls."

He stepped forward, frowning. "Again, I didn't say you had to leave."

"I know."

Then one more step closer. "I don't *want* you to leave."

She blinked, uncertainty in her eyes.

Shit, wrong thing to say. Right? That was that look? He'd just told a woman who had been scared to leave her fiancé not to leave.

Parker rubbed his temples, too damn worried about screwing up—whatever was happening. "Until you're ready. Plan your next move. You're safe here. I've got this place on lock down, with enough security to slow down a hostile takeover, much less a drunk piece of crap like Matt. Scour the fridge. We'll find Bacon some food. Order in, whatever. Stay here until you're ready."

"Why did I have to meet him?" she whispered.

If she hadn't, he never would've set eyes on her, so was this one of those "things happened for a reason" situations? That was a fucked-up thought. He was so far out of his comfort zone that he didn't know what he even wanted to say. "I'm not the guy who's good at… *this*." See, he didn't even know what to call whatever this was.

"At what?"

He scrubbed a hand over his face. "I am what I do. Risk analysis, situational quantification. Ones and zeroes. Code. Cold, lifeless facts. You're fragile and hurt and probably filled with I don't even know what. Feelings. Whatever. I have zero experience with anything you need right now."

"God, that's ironic." A sad smile crept across her face. Lexi tugged at the sweatshirt with his alma mater's insignia. "MIT? I saw your desk, that office in your bedroom. The technology in this place is sick."

Her words made no sense as to why what she'd noted was important. "Computers are my thing."

She laughed quietly. "Damn."

"What are you talking about, Lex?"

"Nothing." She took a deep breath. "You said I was pretty—"

"No, sweetheart. I said you were gorgeous."

The pink on her cheeks intensified, and God, he liked making that happen.

"Gorgeous," she repeated. "No one's said that in a long

time."

Parker shifted, wishing he could fix that. "You deserve better."

Tears welled in her eyes, and emotions scraped through his chest, leaving jagged questions ripping through him.

"Parker…"

"Yeah?" He swallowed the knot in his throat.

"This is going to sound *so* damn stupid."

No stupider than every at-odds thought in his head. "Try me."

"Can I have—can you just hug me?"

And… he… was… *done*.

# CHAPTER FIFTEEN

An explosion of excitement raced through Lexi's body. The tips of her ears tingled all the way to the bottoms of her bare feet. She could breathe with Parker, could feel alive and that unattainable, so-missed feeling of her body sizzling under the intense, smoldering scrutiny of the man she couldn't close her eyes without seeing.

Lexi wouldn't give him the chance to back away. What she wanted more than another breath was to fold her body into his arms. She was just that damn hungry for a human connection. A *male* connection.

For Parker.

A hug sounded simple, but she knew that with as much as was written in his eyes, the intimate embrace would be anything but. He hadn't granted permission, but she didn't care and moved closer anyway. Lexi pressed her cheek against the hard muscle in his chest. She fit in that spot as if their bodies were meant to mesh, and a sigh unlike any sound of happiness she could remember slipped free of her lips.

He breathed her name, and if she could have melted into him, it would've happened at that sound. Slowly, one of his heavy arms wrapped around her back, then the other, as though he were binding himself to her. His chin touched the top of her head, and she closed her eyes, shutting out the world outside his hug. Parker smelled peppery. That same scent had scored itself into her memory when he carried her from her house into his SUV. It was mouth-watering and masculine, and the solid *thump, thump, thump* of his heartbeat in her ear put her into a trance.

She had no idea how long they stood there. Maybe she even fell asleep, standing in his arms, feeling safe and herself. He didn't waver, didn't ask her to let go and give him a little room. Nothing. He was her rock. The start of a new day. Maybe a new life. That was a lot to put on someone who hesitated to hug her, but truth was, he was her catalyst. No matter what came of it, he'd always have a place in her heart for setting her free.

After time slipped by, Lexi stepped back to cast her eyes up. "Thanks. Guess I needed that."

"Me too," he whispered, his arms still locked behind her.

She leaned into his hold, enjoying the warmth that went beyond skin-deep. "Why?"

"I don't have a single answer that is… appropriate."

A shiver fell across her skin and slid down her spine. The earnest look in his eyes was real. Raw. It had a depth that she couldn't understand yet completely accepted.

Parker released one arm and cupped her chin, surprising her heart and making it skip a beat. His strong fingers ran along her jawline, easing her eyes shut as another rush of shivers cascaded down her limbs. It'd been too long since someone touched her with such care. Lips tingling, she embraced the arousal swirling deep in her belly. Her breaths became shallower, and when she opened her eyes, Parker's deep gaze was intent on hers.

"This isn't black and white." His fingers continued to graze her skin.

"Never is."

"But it always is in my world." His quick, unsure smile flashed.

Her skin prickled. She was scared he would release her, but he only inched closer.

"Can we pretend that our worlds don't exist right now?" she asked.

His warm breaths caressed her lips. "I don't think it works like that."

"Please," she whispered then let her eyes close again.

Lexi soaked in all that was Parker. His scent. His strength. The rise and fall of his carved chest and his flat, hard stomach touching hers. Blood rushed in her ears and raced at her pulse. He shifted, and she almost moaned, craving his kiss.

His mouth brushed against hers. The touch was so soft, yet a rush of emotion and arousal tornadoed inside her. She went boneless. His lips were so right, so absolutely perfectly beautiful that she forgot to do more than just exist. She memorized his taste as he urged her to open, letting his tongue tease hers. His hands held her as though she was precious yet unbreakable as his fingers flexed into her back.

Every time she'd dreamed about his kiss, her most spectacular thoughts were nothing like this. He leaned into her, angling her head, deepening their kiss—

Until he pulled back hard, holding her steady.

She gasped, almost crying for his kiss again. "Wh-what?"

But that look on his face—it was the worst. Regret.

"I think we need some space." Parker hated himself on several levels for saying that, but it was the only thing he could do. Kissing Lexi changed everything— it put into action the wants and needs he'd harbored and always ignored.

Beautiful blue eyes broke before him. His gut twisted. Unease that he couldn't articulate flooded his body because everything about her was amazing, but fragile, and he wouldn't be responsible for hurting her.

"But—" she stopped herself.

"Not because I…" He had no idea how to finish that thought. No idea what to say.

Not because he didn't want her kisses and so much more. That wicked tongue of hers would lead them straight to his bedroom, and—he blew out a harsh breath—he wanted it all. He wanted to hear her breathy moans against his neck and feel her come while he was planted deep in the woman blushing before him.

Damn it.

Another frustrated breath burned from his lungs. Screwing her would mess up their situation. When he had her, it wouldn't be because she was lost or because she thought she'd found a savior with a hot shower who'd rescued her from a shitty day. *When he had her?*

Lexi shook her head, blond hair cascading over her cheeks. "That was stupid, sorry."

Her doubt was like salt in the emotional wound he couldn't see but was shredding him. "Don't be like that. I just can't go there right now."

With a tilt of her head, her eyes cast up. Bacon rolled on the ground, making a sound like she was playing dead. So even the dog didn't buy his line. With each passing second, he regretted that they weren't on the way to his bedroom, leaving a trail of clothes.

"Okay." Her eye lashes fluttered, making his chest seize up.

Any more time with her, and he wouldn't be able to hold himself back. "Maybe you should get some sleep. A nap or something. Or dinner? What do you need?"

"A nap or dinner…" she repeated, sounding too sad. But that passed, and something unsteady appeared on her bruised face. "I'm not really hungry. Why are you being so nice to me?"

Her confusion slayed him. "Because you feel the need to ask that question." He inched closer, teasing himself with the idea that another inch wouldn't be too much. "I don't want to leave you alone, Lex, but I don't trust myself. Not with you, not after that kiss."

"But—"

"We've always had a good reason not to cross the line. And now…" He inclined his head. "I think that reason's gone."

She nodded, relief in her eyes, and held up her ringless hand. "Gone."

Parker needed to step away but couldn't force his feet to make the moves. He swallowed, but his throat ached. "I'm trying to be the good guy. Please get some sleep."

She didn't budge, tempting him.

"Or…" He pulled the one weapon he thought he might have. "You can explain how you ended up on my steps, calling my number, if Matt didn't leave you here."

---

# CHAPTER SIXTEEN

Lexi blinked at Parker, more tongue-tied than before and unwilling to share that she'd hacked Matt's phone contact list, got Parker's number, then back-hacked that to see what his billing and mailing addresses were. No one wanted to sound like a genius stalker. The process had taken all of five seconds, maybe longer since she was hunkered at a gas station, piggybacking off the Wi-Fi on someone's phone. But she wouldn't explain any of that. It made better sense for him to think she'd just stolen his info from Matt's phone.

She stepped away, backing up more from his question than anything else. "I forgot, I have to send an email for work."

His eyes narrowed, and he worked his jaw as if he was choking on the word *bullshit*. "Alright."

With that, she grabbed her computer and held it to her chest like body armor. "Then I will take a nap. I really appreciate it."

With that same intense scrutiny, he nodded silently and led her out of the kitchen. At the door of his bedroom, Parker waved. "If you need anything…"

She watched his throat bob, noticing how thick his neck and strong his shoulders were. Whether wanting him made her worthy of wearing a scarlet letter—*no*. She and Matt were over. They'd been done before he kicked her butt then kicked her out. Remembering the last twenty-four hours made her skin crawl. Matt had tossed her around, dragged her upstairs, and thrown her back down. And Bacon. That poor dog had done so much over the last few weeks to stop him. The second Matt had passed out, Lexi ran.

She pulled herself out of her thoughts, vaguely aware of

Parker staring at her as though he'd been speaking.

"Lex? You okay? Need the internet password or whatever?"

"I'm good. Thanks, again."

Kissing Parker, doing *whatever* with Parker was fine. She shouldn't worry about strings or complications. Though the abrupt way he'd pushed away from her had been unexpected.

At least she was safe and warm. She could fire up her laptop without complaints from a nasty drunk peanut gallery. Shadow needed files, and she needed to use her laptop's hotspot to send her broker an update. Parker's house wasn't the ideal place to send mega-sensitive documents, but as long as she could get Shadow the word that the files were heading his way, it'd be okay.

Parker guided through his room and to an alcove off the side of the master bedroom. "You can work here if you want."

His house was large and expansive, *expensive*, and the area he motioned to had probably been designed for some rich housewife to lounge and dress while sipping on some fruity wine spritzer or something. But he'd turned it into a sleek office with more bells and whistles than she could have dreamed of. Some people had food porn, others had real porn, but this was hacker porn. Holy shit. Everything was turned off, and there was a fingerprint and retina scanner. Her pulse jumped from just looking at the four monitors stacked two on top of two and back lit. There were two sets of ergo-keyboards.

She was hiding her inner geek as best she could, but seriously… "This is some crazy shit, Parker."

He rolled the chair back and still studied her. "Here you go, all yours. Quiet work space. Do whatever you need to do."

If it was all hers, she wouldn't let someone else even breathe on the computing power before her. "I can just work on the…" She'd almost said bed. How presumptuous. Except he was bringing her in there to sleep and work. Oh God, now she really was having a hard time taking a steady breath. They were like *the* two most intimate places she could be: in a man's bed and in his personal office—even if it was locked down like Ft. Knox on steroids. That seemed like a lot of trust.

"Feel free. Whatever you need. I'll take this and be out of your hair." He unplugged his laptop from a docking station and tapped the back of his chair. "Work and relax. Deal?"

All in all, she was transfixed by the setup and by the man. "Really appreciate it."

"Alright then."

The room was big enough that he could have put a dozen feet between them as he left. Instead, he walked right to her, his long strides eating the space between them and sucking the oxygen out of her lungs. He tossed his laptop on the bed and stopped in front of her, and Parker gripped her shoulders and slid his palms to her elbows. His thumbs stroked over the sweatshirt, and she would've died had his hand been on her skin instead.

Hoping she didn't show how desperate she was for his touch, she said, "I haven't always been this fragile girl who needs to be saved."

"I know. I didn't meet you today."

Two years of watching him from afar. "I know."

"You might be the most interesting woman I've ever met."

She stepped back, nervous, but couldn't get far because his hold on her tightened. "Why?"

"There are a lot of things about you that I can't explain. I've known you, liked you, been interested in you, but now…"

Her mind raced. She could just tell him how she pictured herself, who she was and wanted to be. What she did for a living, or even her current project. Even Parker might have trouble understanding though. Laymen learned about the zero day market and thought it was illegal. But he seemed on the up-and-up with all things techy.

She could explain her work in vague terms. Given what he'd seen and said so far, he wouldn't tease her or break out the name-calling. No nerd girl titles from Parker, who was up to speed in giving nerd-girl-gasms—because she still couldn't get over his setup.

But her hesitation was still there. Damn Matt for screwing up her head. She just felt so broken. "Well, see, I, uh—"

"Don't." Parker shook his head. "I'm curious. Didn't say I needed an answer now. Just that I plan on figuring you out." His hand cupped her cheek, his thumb sweeping from her cheekbone to the corner of her mouth.

"Oh," she sighed, almost nuzzling his hand like a damn cat.

He took the warm touch away and left her alone, mouth agape and hand wanting to reach out to stop him. Damn. Parker wanted to figure her out? Holy swoonballs! If she was interesting, Parker Black was the most intense man she'd ever met.

Quickly, she went to her computer, trying to shake the tingling feeling that hung in her limbs. Once she was in her email, she typed a message to Shadow.

*Monarch is complete, and Matt and I are done. Big day for me, huh? Thought you'd be proud on both accounts. But because of the Matt situation, I'm on the road and not comfortable transmitting the files. Don't hate. :) Be in touch soon. Xx*

Perfect. She hit send, double-checked that it went through, then powered down her laptop. The reliable machine went silent as it turned off, and she was completely aware of how alone she was in Parker's room. A nap—she needed one and had promised him that she'd try. She must need the rest if he was so adamant she get some sleep.

A nap *in his bed* though. Obviously he didn't realize that would likely mean absolutely no sleep. She'd sooner get rest on the tile floor of his bathroom with towels as a pillow. The man *did* have heated floors in his bathroom, so that wouldn't be a huge hardship.

Lexi trailed her finger along the smooth wood headboard. Parker's bed was so Parker. Dark sheets. Dark furniture. Big, strong, but somehow refined. The carved wood was sleek and inherently masculine. Powerful. His bedroom smelled slightly more of him, but his sheets… her hand slipped from the wood to smooth over the pillowcase and sheets.

God. Her stomach flipped, and carefully, almost as if she were savoring the moment, she crawled onto the king-size mattress and fell into Egyptian cotton heaven, thread count a billion.

There was no way she would get any sleep. Her pulse thundered in her throat, and even now, all alone, she didn't feel as though she could take a deep breath. He'd been gone for twenty minutes at least, and her mind was still entirely focused on Parker. Whose clothes she wore, whose bed she was in, and whose kiss stayed on her lips. Lexi pressed her fingers to her lips. That had been the sweetest, deepest kiss of her whole life, and despite how he'd pulled from her, it was also one of the most empowering moments she could remember.

Her phone buzzed.

Parker: *You're not sleeping*
Lexi: *How would you know*
Parker: *Assumed*
Parker: *Sleep...*
Lexi: *I can't if you keep texting me*

She couldn't break the smile from her face. He was flirting with her while she lay in his bed. In what universe was this happening?

Parker: *Sleep yet?*
Lexi: *Sigh. I'm trying*
Parker: *Buzz me if you need anything*
Lexi: *Thx 1.0E6*
Lexi: *Sorry. Thanks a million. It's a work thing. Never mind. Thx for tonight.*
Parker: *Know what it means, sweetheart. Sleep.*

He *was* flirting with her. Holy shit. But what was her problem, slipping into Silver-headspace when she texted with him? Or maybe she was just becoming comfortable with who she was around Parker.

"I was almost me tonight," she whispered in the dark, Parker's sheets pulled up to her neck.

Her neck and cheeks heated. She was embarrassed by how weak she'd been with Matt, but the world felt full of possibilities just from how Parker made her feel. There was something between them, the kind of connection that made the air feel magnetic, as though it crackled and sparkled the closer they stood.

Her stomach dropped *again,* despite lying flat on her back, and she smiled. Because she was lying flat on her back in Parker's ginormous bed, and he'd set the groundwork for something more than just a kiss.

# CHAPTER SEVENTEEN

A noise clanged, pulling Lexi out of her half-comatose dream. She rolled over, buried in everything that smelled like Parker. She sighed, shaking her head and trying to organize her thoughts. Had that been a doorbell?

The green glow of his alarm clock read a little after nine. Hours had passed since she'd showed up at Parker's. Her limbs were sore, and her face ached. She was bruised and beaten and all of her muscles hurt from Matt. Wait—a doorbell? She shot up in bed. Dread arrived hard and fast because somehow she knew, without a second thought, that Matt was there. Bacon rolled over and whined at the foot of the bed. Dogs always knew what was up, and that whimper said her ex was definitely there.

What was she supposed to do?

She started shaking. Matt would kill her. She was lying in his friend's bed? In his clothes? Holy crap. His violent mood swings had been epic lately. But Parker would protect her. Hell, he wanted to shred Matt to pieces. So she was safe.

The tiniest spring of relief tried to push into her mind. Parker would keep Matt away from her. She took a calming breath and quickly ducked down, burying herself in the pillows and comforter. Maybe her instinct was wrong, and it wasn't Matt. Maybe Parker would lie and say he hadn't seen her. Maybe Matt was risking life merely by approaching Parker. But the more she thought about Matt's jealousy, the more she trembled.

So what to do? Just stay in bed with Bacon? Or she could spy on their conversation. Just a bit of eavesdropping to see what was going on between the men. Anything was better than having a panic attack in Parker's bed.

"What do we do?" she asked the dog that had crawled up to her side.

Bacon's ear pricked up, pivoting as both ladies strained to hear anything. Lexi came up short, but her pup heard something. A low, protective growl came from the pudgy pooch.

Carefully, Lexi crawled from underneath the protective cocoon of the sheets. Cool air heightened her senses, making her feel chilled even though she still wore Parker's sweats. "Stay, girl."

But Bacon ignored her and jumped down.

They inched toward the door together. Butterflies spun in her stomach as if she'd been drinking tequila on an empty stomach, and she grabbed Bacon to feel less queasy. Together, they cracked the door. Hard voices drifted up the stairs, but the words were lost.

"Stay." She pushed Bacon back inside the bedroom then crept closer to the stairs, hoping to hear exactly what the hateful mumbles were. Inches turned into feet, and she stopped at the corner. Their words drifted up the stairs.

"Showing up here isn't the answer," Parker's baritone boomed, making her slide just another foot closer.

Matt's anger resounded though mumbled, probably slurred, words that she couldn't make out.

"Not my problem."

What wasn't Parker's problem? Her? Matt? Their messy breakup? She had twenty questions, and they all revolved around her. Anger rushed through her veins. God, she was just so done. She had to have an empowering I've-taken-back-my-life moment, and this was it, even if there was a stronger likelihood that she would puke from nerves. Lexi stood on shaky legs, ready to confront him, and—what? Would she really tell Matt to leave?

Yes. She'd say get out, that it was over, that he couldn't hit her, hurt her, steal her thoughts for a moment longer. Lexi pushed past the corner, her heart rioting against her ribs, warning her to stop. But it was too late. She couldn't stop even if she wanted to.

Silver gave no fucks about the world, and she was her! Lexi gripped the handrail and forced her legs to take each step down. Her stomach soured. Adrenaline spiked into her blood, and a cold sweat broke out on neck.

When she was three steps from the bottom of the stairs, the men's conversation died. Both sets of eyes were on her, both men with vastly different looks on their faces.

Matt's was familiarly scary. Angry. Harsh lines that didn't come from laughing creased around his eyes. His mouth, which she'd once found sweet, was snarled and rabid-looking.

And Parker normally looked protective and handsome, but there was nothing sweet or sexy on his face now. His strong features were marred with protective concern.

"Are you fuckin' shittin' me?" Matt growled, charging forward.

Parker's arm shot out and caught Matt across the chest. "Chill out."

"Fuck you, and your I'm-not-fuckin'-Lexi bullshit."

Lexi glanced down. Wearing Parker's clothes didn't do her any favors. "Matt, you have to go."

"Get your skank ass outside and in the—"

"No." She stood her ground and shook her head. "We can't do this anymore. I'm done."

"Outside, Lexi."

She wasn't breathing because this wasn't working. What had she expected? If she walked out the door with him… bad, bad things would happen.

"Please—" She swallowed around the lump in her throat. "I left. You knew I left because you forced me out. I don't care if I see you or my things ever again. I have what I need. Let's both walk away."

"Stupid fucking woman. Your things? The only things you care about are your stupid *computer* and that fat-ass dog."

"Time to go," Parker interjected.

"Fine. Fuck it if I care. She's a lazy fuckin' screw anyway. You'll see if you don't already know, goddamn Judas."

His words… her molars grinded, her head exploding. She was *so* sick of this. God! Lexi shook her head, seething. Her fists bunched as she slammed her arms straight. "No one's screwing me, but if they did, from here on out, *they will have to have my permission!* Now get out!"

"Excuse me?" Parker growled, catching her eye then turning to Matt as though he was a hair away from strangling the guy.

"Like you didn't want it." Matt exploded, and he dove at her, hands outstretched like a predator.

Her body had been trained to react. Her forearms covered her face, her hands wrapped around the back of her head. She dropped and curled into a ball, awaiting the punches and kicks that would rain down on her.

But nothing hurt her. The scuffle she heard didn't touch her, and she blinked, surprised, and opened her eyes. Parker had Matt on the floor. When Matt looked ready to tap out or die, Parker dragged him toward the front door. With a quick move, like something out of the movies, Parker flung it open and lofted her ex through it, then slammed it shut. His gaze sliced to her. Their eyes locked, and he stalked over, his hand outstretched.

"You okay, Lex?"

Carefully, she unfolded herself and let him tug her up. They stayed connected at the hand for a minute until his hand came toward her face—not fast but apparently too quickly because she flinched. Hard. Then she cringed because Parker wouldn't hurt her. A guy like him did nice, sweet things. He was strong and tough but had amazing intentions.

"I think..." His jaw flexed in a beautifully pissed-off way. "That it's time to talk."

# CHAPTER EIGHTEEN

Phiber had followed the man he assumed was Silver's boyfriend, hoping to locate the woman. One day she never left the home, the next she was gone, and Phiber couldn't think of a single hacker con she might have gone to. So he followed the guy from Silver's house to this house, only to watch him come out flat on his ass. He'd literally been tossed out, and that guy wasn't small. What was this? *Days of Our Lives*? Phiber shook his head, almost feeling bad. There was no question reject boy was drunk, angry, and had just been dumped.

The question was how could this guy help him get what he needed? He watched reject boy climb his stumbling ass into the driver's seat of the truck that had barely gotten him there alive. The truck's engine revved, and the man hung out his driver's side window, cursing at the house. Phiber opted to stay close to reject boy instead of snooping around Silver's new location. He turned over his ignition and pulled out behind the truck.

They swerved to the local dive bar, and reject boy parked his truck crooked across two parking spots. Asshole. Phiber parked in one spot like a decent human being and followed him in. There was no way, as drunk as the guy was, he would recognize Phiber from one passing encounter at the grocery store. The guy could barely think, evidenced by his turning on his right turn signal only to go left.

The bar looked exactly as he would expect: sparse and crappy with a few folks who looked as though they hadn't moved in days. Phiber sat on the stool next to reject boy and watched him slug back a beer.

The bartender leaned over, wiped the counter, and threw

down a napkin. "What'll it be, son?"

Phiber tilted his head. "Same as this guy."

Reject boy looked over, his eyes narrowing. "Do I know you? You look familiar."

Not too drunk to forget a fifteen-second encounter. "Not yet."

Whatever memory he had tried to grasp faded as he jerked back, swaying on the stool. "I'm no fag. You're barking up the wrong tree."

Phiber laughed. "Nah, man. I like pussy. No worries."

He nodded. "Right." Then he killed the rest of his beer in a few gulps.

Plan was to let him get even more sloshed, then siphon him for info and figure out if he knew where any of the parts of Monarch were or if Silver's new location was permanent.

"Got some woman problems to drink away," he offered, hoping reject boy would take the bait.

"Me too."

That was easy. The bartender put a cheap beer in front of Phiber. "Thanks, man."

"Tab?" he asked.

"Yeah, a tab works."

"Another for me," the man slurred.

The bartender nodded. "Sure thing, Matt, long as you don't cause a problem tonight."

"I never cause problems."

The dude had problems written all over him and needed a friend. Phiber held up his beer in toast. "I blame women."

Matt drunk-laughed. "Amen, my oriental friend."

"Not sure that's the right word, asshole."

"Asian. Amen, my Asian motherfuckin' friend. Cheers to fuckin' stupid cunts. Let's drink to that."

The guy would be a piece of cake. "Cheers."

They raised their beers, and Phiber took a long pull while Matt guzzled.

"What's wrong with your woman?" Phiber asked.

Matt's eyes hung at half-mast. "Computer girl found her nerd hero, and fuck them."

"Yeah." He nodded. "Fuck 'em."

They drank and watched the sports replays on the hanging TV. Well, that actually bored the shit out of Phiber, but he didn't want to rush the guy.

When a commercial hit, Phiber bounced the bottle between his hands. "Computer girl for you? Can't see it."

"Lexi… always got her nose in her computer. Playing games. Working." He used air quotes around the last part.

"She wasn't?"

"Hell if I know. But I do know that bitch fell face first into my boy's lap. Damn nerd boy thinks he's some kind of computer Mozart."

"I could use a new laptop. Get back at the girl. Sell her shit to me, make a couple bucks." He reached for his pocket, ready to entice Matt with easy, revengeful cash.

But Matt threw his head back. "You know what's funny? She left her ring and took the computer. What kind of stupid woman does that?"

Shit. The smart kind. "Where?"

He shook his drunk head as though this all should be clear as day. "To the damn nerd's place. Shit."

Phiber had gotten a glance at the guy who'd tossed Matt clean on his ass. The guy was a big dude, and he didn't look anything like what Matt called him. If anything, Phiber was taking far more offense to nerd comments than the oriental one. Well, actually, fuck him for both.

He needed to get back to where he'd come from. "Alrighty, buddy. Take it easy." Matt nodded, and Phiber threw down a twenty while waving at the bartender. "Heading out."

Time to head back to Silver's new place. His head pounded. Abducting someone wasn't easy for him. He was nervous and trying to make it happen in a way that wouldn't make him rot in hell. Grabbing Silver at the grocery store hadn't been an overly fruitful idea. What, he was just going to sneak her out of the back of the store to his waiting car? Stalking her at home hadn't yielded much. Honestly, abduction wasn't his talent. But the Taskmaster said jump, so he was ready to try again.

He climbed in his car and checked his bag. Laptop, a couple cells, chargers. Nothing to jimmy open a window. He might have a lock-picking kit in his glove box… maybe. He leaned over to check.

"Shit, yes." Phiber made the quick drive back.

All the lights were on. He drove around the block a few times, but no lights went out. They weren't going to bed. Then again, if Silver *was* face first in the guy's lap, they'd be distracted. They'd fuck and pass out. Then he could grab the girl, right? Sneak in while they were occupied and just wait it out. Kind of creepy, but it was a solid plan.

What if… Phiber pulled over and searched his bag for anything that might help. Score. A mini electro-jammer. Instant power outage. The happy fuckin' couple could go to bed, do their distracted thing, and he could slip in. He'd grab whatever laptop looked like Silver's, which would be a bonus, and the girl when they were both passed out. Simple.

# CHAPTER NINETEEN

*Time to talk?* Oh boy. Lexi's mind tumbled. "Um…"

Parker moved around her, sliding his hand onto the small of her back. "Into the kitchen, sweetheart."

Silently, she let him guide her into place. Before she knew it, she was sitting at a table that held a dog-eared technology magazine while he wandered the kitchen—also known as the scene of their first kiss—doing who knew what. "Um…"

"Beer, bourbon, or…" He opened the fridge and made a you'd-hate-it face. "Muscle milk."

"Um…"

A half-smile curved his lips. "That's about all I've got."

"Beer it is." Which she could totally use right about now. "Thanks."

He pulled two longnecks from the fridge and made his way back to the table. He put one down, cracked it open, and slid it over for her. Parker flipped a chair around and straddled it. He opened his bottle then folded his forearms over the back of the chair. His fingers toyed with the two bottle caps, flipping them over in constant, dexterous motion. "I'll start with what I know, and you fill in the blanks."

Biting her lip, she watched his gaze drop to her mouth. The butterflies swirled in her stomach, and her teeth released. No way could she talk about anything he wanted to know while her insides were doing the mamba. Mindlessly, she reached for her beer then gulped a sip while she tried to find the right words.

"Matt's a dick," he offered.

She snort-laughed, taking the beer away from her mouth,

and giggled while slapping her other hand over her mouth.

"Cute." He grinned. "About time you laughed tonight."

"Yeah, super cute. All snorty and stuff."

But the laughter on his face faded away. "Your turn. Say something."

"Matt's a dick. That pretty much sums it up."

"I saw him choke you before. He played it down, and you"—Parker's brow furrowed—"went back."

"Like I said, that was a mistake. I had a bagbiting plan to save Bacon, but—"

"Bagbiting?"

"Oh." Her eyes went wide that he picked that up. "It means—"

"I know what it means. Your plan didn't fail; you just didn't keep yourself safe."

Wariness ran over her. He even thought in the same terms she did. "Right. So faulty strategy. I was stupid."

His head shook slightly. "Nope. I don't buy stupid." Parker grabbed his beer and drained half of it. "If you need to go to the cops or whatever for—" He cleared his throat uncomfortably. "For anything he might've done, I'll be your ride. I'll… be whatever you need."

"Oh …" She had fanatical notes. Everything was written in code, so only she could understand it, but it was there. She had saved a couple of selfies that showed bruises, blood. But showing those humiliating pictures to anyone… she just couldn't process that. "I don't want to. I'm not ready for everything that comes with that."

His jaw flexed as if he wanted to disagree. "You change your mind, you let me know."

"Alright." Because what was she going to say? She'd stayed with a man who hurt her. The floor was suddenly the most interesting thing in the room. She couldn't tear her stinging eyes away as a knot tied in her throat. The hopelessness and loneliness that had strangled her before seemed ridiculous, especially when there were people in the world like Parker, but… she squeezed her eyes shut. Slowly, she pushed through the bevy of emotions choking her and locked her gaze on Parker.

"What do you do again?" he asked, completely off topic.

"Website testing." Her standard answer.

"What else?"

More than he could comprehend. Her standard thought. Yet maybe not. But she didn't trust him enough to even start an explanation. "That's about it."

"You won't leave an abusive home without your computer—"

"It's my livelihood."

"Your dog's name is Bacon Byte."

"She's tiny as a postage stamp, fat as a hog. We both love bacon."

He smirked. "I saw her collar. Byte. With a *y*. You're not making a play off an appetizer there."

Defensive, she pushed her shoulders back. "What's your point?"

"You speak hack and text inarticulations, you recognized bells and whistles in my office, you almost died for a computer. You do more than web security."

Even as he called her on things that most never noticed, she couldn't say the words. She wasn't confident enough in herself to share her true colors with an outsider. Matt had broken her down to this point. Instead of agreeing, she shrugged. "I like the idea of hacker culture. That's it."

And that *was* true.

Parker mulled her words over and nodded. "I get that."

They sipped their beers, her dancing around sharing too much and him likely trying to figure out all of the pieces that put her together. Though why he pushed, she didn't understand.

He ran a hand over his face. "I've never been able to get you out of my head. Before today. Before all this."

Her head pulled back, shocked, on its own accord because she was too busy trying not to pass out. "What?"

Parker's tongue ran over his top lip. "What I don't know is—you." His forehead furrowed. "And why you're hiding that from me."

"I don't mean to." She sucked down a breath as though it might fortify her soul. "And I've thought about you—"

As if Matt had ears in the room, the lights went black. The quiet hum of appliances slowed and silenced. Fear bled into her veins. Matt wasn't leaving Parker's house without her.

# CHAPTER TWENTY

"Nope, screw this." Parker shot up from his chair. The chair clattered on the floor, and he grasped Lexi's arm, pulling her close. The top of her head came to his chest, and when he bent his chin to touch it, the scent of his shampoo in her hair teased him mercilessly while he listened for incoming danger. "Nothing's going to hurt you. God, that fuckin' drunk-ass dick."

But just because Parker wouldn't let Matt hurt her didn't mean the guy wouldn't try. When Parker got his hands on Matt, there'd be no question about where the line was and how far Matt was to stay away from it.

"Parker," she whispered, her voice tinged with fear.

"Give me a second." His ears ached as he listened to the point he could hear his heartbeat. Maybe hers. "One more second."

No sounds.

But this wasn't a regular power outage. The timing was too perfect. This was a drunk dude ripping wires out of his breaker box, though even the act of doing that would trigger an alarm to Titan. What gnawed at Parker's chest was that the backup generator hadn't kicked on. The breaker box and generator weren't together, which meant Matt had to have been hunting around his property. Dude was further gone than Parker initially realized.

As his eyes grew accustomed to the dark, he walked with Lexi to a wall, then carefully, he peeked outside. His gaze ran up and down his neighborhood. The street lights were on, and a few houses had porch lights on or windows lit. Confirmation that this wasn't a power outage.

He needed to assess if there was an immediate incoming assault. Was Matt gonna firebomb his window with a Molotov cocktail? Was he going to shoot at the bedroom windows? What was that asshole going to do?

"Stay put a sec." Parker swiveled to a nearby bookshelf and ran his hand under it, removing a Glock.

"Why do you have a gun in your bookshelf?" she whispered.

He held the weapon down, his finger itching to feel the Ghost trigger, and he moved back to the petite woman shaking in the dark. "Occasional hazards of my job."

"Are you kidding me?" But she clung to him. "Parker—"

"Sweetheart, I need you to give me a quiet second. Okay?"

With no immediate offensive to prepare against, he changed tactics and headed to stash Lexi in the safe room. Then he could pull up the video feedback and disengage the alarm system. Whatever was about to happen didn't need to involve the cops, and he could explain the alerts to Boss Man later. This was between him and Matt.

*Click.*

Parker pivoted toward the breath-of-a-noise at back of the house. Was Matt picking his lock? If so, then awesome. The doors had a built-in security feature that handled petty moves like that. If any door was forcibly breached, the security protocols snapped into effect. The first of which would happen any second.

"Let's go," he said.

They bounded up the stairs and crested the top one when Parker heard a cry of male pain. Matt had disabled the last tumbler in the back door, which meant volts of electricity had shocked him.

"What was that?" she asked.

"The door's wired to give an electrical shock under breach protocol."

"Why does your house—"

He tucked the 9mm into the back of his waistband and snagged a flashlight from the hall closet. "In you go." He scooted her into the reinforced space masquerading as a guest room and turned on the flashlight. "You'll be fine, but I'm locking you in."

"What?" She shook her head. "I don't want—"

"Safest place."

He pressed a kiss to her lips that slowed the spinning world. The seconds his lips seared hers, her fingers dug into his shirt, and he went from shoving her into the safe room to backing her against the wall, kissing to their tactical, strategic detriment.

He broke away—surprised that his body had taken over when his mind would never have allowed a slip like that—and every fiber of his being rioted at their distance. He cupped her face and spent a tick of a second longer than he should have sliding his fingers over her skin and down her neck. "Damn, Lex. You're dangerous."

Then he hurried away before he shut them both in the safe room and kissed every inch of her, from behind her ears to the tips of her toes.

"Focus," he growled. As he hurried toward his office, he couldn't get the taste of her off his tongue. Clearly his self-lecture hadn't worked.

Parker booted up the monitoring system that ran off a centralized battery, cancelled the alerts, and quickly moved through the feedback. A figure who had hidden his face—clearly Matt knew where the cameras were, so the asshole wasn't *that* drunk—headed to the breaker box, then disconnected the generator, and finally headed for the back door. Asshole. The footage showed Matt falling backward then crawling away from the door and running off into the dark.

Pussy. Still, he wanted to check the exterior and reconnect the generator while Lexi was safe. Parker stormed across his bedroom—stopping for a nanosecond to take in his mussed sheets where Lexi had been in his bed—then snagged a backup weapon, just in case. If Matt was still there, Parker would make it clear he wasn't playing games.

He moved through the house to the back door and disarmed the lock. The night was silent as he stepped outside and waited for Matt to bum-rush him from the shadows. "Show your face, asshole."

Silence.

Parker pulled the door shut, engaging the lock from the exterior side, and slid around his home. His body anticipated sucker punches and attacks. He listened for the swish of clothing or a step in the grass. Still, he didn't hear anything other than expected neighborhood noises. He moved past the bushes to the electrical box. The small metal door had been left open.

He glanced in, expecting to see cut wires, but they were intact. Squinting in the dark, Parker angled to keep an eye on his surroundings and still study the box. His wires weren't cut, switches weren't thrown. A tingle of uncertainty fell over him. How had the system gone down? He used the flashlight app on his phone to study the breaker box. Nothing abnormal caught his eye—except. He peered closer. What the—?

A tiny electro-jammer was secured to the back interior wall. He ran his finger over it, confirming that it was exactly what it looked like. He scratched his thumb over it, popped it off the back of the metal box, and crushed the tiny device. The lights on his house blinked and illuminated.

A strong current of apprehension ticked at his thoughts. What was Matt doing with technology like that? The guy was a blow-it-up-question-later kind of guy. Nothing like this. Confusion and concern at what he was missing racked Parker's brain.

He moved back inside, locked up tight, and re-engaged the security system. Then he hit the stairs, taking three steps at a time. After opening the panel hidden in the wall, Parker punched in the code, and Lexi's steel-enforced door unlocked. He twisted the door knob and—ducked as a flash of motion came toward his head. When he looked up, Lexi, nightstand lamp in hand, jerked back, ready to smash it against him again.

"Easy!" Parker stepped to the side, hands up. "Lex, sweetheart, it's me."

She blinked, eyes peeled wide. "Tell me what happened."

"Your ex is an asshole." He tugged her hand, dragging her downstairs behind him. "And we're not staying here."

"Parker."

"Jamming my power and breaking in my goddamn door."

"Jamming?" she repeated, pulling up beside him.

"Since when does that prick know shit about technology?" Parker mumbled, more pissed than making conversation.

Her face fell, all the color fading. "What? Why?"

"There was a—" Fuming and confused at the attempted breach, he shook his head. "Never mind."

"No, tell me."

Then his eyes narrowed on her. He thought about her vague familiarity with technology. "Do you know what an electromagnetic jammer does?"

She nodded, her face saying she was absolutely familiar with the term. "Maybe."

"Well, Matt apparently does too."

Lexi slowly shook her head. "There's no way."

"It didn't get in my breaker box on its own, Lex."

Her face darkened, lines pinching her sweet face. "I've caused enough of a headache here. Can you drop me at my sister's house?"

"Are you kidding me?"

"No. I should go."

"So wait, a sister? Thought you said you bounced around foster homes."

A brief flash of acknowledgment crossed her face. "I just need to go."

"Lex—"

"Will you take me? If not, I think you know I'll brave the elements."

"What the hell is going on with you?" Because if it didn't sound like an idea worthy of a caveman or jail time, he'd tie her sweet ass to a chair and keep her safe.

"I have to get out of here."

His mind turned over everything he knew, and none of it made sense. There were secrets all over her face. His anger and alarm blurred together. He wanted to shake some common sense into her. Wanted to lay down some kind of law that if she was hiding anything from him, she should stop and rely on him instead.

"Haven't I done enough to earn your trust yet?" he asked.

She dropped her head. "Don't be like Matt, questioning what I want to do, when I want to do it. I'm asking you to take me to my sister's. I've caused enough trouble and need to go."

The comparison was like a wave of ice-cold water. He stepped back and hated their distance, but worse, he hated wanting to protect her while she wanted to leave. "Whatever you say, Lex."

But his mind shocked him as he held back the words, "Please don't go."

# CHAPTER TWENTY-ONE

It was well after the middle of the night. Lexi was back in her clothes, and Parker was pissed at her as he drove her to her sister's. Her mind crunched every possible piece of data she had, which only confirmed that she had a problem and needed to go dark after talking to Shadow.

Lexi buried herself in Parker's sweatshirt. She said she'd give it back but planned to steal it. Like it or not, no matter their connection, there was the chance they'd never see each other again, especially given how the night was ending and his understandably frustrated response.

"You sure about this? Did you talk to her?" His knuckles were pinched tight on his steering wheel.

She had already sworn up and down that Meredith was expecting her and that Matt wouldn't think to go over there because of how much her sister traveled. Mere wasn't expecting her, and lying to Parker wasn't the greatest thing to do, but it was the right course of action. "Yes. She left the door unlocked, told me to go in when I got here."

"Okay," he said in a voice so low she wanted to lean toward him. "I'll walk you in."

"No, you don't have to." But if he did come up with her, then she could drag him back into the dark. He could press against her as he'd done when the power was out; he could take her mouth as though neither of them cared who else was in the dark. A shiver ran up her spine as she thought about the power in that kiss.

"You don't have to be so secretive with me, Lex. You get that?"

She tilted her head. “Why do you have guns hidden in your bookshelf? Why is your door electrified?”

He grumbled. “Touché.”

They arrived at Meredith’s swanky apartment building, and Lexi wished the drive had taken a hundred miles longer. Parker shifted his SUV to park and turned his smoldering gaze, so hot that the seat warmer had nothing on him, toward her. With just the strength of his look, he held her stationary.

“Look, Lex, you need to get something.”

God, he made her feel fuzzy from the inside out. “What’s that?”

“I’m not him, and whatever you’re holding so close to the vest? You don’t have to.”

“I do.” She nodded, looking at Bacon, who was asleep on the floorboard.

“So at least you admit that there *is* something.”

“Maybe.”

He grabbed her hand, which she hadn’t realized was fidgeting. “You disappear, I will find you.”

Her blood jumped a few degrees hotter because he’d smiled and said nice things. How messed up did she have to be to simply get aroused from kindness? From the growly quiet and protective manner with which he cared for her?

“I won’t disappear for long.” She unbuckled and jumped out, grabbing her laptop bag and a still-sleeping, snoring Bacon. As she slammed her door, she heard a second door open and shut. Oh, God. Lexi kept her head down and powered toward the apartment’s front door.

His shoes slapped the ground behind her. Her stomach somersaulted. Parker was running after her. Like *running* after her, and she couldn’t breathe.

“Hey.” He stopped in front of her so abruptly that she almost ran into his brick wall of a chest.

Bacon let out a loud snore but didn’t wake, and Lexi guessed that the poor dog was sleeping so soundly because it was the first time in weeks that she hadn’t felt the need to remain on constant safety patrol. Parker’s hands steadied Lexi, then he pulled himself away as though he’d grabbed her too hard. But with him, it was never possessive enough. Crap, she didn't want to leave him. Not yet.

"Wait a sec. Okay?" His breath came out as a cloud in the cold.

"I should go inside."

"I need you to stop." Hesitation was written all over him, as though he had no idea what he was doing, and that confusion in and of itself was baffling.

"What are you doing?" she whispered.

His palms went to his face, running his fingers into his hair, where they knotted. "I want to—I don't want to hurt you. I need to grab you. Hold you. I want to feel you. But damn it…" Uncertainty danced on his face. "I'm not the guy who knows how to help with whatever you've been through. I don't regret much, but I already regret ruining the chance."

His words made her boneless. Standing was a challenge she didn't think she could meet for much longer. "The chance at what?"

"At you, sweetheart."

*Oh God...*

As though he were inching through a minefield, he closed what remained of the distance between them. "I work with numbers. With code. You know I went to MIT but then I became a Marine. Now I'm Titan. I call what I see. It's either black or white. One way. One order. One goal. So that look on your bruised face, coupled with trying to make sense of today? I want to drag you back to my car. I want what you *do not* need. And if I let you go, I'm sure of it, you'll be gone. It's that simple."

Numbers. Code. He couldn't have said anything more perfect. All those words translated into one phrase: no bullshit. He spoke her language, and he could also read her mind, maybe her soul.

"You speak code?" she said. "I speak similar. All of which is far easier to understand than what I'm trying to figure out…" With Shadow's concerns, Phiber sightings, just everything.

His throat bobbed. "The more I know about you…"

"Same…" His unfinished thought mirrored hers exactly. "What's Titan?"

"Nothing. A job. My world. A lifestyle. It's complicated."

The sound of the apartment's front door opening interrupted them, and Meredith's doorman approached from behind Parker. "Can I help you, Miss Dare?"

"Hi, Malcolm."

"Your sister is n—" He cut himself off as her pinched face begged him to shut up. "Can I help you with anything? Bacon, perhaps? And your bag?"

Lexi transferred her snoring dog into his arms. "Thank you."

"Your bag?"

"No, I'll keep it."

He nodded. "We'll be inside."

"Thanks."

Parker stepped close to her again. "Won't let go of that bag."

She shook her head.

He stepped closer until their stomachs touched. "It doesn't feel like you were on my steps hours ago. Feels like a lifetime has happened since then."

"A lot has." She nodded. "Matt showing up, someone trying to break in."

"Me kissing you."

The pounding of her heartbeat nearly drowned out his words. "Yes," she whispered as the memory of his tongue in her mouth became vivid.

His eyes flared, and he licked his full lips as though he were also remembering. Parker pressed against her until there was only a slip of air between them. His hands took her waist, and his warm breaths in the cold were her undoing.

"Please…" *Kiss me, touch me, save me…*

His mouth claimed hers, and walking her back toward his SUV, he kissed her as though she were leaving him forever. Her back hit his Range Rover, and despite wearing his sweatshirt, the metal froze her body. She hunched into his arms as his lips moved to her neck. The length of his hardened shaft pressed against her through their jeans, and holy crap, Parker was impressive.

He opened the back door, took her laptop bag, and tossed it onto the floorboard. Then Parker leaned into her and scraped his teeth along her neck until she moaned. God, his sinful, talented tongue worked her skin until her hips writhed against his erection to the point that she should've been embarrassed.

"Get in the car, Lexi."

He barely let go of her. As she fell on her back across the seats, he climbed on top of her, shutting the door and leaving the frigid night behind them. She was pinned beneath his weight, his arms around her. One of his hands held the back of her head, and the other wrapped around her torso, under her shirt, smoothing up to the clasp of her bra and down to the edge of the pants that she'd die to take off.

"Please," she whispered. "I haven't felt like this… ever."

He flexed his hips, and the tips of his fingers dipped below the waist of her pants.

"God, I'm begging, Parker."

"You don't have to do that." His mouth was on hers again, his tongue licking the seam of her lips until they tangled in a kiss. But he stopped and shifted, dragging her into his lap and cradling her. "You're the only person that makes me do what I'm not expected to."

He unsnapped the button on her jeans and dragged the zipper down so slowly she couldn't help but shift her hips up. His eyes locked on hers as his palm went flat on her belly. His touch was strong, and holding her gaze, he slid past the lace band of her panties and pushed deft fingers between her legs.

"God," she moaned.

He grazed over her folds, and Lexi inched her legs apart, breathing heavily, as though oxygen was in short demand.

"So soft," he growled quietly.

He hadn't done more than press against her, and she was pulsing for more. "Parker…"

His fingers spread, finding her clit and stroking. Her head dropped back, but he held her in place. "More?"

She couldn't talk. "Hmm-hmm."

One finger pressed inside her, then he added another, drawing them in and out. This was heaven. Her nipples ached for his mouth, her body begged to be stripped down, and the building sensation promised to be catastrophic. Just his fingers were better than anything she could remember. Ever.

Still, he watched her face. His eyes studied her, maybe memorizing the cues to what made her moan and gasp his name.

"Parker, God."

His hand moved deeper, stronger, working her as though he'd been born to make her beg. She gulped breaths and watched his jaw tick, his brow furrow, his tongue lick those lips she'd just kissed.

"I'm so close," she gasped.

He bent over, pressing his mouth to hers and delving his tongue deep, like his fingers. Her body went rigid, her back arched, and she ground down on his hand while crying out.

"God, Lex. You're fuckin' beautiful when you come."

The world spun, and she disappeared into a climax-soaked oblivion. This was too much like a dream come true.

The trembles of her innermost muscles slowed their spasms as she came down off her high. His hand went lax and his kisses went lazy as she lulled through the high and low of climax. This was a euphoric cloud, and she was completely surrounded by all things Parker. His scent. His taste. The way he made her fall apart.

"Hell. You're always beautiful."

A blush hit her cheeks—she felt its heat almost as much as she could still feel him touching her. "Thank you."

He chuckled and rumbled around her, righting her pants, and pulled her to sit up in his lap. "None needed."

"Look at you, all gentleman-like."

"Sweetheart, I just finger-fucked you in the back of my car. Not a raving sign of chivalry. But…" He directed her face up toward his. "I think maybe it's the first time in a while anyone took care of you. So I'll take that."

Nodding, she bit her lip, tugging at his belt. She wanted to return the favor as much as she wanted to taste him. That kind of desire was liberating. It was also a sign that she'd been with the wrong guy, even before Matt had ever hurt her. Because never had she ever wanted her mouth on someone as she did at that minute.

He stilled her hand. "You don't have to."

"But…?"

"You left your fiancé hours ago. Your face is bruised. As much as I want your tongue stroking my cock, Lex, not like this."

Her eyes drifted from him to the apartment building. She didn't know what to say, but emotions choked her tightly. He was obviously trying to put her ahead of his own needs.

"I don't want you to go, but you're going to anyway." Parker pressed his lips to her forehead. "Run away. Whatever you're keeping from me, that's yours to hide. But when you're ready, I'll be there. Deal?"

Her stomach flipped. "You're for real, aren't you?"

He gave her a short chin lift to say yes. "Real enough."

"I'll call you when I'm…"—*safe*—"when I've had time to figure out what I need to."

"Do your thing. Call me later. Maybe explain the big secret on how you knew my number and where I lived."

Her cheeks heated all over again. "Maybe."

After another quick kiss, Parker opened the back door. "Looking forward to it."

Though her spaghetti legs and squishy-filled chest worked as she moved from the Range Rover, she couldn't help but be unnerved with the casual way he seemed to accept everything she'd tossed at him today. Well, other than him not wanting her to go to Meredith's. The guy seemed chill about almost everything except for her, and that made her happier than she'd been in a long time.

# CHAPTER TWENTY-TWO

Lexi pushed through the apartment doors to face the doorman and Bacon, who was now groggily awake. "Hey, sleepyhead."

"Do you need a hand upstairs, Miss Dare?"

"No, Malcolm. Thank you."

"It's nice to see you around again, especially when you're smiling. Have a good night." He handed her the leash.

"First time I've felt like smiling in a while. Does that all-hours coffee shop across the street have a problem with pets?"

He shook his head. "Very pet friendly."

"Okay, I'll be back." She went back outside and tried again to reach her sister.

Meredith's phone once more went to voicemail, and Lexi was certain the likelihood that she would come home tonight was nil. Meredith liked to save the world, doing volunteer trips or whatever, hoping that she could help foster kids that had it worse than they had. To each their own. Lexi donated money to the cause while Meredith liked to be hands-on in the system. It actually made her a much better person than Lexi, because Lexi wasn't sure she could stomach some of the places Meredith had grown up.

The cold air crushed her as she ran across the street with Bacon huffing and puffing behind her. When she pulled the heavy door, her stomach rumbled at the sweet scents of coffee and muffins. Even the pup grumbled for food.

"Okay, you get something too," she told Bacon.

After looking over her shoulder to be sure no one was watching her, she ordered a vanilla latte, chocolate croissant, and a slice of carrot cake for Bacon. They hunkered down in the back corner, and Lexi punched the Wi-Fi password the cashier had given her into her laptop. She pinged Shadow as she waited for the latte to cool.

Shadow: *Got your email. All looks good.*
Silver: *You said you had some concerns before. Someone wanted what I wouldn't sell too.*
Shadow: *Yes*
Silver: *So that's all taken care of?*

She tapped her finger, waiting for Shadow. There could be a dozen reasons he wasn't answering immediately. She had no idea where in the world he was, if he was alone, in public, or on the phone. But as the minutes ticked on and she sipped her latte, Lexi knew there was a problem.

Silver: *Shadow.*
Silver: *??*
Shadow: *Not all taken care of. Why?*
Silver: *Went to a friend's, someone broke in. Power was cut with a jammer*
Shadow: *Where are you?*
Shadow: *Don't answer that. Go off the grid. Now.*

Her fingers hovered over the keyboard as she typed out and deleted the same questions more than once: *What is the problem?*

Shadow: *I still see you. So can the world if they're smart enough. Shut down and move. See you when and where we planned for the auction.*

Then he went offline. *Shit.* Lexi looked around. Everything seemed benign. But she'd never had Shadow talk to her like that before, never felt the sense of dread that had started with Parker mentioning the jammer—which meant the person who'd tried to break into his place was most certainly *not* Matt—and now Shadow's demand that she go dark for weeks.

If there was one person she'd listen to, it was him. And maybe Parker. Perhaps BlackDawn… she wondered what his take on Monarch would be.

She shut down and packed her computer, shoved the croissant into a bag, and guzzled the rest of her super-hot latte before she tugged Bacon to fall in line behind her. This would be a long night, and for the time being, she had no idea where to go or how to get there.

*Actually...* she had transportation. The old Lexi surged in her veins. She knew exactly what her next move was. How had she even forgotten?

Her cell phone buzzed, and a dooming thought pricked at her. Buzz kill. Was Matt texting her? Maybe it was Shadow telling her that going dark meant turning off her cell? God, going dark wasn't her thing. She needed a checklist.

Pulling the phone free of her back pocket, she hesitated before swiping the screen. The digits rang clear and familiar. Parker. She hadn't saved his number, but there was his text, waiting. Damn near giddy, she swiped the screen again to read it.

*Hope you're dreaming. Gnight.*

Holy shit. Her entire body swooned from four words. So sweet and almost intimate. He didn't write that he hoped she was asleep. But dreaming…

Stepping onto the sidewalk and not feeling the bite of the cold wind anymore, she imagined what she could dream. He'd given her a lot to remember. Lexi bit her lip as a heat blossoming in her chest made her light on her feet. Bacon trotted beside her as they hustled back into the apartment building. As soon as Monarch sold, maybe she could show up on Parker's doorstep again and pick up where they'd just left off.

She pushed inside, and Malcolm greeted her. "Miss Dare."

"Can you do me a huge favor?" He'd done it before, every time she needed to get Bacon safely stowed when she traveled for work.

"If it has to do with my furry friend, I would love to."

Lexi jumped up on her toes and hugged the guy. "Thank you."

He chuckled. "At your service. But truly, Miss Dare, I'm happy that you have a smile."

"Thanks." She bent down and ruffled Bacon's fur. "Be a good girl. Thanks again."

Then she rushed to the elevator and headed upstairs. A few floors up, Lexi, infused with excitement, headed to Meredith's apartment. She grabbed the front door key that Meredith stupidly left under the mat and let herself into the empty apartment. It was cold and dark, looking as though it hadn't been lived in for a few weeks. Yeah, her sister was off somewhere, and if Lexi was a halfway decent sister or friend, she would've known that. It was insane how deeply she'd been sucked into Matt's world.

Enough of that. Because Parker wanted her to dream.

She smiled in the dark then moved to the kitchen and shuffled through the junk drawer. Bingo. The key to her Gixxer. Excitement surged through her. This was a big step to becoming herself again.

She headed to the bedroom to borrow clothes and anything else that could get her through the next two weeks. There'd be a bag in the closet and pajamas in the dresser. After tossing a pile of socks and PJs on the bed, she pulled open the walk-in closet door and flipped the switch for the light. On the closet shelf, right smack in the middle, was a cardboard box labeled LEXI, as though Meredith had known that one day, Lexi would be staring into her closet.

"Oh boy," she breathed then went on tiptoes to pull it down.

Lexi kneeled next to the box, tugging the flaps free. Her clothes were folded neatly in even squares. They were all things she thought she'd tossed or given to Meredith when Matt had started to make a fuss about her wardrobe, saying she stood out too much, acted too sexy. The thought of that made her laugh. How had she transitioned from this—she unfolded a pair of tight leather pants—to the boring jeans she wore now?

Though the unflattering jeans hadn't stopped Parker…

But, God, she loved the pants in her hand. The ones that Matt said made her look like a biker slut. The ones that were her absolute favorite. Reverently, she placed them next to her and kept digging through the box. Shame poured over her at how she had abandoned the very fiber of who she was for a man who'd promised never to leave her. Surely she was a slam dunk for therapy. But it was nothing she couldn't figure out on her own if she really worked on it.

Lexi pulled outfit after outfit from the box and transferred them to the bag she was borrowing. Finally, she slipped out of her generic, blend-into-the-crowd clothes and into the everyday version of what Silver would wear in public.

A thrill ran through her. She walked over to Meredith's bathroom, raided the makeup that had been left home, and when she was done, though it was the middle of the night, Lexi's ice-blue eyes were smoky and her lips were glossy. Her clothes were so… *her*, and she took a deep, soul-resetting breath.

Returning to the closet, Lexi found a jacket that she'd have to remember to give back to Meredith, and she twirled in front of the wall mirror. *That* girl, even in the dark, felt like coming home. She didn't know where she was headed. Literally, she had no plans except to go back to the coffee shop and buy them out of muffins and scones. Then she could disappear.

Lexi grabbed the eyeliner and wrote a note to Meredith on the mirror. She stared at the simplicity and truth of her words.

*I'm back. xo, Lex*

Bike keys and bag of clothes in hand, Lexi secured her laptop in a messenger bag strapped to her back and walked out with a renewed sense of who she was and what she was doing. This was the old her, reborn.

# CHAPTER TWENTY-THREE

"You tap into that comm system yet?" Jared's voice carried before he walked into Parker's office.

"Yup. Boring-ass shit, but soon as something decent pops up, I'll let you know."

"Alright." Boss Man cracked his knuckles, pacing. "Dig into the recruit files?"

"Yeah, I'd say three of them are solid Delta material."

"It's not for Delta."

Parker spun in his chair. "Yeah?" Because none of the guys would fit on any other team Jared had. If they weren't for Delta—but they could be for…

"With the girls all pregnant and their husbands asking about paternity leave, seems like a good time to bulk up the main team."

Holy. Shit. Titan was expanding. Parker grabbed the jackets for the three men that he thought would pass muster. Jax Riddle, Bishop O'Kane, and Locke Oliver. "Then these three are solid Titan."

Jared glared. "Any of them have baggage?"

"Nothing that's out of the ordinary for us."

He nodded and took the folders. "Right. Well, if there's nothing sketch, I'll give these guys to Rocco for a look. What else is going on?"

Parker thought about Lexi and how she'd disappeared. He'd even checked a few sources—not like he was trying to be an overbearing stalker asshole—but the girl hadn't used any credit cards or her cell phone in days. Checking up didn't make him a creep. Except it sounded like it did. Fuck. He was in way over his head and had no idea what to think about anything. "Not much."

Jared slapped the folders against his palm. "What's going on with that side project you picked up?"

"The Monarch security check?"

He nodded. "Yeah."

"Nothing. Dude hasn't given me much, and what I do have isn't turning up shit."

"Waste of time?"

"A favor owed that will be returned."

Jared nodded as though he appreciated the behind-the-scenes, underground world Parker utilized. "So it's almost wrapped?"

"Almost. Shadow's got an in-person meeting in a week or so. Wants me there as more of an extra body than anything else. But other than that, the project is done." Not that Parker was going to blow off what Shadow was asking, especially if he could help Silver, but Silver had been MIA, likely preparing last-minute details for the auction, and Shadow was hell-bent on being vague.

Winters and Rocco walked in. Rocco had dark circles under his eyes and coffee in hand.

"Long night?" Parker asked.

Rocco scowled, and Winters laughed, slapping Rocco on the back.

"Babies are a fuckuvalot of work." He guzzled coffee. "Cat's got it down, but man. Not easy."

Jared pushed the folders at Rocco. "New guys. Thumbs up or down by the end of the day. We'll make arrangements soon as you say go."

Both men's eyes went wide. Rocco put his coffee on a console.

"Hey, jackass." Parker moved the cup. "Spill that on there, and you and I are gonna have problems."

"Yeah, yeah." Rocco's exhaustion was gone, replaced by curiosity as he went through the jackets. "Fuckin' hell. These dudes are solid."

Winters peered over Rocco's shoulder and nodded. "I know that guy."

"This one?" Rocco lifted a head shot.

"Yeah. Man's good. Was deep in a weapons trafficking cartel, right?" Winters turned to Parker.

"Right," he confirmed.

"Alright, assholes." Boss Man headed out. "Gossip later. I've got to get Sugar's sweet ass to a doctor's appointment."

"You going to tell us girl or boy yet?" Rocco called after him then mumbled, "Totally going to be a girl. The man is destined to be surrounded by women."

Winters laughed. Then they both looked expectantly at Parker.

"Nope." Parker turned around, pulling up screens of nothing to look busy.

"Do you know what the baby is?" Rocco asked.

"Have you looked?" Winters pushed. "Do some hacker magic and give us a confirmation. We'll go paint the place camo-pink."

Parker shook his head. "I do *not* have a death wish."

Rocco shook his head too. "Nah, Boss Man'd get over it."

"Shit, Boss Man isn't who I'm worried about."

Winters and Rocco both made agreeing noises. Jared was one thing. Sugar, on the other hand, was just scary when she wanted to be.

"So how's Lexi Dare?" Winters changed the subject.

Parker glared. "If you girls are done gossiping, out."

Rocco grabbed his coffee and perched on the edge of a table. "Must be going good?"

Winters raised an eyebrow. "Or is she still with Matt?"

"No," Parker growled, not interested in sharing, especially since she'd disappeared and he was doing his best not to care too much. He'd had one day with her—even if he had made her come on his hand and moan his name. One single day. His gut churned that she was gone. *Again.* Second time she'd left him after he'd saved her. He thought she needed help with… something but had no idea what.

Parker did, however, know where Matt Pindon was almost every waking moment. If that fucker did anything that looked like coming after Lexi, Parker would kill him just for the sport of it. Shit. He rubbed a hand over his face.

"Going that well, huh?" Winters joked.

"She's with her sister."

"So you and her…?"

Rocco sipped his coffee. "Obviously not. Dude needs to get laid."

Parker glared. "Would you two fucks shut it?"

Both laughed, but Winters shook his head. "No joke, girl seems like she's a good catch."

"That's her, right?" Rocco nodded at the desk, where the print-out from her sister's security footage was.

Yup, that was her. So her. Hotter and sexier than when he'd dropped her off. The shot was of her walking out only an hour later. She was on the way out the front door, with her back to the camera, but she was looking to the side. Her platinum blond hair looked nearly white in the black-and-white footage, and that *wasn't* what he'd left her wearing. Because if it had been, he'd never have left. That image showed classic Lexi. The one who had all but disappeared. "Uh… yeah."

"Not creepy at all, dude." Rocco laughed.

Parker balled his fists. "I don't know where she is."

Winters stepped closer. "So use your boy genius powers and find her."

Parker pinched his eyes closed, trying to think of any way to track her down without being a super-sketch privacy invader. "Some things you're not supposed to do."

Winters grabbed the paper. "Like finding her on security footage."

"Asshole." He reached for the print-out. Parker had stared at it forever. Even in the almost-grainy picture, she was clear. She wore a killer shirt along with tight black pants and fuck-me boots, and from the visible slice of her face, her dark eyes were made up like a rock star's. He could describe that outfit in detail, could almost feel it against his palms he'd studied it so hard. She looked like sex and cotton had collided, making it the world's most teasing security footage shot ever. It had to be less than fifty degrees outside, and she was dragging what looked like a leather jacket. Parker closed his eyes but could still picture her vividly.

Winters took the paper and stared. "Damn."

Rocco nodded. “Babe’s hot.”

“That’s a Sugar lookalike,” Winters agreed. “*Not* the girl I met with Matt. This one is a total badass.”

“Same girl. More like who she was before that asshole got in her head. But yeah…” Parker blew out a breath. “She kinda is.” Then he dropped his head forward, trying to ignore the hurricane of emotions: anger, arousal, worry, frustration. “My problem is, she’s totally gone.”

# CHAPTER TWENTY-FOUR

Morning light poured in from windows high in the cathedral-height ceilings. It had been two weeks since Lexi had walked out of her sister's apartment and gone dark. Slipping from one extreme to the other, Union Station was about as public as she could get. She leaned forward, balancing on the front two legs of her café chair. Noise echoed, and people in business suits rushed around.

This wasn't her scene. Really, Washington, DC, as a whole, wasn't either. The people were useless. They liked to hear themselves talk too much—as evident by the several self-important types on their phones while ordering coffee, talking as though they held the keys to world peace—and they all looked the same. Dark suit, red or blue tie, cuff links, and smartphones attached to their ears.

She didn't blend in at all in her form-fitting T-shirt, leather pants, and boots, which made the phone-stuck-on-ear folks either avoid her or stare. Clothes weren't a cure for losing one's self, but they'd been the catalyst. As each day passed, and with every silly self-help book she'd read, Lexi had become more confident and more her.

"Are you using this chair?" The man was already moving it, cliché phone stuck against his head.

She hooked the chair with her boot, fighting the submissive urge to agree, and kept it close as she waited for the barista to call her second latte of the day. "I'm waiting for someone."

The man nodded as though it wasn't a big deal. Because it wasn't. Only Matt would've thought it was. Lexi channeled one of the pages of the many books she'd read while off the grid. *I deserve to feel great. I am worthy of being safe. I can say yes, no, or maybe later. My thoughts and feelings are allowed.* She took a deep breath. Thinking simple, common-sense thoughts helped. Go figure…

She thought back to her time off the grid. No computer usage. No cell. Nothing to do except hit bookstores and coast by libraries. Reading and journaling passed the time. She wanted to understand herself. Like, she *knew* herself but didn't *get* herself. If that made sense. Even now, sitting in the middle of a commuter hub, she didn't totally understand the difference, but the weeks alone had helped. Connecting the dots from her foster home roulette to standing by Matt the abuser hadn't taken much thought or energy; it had just taken self-reflection.

And now… she wanted to see Shadow, to show off her newfound old self. Not only would he notice, but he'd be proud. That excitement was one of the reasons she'd arrived early, just in case he did too. She also wanted to call Parker the second the auction had wrapped up. With all the time on her hands, she'd thought about him to the point of exhaustion. Or exhilaration.

The vaulted ceilings and marble floor amplified every sound. The throngs of people made her itch to get back on her bike and fly away. Just give her a laptop in the middle of nowhere. Maybe give her Parker in the middle of nowhere…

Jittery, Lexi tapped her nails on the table. Maybe she shouldn't have ordered a second latte. Though she didn't have to actually drink it. *Okay, just calm down.*

Lexi pressed her fingers onto the table. She was at the right location on the right day. It was time to come in from the dark in the electronic sense. She flipped open her laptop and logged on to the device that hadn't been booted up in weeks. Emails, messages, and everything else had piled up. After a few seconds, she disabled her Wi-Fi and turned off anything that would track her location. As she scanned through, one codex message from BlackDawn caught her attention. What had that guy learned about her? What did he think about her sale? Did he notice she'd gone silent? She would notice if he disappeared. Watching him work had entertained her for hours.

He challenged the way she thought about her job, the world. Black was by far the smartest, most talented of the elite she knew.

Knowing that his request was outdated, she opened the message anyway.

BlackDawn: *Dealing w/ a salted, brute-force hash attack. Got any plain texts I can pull from?*

Then in the same thread an hour later.

BlackDawn: *Never mind. Got it. You alive?*

Why had he asked that? Had Shadow told him that she was physically in danger? Or was that rhetorical? Of course it was. Overthinking much?

She needed to say something and probably give him a virtual fist bump because over the last two weeks, she'd used a few tricks he'd showed her over the years. Nothing too complicated, just things she never would've guessed she would need to know, like accessing her bank accounts without a trace and erasing records of her staying at cash-only motels. Those had been her off-the-grid tools. Funny how life went full circle.

She powered on her phone to ping Shadow while simultaneously reaching back into her memory, trying to pinpoint the moment her path had first crossed with Black's. Sometime in her teens, when she'd been too much of a punk and trying to prove to the world that she was as good as she thought she was. Black had seemed to be doing the same—though they had distinct specialties, hence the partnership.

*Bzz.* Her eyes shot to the phone on the café table as if it was a lit line of dynamite. Wow. Maybe she should've gone with decaf. She didn't know the number but assumed it was her broker. The guy had a new phone almost every day, which was a pain to keep up with, but she didn't blame him.

"Shadow," Lexi answered as her gaze darted through the crowds milling through Union Station. "I'm here super early. Are you?"

"Not yet. Just checking on you." The apprehension in his

voice made unease churn in her stomach.

"Everything still a go today?"

Shadow cleared his throat. "That buyer that I was… concerned about, they're offering to triple, maybe even quadruple, the best offer you'll get from any NATO country."

*What?* "No. You have my list of approved bidders. Why are we even talking about this?" Last thing she wanted was her exploit to be resold to some third-world despot or terrorist leader who would do a lot worse than cyber spying.

"I just want you to think about what you're turning down."

This was about money? "What I'm turning down for both of us? Is that it?" She shook her head. "Since when do you care so much about your fifteen percent?"

"I don't, Silver. But—"

"Then why are you acting so different?"

"I just want to be sure," he mumbled.

"I care about what happens to the world. Selling Monarch willy-nilly isn't a good thing."

He huffed. "And I care what happens to *you*, Silver."

"So this is still about the break-in?"

"Maybe. Alright, be there soon. We can talk in person."

No, she wanted information now. "Is someone trying to stop the auction? And what did BlackDawn find?"

"Does *in person* mean anything? As long as the program is still saved in more than one place—your standard operating procedure—everything will be fine."

She bit her lip. "You've scared me. You ask me to do what you know I will never do, and I still don't know the details of your concerns."

"Silver—"

"What is it?" she hissed. "Just level with me. Someone's going to try to steal it from me physically?"

Shadow cleared his throat. "That was a concern. Which is why I asked you to go dark."

"And you said you'd fix it." She tried to keep her voice low, but she was exasperated—and scared.

"I did. I hired help."

"You did what? How many more people are you going to bring into this? First, another hacker nosing into my business, and now, what, an armed guard or something?"

"It's our mutual friend."

She shook her head. "I don't have a friend like that."

"You do. Black does security in person too."

"What?" She closed her eyes, trying to piece everything together.

"He's a client. Just as you're a client. He did a generic security sweep for me, and he has no problem getting physical. It all works."

"I don't want to meet him! No one knows Silver. I don't want to meet *anyone.*"

"I know, but desperate times call for—"

"Now we're desperate?" she snapped.

"When your safety's an issue, yes. He'll find you if I don't see you first."

BlackDawn would find her? If there was anything she knew about Black, it was likely he already had.

# CHAPTER TWENTY-FIVE

Parker tugged down a ball cap and held a coffee cup from the first café he saw. There were a couple of places to grab coffee in Union Station, and even though it was probably coffee blasphemy to bring a cup from Grinds into Grounded, he wasn't going to waste time determining there was no Shadow at the first place without buying a cup of joe.

This wasn't a typical Titan job; it was a favor. Shadow had helped him over the years, and while he didn't need a broker on the regular, the man was a source of information and a trusted ally. As it turned out from their brief conversation, Shadow was more worried about the Monarch auction than he had initially let on.

They'd never met in person, but Parker had always felt he could pick a hacker out of a crowd. They had a look, and it wasn't cliché flannel shirts and hipster pants. It was more a look in their eyes. As if they knew that cameras were watching, bank accounts weren't safe, and identities were easy enough to steal. Add on the nerves he'd picked up when Shadow reached out for security, and Parker felt positive that he could easily pick out Shadow. He'd be older, concerned about a deal, and discreetly look loaded.

There was a bonus to this job. Parker wanted to see Monarch before it was sold. Simple curiosity had made the trek into DC worth it.

Taking a pull from the coffee, he dropped into a chair along the wall and assessed the open area of the coffee shop. Suits talking business, and tourists snapping pictures, begging to get pickpocketed. None looked like he'd guess Shadow would.

"Silver. Order up."

Like Monarch's Silver? What were the chances…? He assumed he'd find Shadow first, but meeting Silver in person would be interesting. Parker's eyes shot to the barista pushing a drink onto the counter.

In a split second, everything he knew about his world shifted. A chair pushed back, and a Lexi Dare lookalike stood with her back toward him. He knew that hair, that body, and the clothes similar to the security footage. What was she doing there? After she'd never responded to his text the night he dropped her off? And what was she doing… now…?

Parker watched her walk to the coffee called out for Silver.

"Round two, huh?" The barista laughed.

Parker's eyes tracked to the small table she'd left within her reach, with another coffee cup and the laptop Lexi had been so protective of. She hadn't seen him, and he couldn't register the woman in front of him, with those pouty pink lips, who joked with the barista. She was sexy like he couldn't comprehend. She wasn't doing a damn thing other than walking back to her table, coffee in hand, but the sway of her hips, the perk of her breasts…

"Fuck me," he whispered and stood, scraping his chair loudly enough that she looked up.

Their eyes locked. Her lips twitched. Not a smile. Nowhere close to a hello. The leather-clad rock-star lookalike apparently was as shocked as he was. Parker didn't speak. Didn't move. Until he did, bounding over to her and strangling the urge to grab her, kiss her, and drag her to a back room where he could have his hands and mouth all over her.

On a scale from one to smokin', Lexi was nuclear. With wide eyes, she tilted her head to look up at him. There was little room between them, and if he could erase the inches without looking like some overeager fuck, he would.

"Parker, hi." She bit her lip, looking as if she'd been caught red-handed. Her cheeks pinked, and her eyes danced, wary, searching around him.

For what, he didn't know and didn't care.

"Nice to see you." She turned and shut her computer.

"Can I join you?" he asked.

"I can't."

"You can't, what?" He wouldn't take no for an answer, completely mesmerized and almost forgetting his confusion about the Silver coffee questions.

Again, her pupils danced. "I'm working."

"Same." He pulled out the chair at her table then sat down.

"That seat's for my co-worker. He'll be here any time now. You should really go." Lexi twisted her coffee cup.

The scrawl of the name on the cup caught his eye and disappeared each time she moved it. But it read Silver. He hadn't heard wrong, hadn't lost his damn mind. Anxiety prickled down his spine as all the pieces lined up. The collision of his two worlds was explosive. Was he wrong? No, there were too many coincidences that he should've picked up on already. His hand clapped on top of hers.

Slowly, she pulled in a quiet breath and tried to tug her hand back, but he clasped it and didn't let go. "Parker, you have to go."

Shoving emotion aside, he ran through the facts. She'd gone back to a dangerous, abusive relationship for a computer? The unexplained jammer that he couldn't figure out how to blame on Matt? Shadow calling with a security concern about Monarch, and Lexi sitting here with that coffee cup? All the dots lined up. "No way…"

Her forehead pinched. "What?"

"You're Silver."

Color drained out of her face as her smile went flat and paranoia exploded in her icy blue eyes. She dropped her gaze to the scrawl on the coffee cup. "I don't know what you mean. It's just a nickname for a coffee shop."

He leaned forward to study her lying eyes. "Damn, Lex."

"No," she whispered, shaking her head in the most unconvincing manner. "I'm not."

Despite the leather and eyeliner, she looked as delicate as she had in his sweats with towel-dried hair. Parker's heart pounded as the magnitude of their extensive relationship formed, all the things Parker had assumed simply by never asking. What he'd known was Silver was a code-breaking *dude*. A trusted, competitive contemporary who Parker could find in the middle of cyberspace, run a hack with, try to one-up, and say see ya until later. That was Silver. The winter princess scowling at him? Not Silver. But yet it all made sense. "You're…"

"Busy," she mumbled, refusing eye contact.

Parker rubbed his temples. How could he know a guy for a decade plus, when the guy wasn't even a guy? "You can't be…" You can't be *him*.

"No idea what you're talking about." She stood, shoved the laptop into a messenger bag, and tossed the full coffee cup with Silver scrawled across the side.

"Wait. Don't leave."

"I have to work." Then she ducked under the table and retrieved a *motorcycle helmet*. "Nice seeing you. Thanks for everything before."

With a toss of the bag over her shoulder, she tugged her thick ponytail from under the strap of the bag. Damn, it was the kind of hair that a man could wrap a fist around.

What he knew and what he saw didn't mesh. Lexi was a wisp with icy blue eyes who had thankfully left her shit fiancé, and Parker had a major hard-on for her. What Lexi did not look like was an elite hacker who had bantered back and forth to him in code for a third of his life.

He remained frozen to the table, remembering the weekend that Matt had met her. Bachelor party for one of their boys. Parker had been able to write off almost the whole thing on his taxes because there was a technology conference at the same hotel, including a hacker competition. Holy shit.

Lexi Dare was, without a doubt, SilverChaos.

# CHAPTER TWENTY-SIX

Parker abandoned his coffee and jogged until he came up beside her sweet body speeding through Union Station's wide corridor. "Give me a second."

"Nope. Bad idea."

A wave of men's glances followed her. Not a single man could walk by without staring, and she didn't seem to notice. She hit the escalators, and Parker stayed with her as a new rush of people departing from a train swallowed them with briefcases and rolling suitcases. Lexi quickly moved to another platform then slid behind a black gate, ignoring a large red-and-white "Closed to Public" sign. Parker stayed on her six as people bustled around.

"Lexi, come on."

"Leave me alone."

But he didn't. Wouldn't. Suddenly they were alone in a maintenance hallway. She pushed through another door covered in dust and cobwebs that creaked when it opened into a service alley. It was dark, dank, and dirty. They were somewhere between the rails and a garage. Exhaust and the smell of metal hung in the air. Lexi never slowed, an old pro in the back tunnels of Union Station. That didn't thrill him.

Enough. He reached for the sharp angle of her shoulder. "Where are you going—"

The little blonde spun on him, helmet in hand as a weapon, and smashed it toward his face.

"Seriously?" Parker ducked, grabbed her arm, and spun her around so that the sinful round of her backside was pressed against his thighs. "Don't be like that."

Sweet citrus drifted into his nose when she reached back and ran her hand into his hair. She didn't pull, but she didn't let go either. "I need you to go away."

Parker belted his arm across her chest while he kept her helmet-wielding arm down. His lips brushed her ear, and at that moment, the citrus struck him. "You *don't* need to take a swing at me."

"You follow me into a back alley?" she whispered. "I can hit you if I want."

He chuckled into her hair. "I'm not Matt, and you *are* Silver."

"God." She twisted in his hold, her lips coming within inches of his. "Leave it be."

"Why would I want to do that?"

The brim of his ball cap pressed against the side of her head, sheltering him, giving him a moment to savor her. She smelled like lemons. Sweet and tart, which was exactly what she was like. Why he noticed and why he cared jumbled together. Truth was, knowing Silver, the way the hacker could work a job, how intelligent Silver was, how much of a challenge… it all shifted what had already been extraordinarily hot and full of potential to something with years' worth of gravity and depth.

Their tension multiplied the sexual charge that had been there in spades. Whatever he'd ignored after he'd driven away that night weeks ago was nothing compared to the lightning pulsing between them. She felt it too—he knew that without a doubt.

"You were here to work," he whispered. "I was too."

"Good for you, Parker."

And that was his in. "Try BlackDawn."

Her head whipped up, her glare disbelieving. "Excuse me?"

He smiled as he watched her process his screen name. "Now we seem to be on equal footing. Everything I didn't get before makes sense."

She rolled her tongue over her bottom lip before catching it between her teeth. She didn't steal away, didn't look away. Just blinked and tried again. "You're still holding me."

"I know." He squeezed her tighter because God, did he

know he was holding her. It'd been over two weeks since he'd had her in his arms, and with her smelling all woman and dressed like sex in leather, there was no chance in the world Parker would release her. "If you didn't know, it's one of my favorite things to do."

Her pink glossed lips parted, but nothing came out.

"I like the new look. Old look. Whatever."

She blinked darkly shaded eyes. "You remember?"

"Something like this? Shit, sweetheart, etched into my memory."

Slowly her body softened. "Shadow hired you?"

He nodded.

"You're BlackDawn?" She sounded breathy and gave another slow blink.

Yeah, a little breathy and a lot bothered. Maybe angry and confused. Who knew what else? Mostly she sounded like he felt. Totally mind-fucked and turned on.

Trains clanged in the background. Horns blared from distant streets.

"Yeah." A lump formed in his throat as he released her, dropping his arms and letting her step back.

"I can't process any of this."

"What's there to process?" But even he knew that was a lie. All of this was confusing. How he felt, how she looked, what they thought about the tension they couldn't ignore, and the work they'd done together for so long without knowing. Silver was anonymous, and his work at Titan was classified. None of this should converge.

He grabbed her hips, and she slammed her open palms against his chest.

"Why are you angry, Lex?"

"I just am." Her fingers splayed then clutched his shirt.

He jerked her close, and her mouth went wide. The passion in her icy blue gaze rocketed through him. He shook his head. "No reason for that."

"Go away. I need to think. I thought I had my head right, but now—God!"

His eyes dropped to her hands fisting his shirt. "You're holding on to me, sweetheart."

But instead of pushing him away, her fingers bit tighter into his chest. He spun them around so her back was against the wall, his chest pressing against hers with her clenched hands sandwiched between them. Her breaths came quicker. Her tongue darted out and licked her lip, and he groaned, flexing his hips into her.

"You still haven't let go," he breathed against her lips.

"I don't want to."

His mouth collided with hers, his tongue plunging into her mouth as she gasped and moaned. Her hands tightened, trying to pull him closer though it was impossible. Whatever had happened in Parker's kitchen was sweet, and even in his Ranger Rover's backseat, he'd been careful with her. This wasn't like that. It was harsh and rough and hungry.

Lexi's legs crawled up his thighs, and he pressed against her, giving her his weight, making sure she knew that all the blood in his body had rushed to his cock. He moved to the slope of her neck, kissing and scraping her soft skin with his teeth. His tongue licked, and as he savored her skin, her hips started a sinful rhythm.

"Wait." Harshly, Lexi released her grip on him. "Parker, God. Wait… work. I have—" She gasped when he ran his lips to the spot behind her ear. "Work."

Who cared? He needed her alone. Not in an alley but a bed, where he'd strip the leather off her legs and kiss his way higher until he could delve into that pussy and make her come. But damn the look in her eyes. The second he let go, she would run. He didn't know why and couldn't push her to stay.

"Parker, please."

He had to release her, though not without a warning. "This isn't over, Lex."

As he set her down, her eyes squeezed shut, and her erratic breathing might as well have been a stroke to his swollen shaft. He didn't want to stop, and with her panting like that, those kiss-swollen, pink lips of hers teasing him… he shook his head. He was lust drunk and nowhere near ready to think about the Monarch job.

"I have to go," she whispered, retrieving her dropped helmet.

"We'll talk about this later."

She bit her bottom lip then spun away. Parker let her go, watching as a tightness hit his chest. His arms were empty, and for the first time, his life felt empty too, devoid of a partnership they didn't even have. Yet. He wanted her friendship, wanted her in his bed. He already enjoyed working with Silver. What a wild combination, maybe making him acknowledge for the first time how much he wanted something substantial outside of Titan.

She hopped over a low cement retaining wall, then she was gone. He was alone in the middle of a maintenance alley. Trains clanged and echoed around him. The exhaust replaced the lemon scent that had made his mouth water. Even as she disappeared from sight, his boots wanted to chase her down. Seconds later, the growl of a motorcycle roared to life then faded away.

Time was drawing near. Monarch would go to auction soon. So even if Lexi ran, Parker knew Silver well enough that there was no doubt she'd be back inside for the auction.

Silver was Lexi was… *his*. That put a smile on his face.

# CHAPTER TWENTY-SEVEN

Lexi couldn't shake the feeling that someone was watching her. Parker? Phiber? Matt? She needed to get back inside the station. The auction would start on time whether she was next to Shadow or not, but did she really want him to give her hell for showing up late? Nope. Not at all. But then she'd see Parker, and she felt like a damn fool. Running away from him? What was this, sixth grade? But she was overrun with emotions, and instead of crying or screaming, she ran.

Parker and BlackDawn were one and the same. So she'd trusted both without question.

She revved the engine then rode around another traffic-filled corner until she hit the next red light. The unsteadiness in her stomach churned. Looking for whatever made her feel hunted, Lexi checked her mirrors and saw nothing.

There was less than an hour until go time. Less than sixty tiny minutes to replay everything that had just happened with Parker. She let his name roll in her mind. When his brooding eyes had landed on her in the coffee shop, she'd wanted to run. To him. From him.

She shook her head and rested her boots on the asphalt, waiting to move through the gridlocked light. "Come on."

The light turned red again, and no one had moved. She dropped her head then gave up waiting, forging a path down the street. Cars honked. Taxi drivers edged closer. She didn't care and couldn't stay put.

One turn, then a shortcut through an alley, and the arm of the Union Station parking garage gate lifted after she grabbed her ticket. She parked her bike as a text message buzzed her phone. She didn't look at it, knowing it had to be Shadow and wishing it was Parker. She headed through the cold garage, jogging down the escalators then skipping past the regular entrances to a back door.

She opened the door labeled "Authorized Entry Only" then walked down a poorly lit corridor, where she read the text.

Shadow: *Where are you? Thought you were here early. I want you to meet BlackDawn.*

That made her snort-laugh. Today was going to be absurd or epic. Her money was on a little bit of both.

Parker settled in diagonally from Shadow after discreetly nodding hello. Shadow had a good instinct, but what he didn't know, or hadn't shared with Parker, was that there'd already been a piss-poor attempt to steal the hardware—at *his* house. He wanted to shake his head and growl at the guy who should have read him in on all the concerns.

Jared had barely signed off on the job. Shadow was a good point of contact, though right about now, he was on Parker's shit list. He shifted in his seat, resisting the urge to text Lexi, and instead he tapped his fingers, unsure of how much leeway to give Shadow for not sharing all pertinent intel.

A race of excitement slid down his back as he heard the click of her heeled boots. His muscles bunched, and his hands clenched. Staying seated was a task when all he wanted to do was drag her to him. Her ass swayed as she walked to Shadow. There was a gentleness in her voice as she said hello and gave him a half-hug, making Parker jealous of the old bastard who had her attention.

Shit. He needed to focus. On something beside her voice, her walk, the memory of her taste and how she smelled. Parker groaned.

Shadow nodded as if he were signaling to Parker who the woman was. He could read her expression somewhat. Nervous curiosity. Apprehensive excitement. Lexi shifted in her chair, casting her eyes across the crowd. She was looking for him. God, he liked being the person she wanted her gaze on.

Shadow motioned discreetly, and Lexi pivoted, landing a sexy glare on Parker. The heat in her eyes reached his groin. Even his heartbeat picked up the pace. But he kept all that to himself as he casually acknowledged her with a small chin lift.

As if she'd been caught, she dropped her head and fidgeted. Her fingers knotted then retied. Was she still mad? Why was she nervous? Because of him or the auction? Their security threat? His nightmare was her in danger, but the threat would soon be over. After all the Monarch file transfers were complete, it'd be magic. Threat averted. Poof, danger gone. Someone else would be in possession of Monarch, and their worries about stolen technology, or worst case, a kidnapping where she'd be forced to reveal the coding behind the exploit, would be over.

Assuming he knew everything he needed.

Which he didn't. If he knew everything he needed to know, Parker could've put together a statistical likelihood of almost any situation happening. But nope, not with the limited intel shared. He bunched his fists. Everything about this job had changed now that Silver was Lexi.

Parker picked up his phone and sent her a text.

Parker: *I didn't say before, Monarch's incredible. Proud of you.*

Her fidgeting hands picked up the phone, then her head shot toward him. He wanted to laugh. No one had apparently told her the intricacies of not drawing attention to the undercover guy. But then a smile she tried to hide rolled onto her lips, and her fingers worked the phone.

Lexi: *No one has told me they are proud over anything I've done. Ever. Except maybe Shadow but he doesn't count. ;)*

His heart seized, then his phone showed another message from her.

Lexi: *So thx. That means a lot.*

He kept his eyes up but responded.

Parker: *Second time it's come...*
Lexi: $2^{nd}$ *time what?*
Parker: *That I learn you haven't been told what you should.*
Lexi: **blush**
Parker: *Prepare yourself, sweetheart. That's all about to change.*
Lexi: *Oh yeah?! :)*
Parker: *You should know, you're...*
Parker: *Smart.*
Parker: *Gorgeous.*
Parker: *Sexy.*
Parker: *Crazy intelligent <— guess that's smart, huh?*

He watched her stifle a laugh and Shadow give her a questioning glance.

Lexi: *It's easier for me to talk like this.*
Parker: *I get that*
Lexi: *I've msg'ed you a thousand times.*
Parker: *Yup*
Lexi: *Sorry I ran out on you earlier.*
Parker: *Are you gonna explain??*
Lexi: *Shadow's looking at me funny*
Parker: *Let him look*
Lexi: *Everything I ever wanted was so close. I never saw it.*
Parker: *The auction?*
Lexi: *No*
Parker: *Monarch?*
Lexi: *No!*
Parker: *Hanging w Shadow, drinking crappy coffee?*
Lexi: *No!!*
Parker: *What then?*
Lexi: *YOU*

Parker: *;) I know...*

She laughed out loud then texted him a smiley face. Now it was his turn to smile, but he hid it from the world while sipping his coffee.

Lexi: *Yeah, this is easier*

Parker: *For some things. Agree. Tell me what you're not telling me IRL*

Her head tilted, and she put the phone down. Picked it up. Put it down. Then she typed out something. Nothing came through though.

Parker: *Hit send, sweetheart*

She picked up the phone to read the text, and he took his eyes off her to gaze around, looking for who knew what. Shadow really should've given him more of a heads-up, or even an idea of what was really going on. His phone showed a text message from her, and he opened it.

Lexi: *I've so fallen for you*

His stomach jumped into his throat. But he had an easy answer for her.

Parker: *Good. Glad ur right there with me. Cause I'm in deep.*

He checked the time. Shit. Thirty minutes out. He really should be on patrol for whatever lurked.

Parker: *Eyes up, stay alert. After this is over, I'm taking you out to celebrate*

He saw her nod, and he powered away thoughts about just how he'd show her a good time. Parker powered on his tablet and opened the app to monitor all nearby electronic communication and external cyber activity. He tucked his chin and kept his roaming gaze on the lookout, watching and waiting, ready for who knew what.

# CHAPTER TWENTY-EIGHT

Giddy and warm under Parker's stare, Lexi didn't know how many hours passed as Shadow played auctioneer on his laptop. It was a long time to sit in a coffee shop and watch his wheeling and dealing, especially since never once did she feel Parker look away. Squirming in her seat, she occasionally cast a glance at him and saw his smoldering, protective blue eyes were locked on her. It was enough to make her starstruck.

Shadow's fingers banged furiously on the keyboard as he ran bids and countered offers from across the world. "So do you two have a thing I don't know about?"

She choked on the unexpected question even though they were eyeballing each other like horny teenagers. "I was engaged until just recently."

"And we both know what I think about that piece of shit. Is Matt bothering you?"

She shrugged. "I've been dark. No contact with anyone, even if they reached out."

Shadow stopped and twisted the pivoting screen. "Looks like we're finishing up. Yay or nay?"

Her focus zoomed in on the screen. The UK had bowed out then started lobbying Shadow to sell Monarch to the Americans. Back and forth the French and US governments bid. The US government was the highest bidder, and the time between bids was lengthening. The dollar amount was absurd.

"Yay."

"Good. We have a deal." Shadow gave her a thumbs-up then went back to his keyboard. Seconds later, the burner phone on the café table rang as his hand was already moving to it. Without pleasantries, he answered and said, "Process the wire transfer immediately. You'll have Monarch by close of business tomorrow."

The deal was done. Finally, Uncle Sam won the auction, paying *big* money. She hadn't expected that high. Not at all. A quick look at Shadow showed he thought the same thing. The guy had just made *beaucoup* dollars.

"Job well done, Silver."

She nodded. "No kidding, right?"

"Pull another one like this off in the next year, and you'll be my most profitable client."

She already knew she owned the top of his client roster but didn't let that slip. "Already working on something, though I don't see how it will beat this one."

"Alright. Let's get ready to transfer the files so you can get out of here. Maybe go talk to Black, who can't take his eyes off you. That might do you some good."

Heat crawled up her neck. It was almost unbearable. She'd never been so distracted, so consumed with lust-soaked thoughts. "You hired him to *watch* us. He's doing his job."

Shadow chuckled. "The job's done. He knows it. Auction went off without a hitch. Not the first time he's worked jobs like this. Auction ends, he leaves. Simple."

She shifted to take in Parker. "Nothing's simple about that guy." She hesitated. "At least by the look of him." Because she wouldn't admit to knowing him in real life. Ha. She wouldn't even admit anything to herself at this point.

"Go say hello. Introduce yourself."

She grimaced, not wanting Shadow to see that side of her. "Small talk isn't my thing."

"You guys are old buds. Go say hello. I'll upload the last part of Monarch, and we'll be done here."

Then the threat would be over, and Parker could stop his scorch-the-world protective scowl. She withdrew a flash drive from her back pocket and slid it across the table. "Last piece of the puzzle."

He took but didn't plug it in. "Silver, go say hello already."

"Maybe. Well, truth… it turns out we've… known each other."

Shadow's jaw flexed as he studied her. She was familiar with that look. It sprouted on his face before he felt the need to impart fatherly wisdom. "I know you don't have…"

"Any father figure," she finished for him.

"Anyone who has held that role." He nodded. "Except me. I'm always around as a set of ears you can trust."

Lexi regarded the man she'd been in business with since her late teens. "He's a good guy, isn't he?"

Shadow nodded but said nothing.

"I'm not sure I trust my judgment." She sucked her teeth.

"Well, if that's it, shake it off. Check your bank account tomorrow then go to an island somewhere and have a drink. Bring Black."

"Ha," she snapped, her cheeks lighting on fire.

"Go to Barbados. Hit the Virgin Islands. Something. Lay low. Forget about Matt the dick and…" Shadow flipped the thumb drive in his fingers before plugging it in. He paused, staring at the screen, and she waited for him to enter the string of codes that would combine the files. When his fingers stopped moving, his eyes tightened as he reread, then he smiled. "And trust your judgment. It's gotten you far in life with things like this." He tapped the side of the screen. "I—"

A burst of movement made Lexi jump back, knocking over her coffee and sending it spilling. A blur of a person swooshed by and grabbed Shadow's laptop.

Shadow's chair clattered as he jumped up. "Motherfucker!" Running as if he had any chance to catch up with the guy, Shadow panted as he sprinted across the café. "Damn, Black. Go!"

But Parker had moved toward her instead. His worried eyes tightened on her as an arm wrapped around her neck from behind. The rough fabric of a muscled arm caught her throat, choking her.

"Let's go," an accented voice growled in her ear. "Move fast."

She was surprised and stupefied, but she snapped out of it as she saw Parker clawing his way across the crowd. Lexi struggled and kicked, slamming her head back. Her gaze tracked to Parker as he threw tables and chairs away to get to her. His hard body leaped, and the massive weight of him slammed onto the man at her neck, dragging her into the throes of Union Station.

Lexi hit the ground. The thud of fists clashing bled through her ears as the crowd screamed and scurried. People ran, some shouting for the cops, some shouting just because. Parker's punches rained on her attacker. Two security guards descended out of nowhere, struggling to get the pit bull off his victim. They hooked arms around Parker and struggled to pull him back.

"I'm good, I'm good." Parker's muscles bunched as he paced in a tight circle, and she saw his mind working over what had happened.

Shadow was gone, stupidly chasing the laptop, not that he would walk back over with cops around. Parker's face registered what she was realizing. Whoever had wanted Monarch was still on the hunt. She wouldn't be safe in the custody of Union Station security or Capitol Hill police or whoever these guys were. She needed to get back off the grid, and she needed to do it *now*.

Parker wiped his bloody fists on his shirt, his eyes stuck on hers, and she was certain he was trying to impart a directive. Or was he? Maybe he was out-of-his-mind angry, and that's how it registered on his intelligent face.

Nope. *Trust your judgment*.

She dropped her eyes to the marble floor. The unconscious man wasn't Phiber. Neither was the one who'd stolen the laptop. The officers were attempting to question Parker, but his attention was on her.

Ignoring everyone clamoring for his attention, he tilted his head. "I'll find you."

The cops turned toward her. Their questioning eyes still weren't sure what had happened, but now they were clued in to her. Soon they'd watch security tapes and see that the man had grabbed her. But for now, she needed to disappear.

Her pulse thundered in her neck, and that booming sense of dread was going to make her hyperventilate. Parker would be arrested. Shadow would have a damn heart attack running after her stolen project—and God, she needed Monarch back. It was too dangerous to be on the black market.

Parker pulled back hard when a guard put a hand on his shoulder.

"Calm down, son," said one uniform as the other approached her.

"Ma'am, can we talk to you?" the other officer asked.

Parker shook his head hard. "Go, Silver."

*Go*. She snapped into action, sprinting through the coffee shop's chaos to the back room, then she hauled ass down an industrial hallway. She heard the voices ordering her to wait and replayed Parker's promise to come find her. But hadn't she caused enough problems? Less than a minute later, Lexi kicked through the fire door, ran through an alley, and scaled a barrier to the garage.

Tears streamed down her face. She didn't even know why. Shock? Anger? Terror? Worry? Running from who knew what or who. Monarch had been stolen, *she'd* almost been stolen, and Parker was likely to be arrested. Blood rushed in her ears, and adrenaline was about to make her heart explode.

With one long, deep breath, she jumped on her Gixxer, revved it, and rushed out of the garage with no idea where she wanted to hide, but knowing she needed to get there now.

# CHAPTER TWENTY-NINE

An hour after Parker had been unceremoniously released, he hovered over his keyboard, pulling the security footage, trying to get a better look at what had happened. It'd taken Titan less than two hours to find him in the system and have him released, but in that time, a lot had happened. Most notably, Lexi had disappeared in broad daylight—thank God—but now he wanted eyes on her.

He pinged Silver's screen name and called Lexi's phone. He waited a couple of minutes and did it again. Nothing. Her cell was turned off, so he couldn't triangulate her. Despite the tracking software he had that could handle problems like that, he was coming up empty.

Parker's gut twisted tightly as he called up another angle of security footage and scrolled through frames rapidly. Nothing… his fingers flew over the keyboard, pulling up video feeds from traffic cameras, running a program that would search for a motorcycle. That was all he had. He wasn't even sure what kind of bike she had. Wait—there.

A slender figure on the back of a bike weaving through traffic, heading toward Virginia. The feedback was stilted, but she flowed confidently, maneuvering through DC's heavy traffic until she exited onto the GW Parkway.

He sat back, letting the soreness of his knuckles drift over him. Felt good. Fury he hadn't realized he harbored had exploded when that man put his hands on her. Whoever he was, he was in the hospital now. Never had Parker been more certain that he needed to help her, and never had he been terrified that she needed his help.

Without intel, he was useless. Normally he totally owned cyberspace, but right now, he knew crap. No—no, he knew she was heading to Virginia and that it didn't look as though anyone had followed her.

He needed to remove his emotional response and think about this as if it were a job. Because it was. Even if it was so much more than that. He actually had several things going for him. Lexi didn't seem like she was avoiding cameras, she was safe, and she hadn't been trained to disappear beyond just going dark on the web. Even if SilverChaos was a sly fox online, Lex hiding in the real world was out of her element. And she knew he was coming for her.

Fast as his mind would work, he sent out coded messages to various places where she might check in. Only she would know who had sent them and what the encrypted words said. Only Lexi would know that as his fingers slammed on the keyboard, his short orders were laden with a desperation unlike anything he'd ever experienced. *Get a hold of me. Find me. Call me. Tell me where the hell you* are.

No responses to any of them came as he sat and waited.

In over her head and incommunicado, what would her next move be?

Parker bent over and rubbed his head. Until she reached out, he'd work the other angle. With a few key strokes, he hacked into DC General's medical records and pulled up the John Doe admitted semi-conscious earlier today. There was nothing noteworthy in his medical charts, but what was interesting were the notations about his unwillingness to give a name and checking out against medical advice. Definitely didn't want to be there.

Parker clicked a couple more screens, finding nothing, then went back to the original screen.

**Error. Page you are trying to reach does not exist.**

Parker's head tilted as he studied the screen, then he cued up the search function for the hospital's database and typed in the patient ID number.

**No patient with that ID number found. Please try again.**

His eyes narrowed, and his sixth sense tingled. Someone else was in the system at that same moment, hacking this info and erasing it.

What the double fucks was happening? This info was so in the weeds that it was almost pointless to remove it. It was a complete clean sweep, and he couldn't grasp which player would risk grabbing Lexi. None of the bidders would. If they were legit, they wouldn't arrange for an abduction, and if they weren't, they'd hop town and fly home. No need to hack the medical records.

Who wanted both the program *and* Lexi? Who needed to cover their tracks, unable to hide behind the protection of foreign diplomats or bullshit political agreements? Parker's throat went dry as his mind focused on one dangerous hypothesis. A terrorist organization interested in a cyber-attack could want both the niches, social media centric technology and the mind behind it. Wouldn't be the first time they'd pulled something like that.

His fingers tapped the desk as he pulled up Monarch's social media site and dummied an account for the social network. It was like Facebook, except specifically for women, catering to military families. He opened a different browser to read Monarch's corporate user stats. Nothing he couldn't guess.

Now that he was logged in as a new user, it automatically prompted him to enter entirely too much information: home address, work address, family names, ages, where they worked, what they did. No wonder Monarch was such a heavy hitter. They had tons information they could sell to advertisers.

Entering his BS information, he clicked to the next screen. *Groups to join.* A cartoon caterpillar was guiding him through the process. As soon as Parker clicked one interest, another page with more groups appeared. Users looked at it as Monarch offering community support, but Parker looked at it through the deviant goggles of a malicious third party. There was far too much easily accessible information.

He shook his head, his stomach dropping at all the information a terrorist could get their hands on with one simple program. The caterpillar inched across the screen, urging him to pick a group interest to find his *home to flourish.* Shit. Automatically, he picked Military: Marines. Hundreds of Marine Wives and Family groups popped up.

The gnawing nauseated feeling he'd had before exponentially increased as he joined group after group. Within minutes, he had a social network of several thousand and a reach of hundreds of thousands, all "fellow" military wives. All posting their husband's rank and location, the change-of-command photos, their well-wishes and concerns, the missed birthdays and postponed homecomings. There was so much emotion on the pages, so much shared with each other, that for a second, all Parker could do was feel sick over the sitting targets in front of him.

Terrorists didn't want their fight abroad. They wanted it here in the US and in allied nations. Monarch gave them pinpoint-level accuracy on where they could show up and wreak havoc.

They were bringing the fight here…?

But it was only a theory based on instinct and assumptions on what was happening in the world and the international political climate. He had nothing hard and fast to base his theory on, but Parker had no doubt what was happening. Even though there wasn't much in the terrorist chatter and there had been little given to soldiers' families in terms of warnings—simple things like don't post pictures or friend people you don't know—truth was, no one had told people to stop posting their lives online. And it was finally going to come back and haunt them.

Parker picked up his cell and called Jared.

Jared answered on the second ring. "If this has anything to do with that Shadow security thing that you promised me was a 'simple job,' I'm not in the mood."

"Think it's bigger than that." Parker's eyes narrowed as he continued to add friends and expand his Monarch network. The caterpillar was gone, and a butterfly had taken its place, promising him he was ready to fly.

"Yeah, how so?"

Parker kept clicking. The butterfly sent him a notification that it was hungry. What the hell did that mean—oh, he needed to join more groups to keep his stupid butterfly happy. The site was genius if it wasn't so damn dangerous.

"Parker," Jared snapped. "What the fuck do you have?"

"It's a theory, but I may've scratched the surface of a terrorist plot."

He groaned and cursed. "Be there in five."

Shit. Okay. This was what he did, what Titan handled. But he also needed to find Lexi and make sure she was safe. For the first time, the right move wasn't analytically clear—no, wrong. It wasn't the first time thinking about her had altered his decision-making process.

Parker rubbed his temples. He needed to see this idea through, to investigate what he thought. But at the same time, his mind searched for the woman who made him want to question his standard operating procedure.

Jared stormed into Parker's tech-lair. "Explain."

So he did, spending twenty minutes walking Boss Man through the site and his thoughts. Jared rubbed his face, looking over everything the screen said and analyzing the limited intelligence they had.

Finally, Jared shook his head. "Seems extraordinarily complicated for micro-targeted attacks. If the fuckers want to come over here and cause havoc, why not ping people off the street? Attack random homes."

Parker pulled up a page of his Monarch groups, noting the obnoxious, already-hungry-again butterfly. "All military."

"I got that." Then Jared's brows went up as his eyes narrowed on what Parker was certain was a list of deployed wives support groups. "Shit. Fuck."

"Right?" Parker nodded solemnly. "Those fuckers come over here and hurt families, *kids*, while their dad and mom are overseas? If there's no rhyme or reason to the attack—" He scrolled down the list. Young and old. Every part of the country. There were too many people to protect at once. Thousands of vulnerable possibilities. "Screw low morale—a lot of those soldiers will do what it takes to protect their families. And those who don't do something will be distracted and dysfunctional."

"Fuck." Jared cracked his knuckles. "Alright, I have a couple calls to make. What's your next move? Where are you digging on this?"

"Back hack the IP of a lead in the DC General's server. Look at the hole in Monarch's site and see what it really shows, then trace the security footage to follow the stolen laptop."

"Good. Do it."

Parker's fingers were already flying on the keyboard. "It'll take time."

"If that thing is on the run to God knows where, we don't have time."

No time and not enough manpower. Lexi had to keep herself safe, at least until they made progress.

"And, Parker?"

He looked up, still typing, still worrying about his woman.

"If this is what you think it is, then I need to turn it over."

Parker nodded, not feeling territorial at all. "No problem."

Boss Man's brow furrowed. "Why?"

"Why what?"

"You fight to keep every project under your control, and the possibility that this mother bear might be the greatest looming threat out there, you're cool with passing it along and not asking to stay with it?"

He paused, thinking over the absurdity of what Jared had just suggested, then he nodded. "Something like that."

"What's going on with you?"

He took a deep breath before sharing how his personal and professional lives had crashed together. "Silver is Lexi."

Jared's jaw worked side to side. "I'm not exactly sure what that means."

Parker had never not shared everything in minute detail when it came to his concerns, ideas, and solutions, and Jared always listened, even when Parker went a little too deep in the weeds. So this was different. They both seemed to feel it too.

"You have a problem with asking for help?" Jared asked.

"No."

"Alright then. Ask when it's needed."

"Ten-four, Boss Man." Maybe. She was so guarded that Titan storming after her might make her run deeper. He was at a crossroads, torn between following after a terrorist threat or chasing down his woman on the run.

Jared pulled his phone out, already dialing, when he paused and turned around. "Don't make me pull you out of custody again."

"No worries for that." Parker kept his face stoic and unreadable, but on the inside, he'd already decided Lexi was his priority and changed his mental operations to focus on a missing-person job. Soon as he had anything to go on and Jared had turned over the threat concerns, he'd be out the door.

# CHAPTER THIRTY

Parker pinged Lexi-slash-Silver again every way he knew how and went back to tracing her through camera footage, searching for her motorcycle. A quick blip of a reply, nothing more than a symbolic hello, came across his phone, and his chest tightened, possessive concern eating him alive. Parker studied his cell phone then replied with digits and a message that it was a secure line. Then he stared. And stared. Waiting.

The screen lit before it rang, and relief broke through him as the unknown number flashed on the phone's console. He swiped the handset off the desk. "Where are you?"

"You should leave me alone. *You* told me to go dark," she whispered.

"I also said I'd find you. It'd be easier if you answered when I reach out." His fingers flew across the keyboard, trying to pinpoint her precise location. It might have been secure on his end, but she was still flailing in the wind. Time wasn't on his side. *Eastern United States.* Alright. Getting somewhere. Lexi was at least still on his side of the country.

"Stop. I know what you're doing, Parker."

"Of course you know what I'm doing." Though he could tell she'd gone through a lot of hoops to hide where she was when she called. Not that that would stop him. He hit a cyber-wall. Shit. Backing out, Parker tried another way, searching for a hole, something she wouldn't have anticipated. He ran a hand into his hair, growling at the screen. "What I don't get is why I have to."

"I've created this mess. I don't want you to get hurt. I don't want you to get in trouble with the law. I don't want you to accidentally murder someone on my behalf."

God, she had no idea. "Don't be like that, Lex. Where are you?"

The next line of code got past another one of her barriers. His search narrowed as he triangulated. *Virginia*. Okay, so she hadn't gone too far.

She sucked in a breath. "Don't use my name."

So quiet. Too quiet. Her words stabbed in his chest, building pressure that he wasn't used to. She was scared, and he needed to fix that.

"We're past the point of being concerned over a name-handle connection," he said. "You're in trouble. I can fix this. It's what I do."

She remained silent.

"Goddamn it, Lexi, where are you?" He went back to the first screen that had started his initial search. Inside Union Station, she was just walking into the coffee shop. Even in that simple, grainy picture, she was so damn beautiful that he almost couldn't take his eyes off her.

"Just let me stay dark for a while, and I'll be back."

"It doesn't work like that, Lex."

"Everything will be forgotten."

"There's a whole lot I have no intention of forgetting." He'd almost pinpointed her. She was in northern Virginia.

"You can't just beat up your way out of this. I'm causing trouble for everyone—God, were you arrested?"

"You have no idea what's going on. You need a safe house and security."

He should've told her more of who he was, what he did for a living, how he was more than a set of hands and a brain that could turn her world upside down. He should have sworn that he was her protector, and that he would kill himself to make sure he was holding her at the end of the day—God help anyone stupid enough to try to come after her again. Damn it. He should've said more than Titan was complicated because Titan was his authority to scorch the earth until he found her.

"I have it under control, and I'll call you later."

The line went dead a half second before he could pinpoint her location.

"Fuck!" He slammed his phone receiver down and pushed back from the desk.

Breathing hard and mind racing, he didn't know the next move and couldn't make heads or tails of what he was supposed to do. He had a decent area with multiple modes of transportation and several interstates. Not a lot, but the data was a starting point. Parker snapped out of his stupor and worked the remnants of her signal, hoping to find some regional bread crumb.

A throat cleared behind him. His head turned and took in Winters leaning against the wall, arms crossed.

Parker blew out his frustration. "Busy."

Winters took a step forward. "What the fuck was all that about?"

Anxiety, confusion, and a thousand things in between skewered his judgment. "Nothing."

"Parker?" he tried again.

Parker ran his hands along his desk to try to let the smooth surface calm his nerves. His work area was icy cold. They kept it that way for the electronics. The lights were dim, and the room hummed. None of it gave him direction, none of it centered him, and finding no answers, he dropped his head farther, rubbed his temples, and cursed.

His buddy laughed quietly. "You want me to guess what's wrong with you?"

Parker shook his head. "I am fucked."

"Nah, you're never one to get into a position that screws you. Though you almost landed your genius ass in jail today, so what do I know?"

"A friend of mine found herself in deep and doesn't know how to get out. She thinks she has it handled, and she doesn't."

"You realize you're being vague and talking in circles?" Winters scowled.

Parker sighed. "It's a long story."

"Is there a short version?"

Short version… there wasn't one. Other than the one-sentence summary he'd given Boss Man. *Lex is Silver.* Jared just walked back in, so the conversation had the potential to get much worse.

"They're running with your intel. Looks like you're right," Boss Man grumbled then tilted his head. "What the fuck is that face for? Thought you had your thing to do."

Winters gave Parker a look and a moment to answer Boss Man, but Parker didn't. Winters turned toward Jared. "Parker's got problems."

Parker scoffed, internally agreeing. "I don't have damn problems."

Winters laughed. "Then he has a chick with a problem."

"Thought we'd been through this already." Jared's eyes sliced to Parker. "Fix it."

"Yeah." Parker turned back to his computer, his eyes catching on the screen where he'd left Lexi frozen in place. He couldn't look at that and play dumb to the extent of his interest in her, so he pushed away and stood. "Working on it."

Winters made a wry noise, his mouth down-turned as though he was trying not to laugh. Jared raised an eyebrow at Winters. Parker wanted both men out of his office.

"This problem," Jared pushed, eyeing the dynamic between Parker and Winters. "Fixed soon? Fixed when?"

Parker rubbed his temples. "Think I need some time off."

Jared's raised eyebrow dropped, and he glowered. "You need time off for a problem connected to a terrorist cell with a chick I just learned is involved?"

"Yeah. Basically." Though when it was laid out like that, it had a problematic vibe that Boss Man wouldn't deal well with.

"Wait, she is?" Winters asked, dumbstruck.

"No." Jared's boots turned, and he pounded out of the room, growling as he went. "No time off. Work it from here."

The headache punching at Parker's temples worsened. "Alright, wait."

Jared glared. "You have twenty seconds to try again."

Winters leaned against the wall. "Might as well explain everything, 'cause I'm confused as all hell."

"Shut it, Winters," Jared snapped. "This isn't gossip central. But, Parker, man, you're screwing shit up."

Parker pulled in a breath through his teeth. "A hacker I've known most my life—" Explaining the intricacies of something Jared didn't care wouldn't help his case. "Turns out is the same person as the woman I'm... seeing."

Winters laughed. "Now there's an upgrade."

"Would you shut the hell up?" Jared growled.

"What am I missing?" Winters asked.

Jared paced. "The hacker and the girl are the same person, and there's a terrorist cell that the ARO implanted in the States, and they've set their eyes on a niche attack on US soil."

The ARO? Parker's stomach dropped. Shit. Worse than he'd expected. Jared's contact had worked fast. Bad news all around. The Arab Revolutionary Organization was smart and wanted headlines.

Winters ran a hand over his face. "What's Lexi have to do with them?"

The line between Boss Man's brows deepened as he stared at Parker. "You didn't see this coming?"

"Why would I have seen this coming?" He turned to Winters. "You've known the girl as long as me. You know she was into this?"

Winters shook his head. "Nope. Lexi, one. Boy genius, zilch."

"Jackass." Frustration wasn't making Parker's explanation any easier.

"Thought you were smart." Jared shook his head. "Fuck me, I was wrong."

"What?" Parker asked.

"Man, you do not *think* you need some time off. Something looking like Lexi running free with some attack dog after her? You say, 'Call up the fuckin' troops, we've got work to do.'"

Parker blinked. "This is off the books."

"Everything's off the books."

"This doesn't pay."

"The best jobs don't," Jared replied.

Parker dropped to his chair and leaned back, rubbing a hand over his jaw. "I'm not sure what I'm getting into. Titan doesn't need that."

Jared shook his head. "If there's one person who knows what shit Titan gets into, it's you." He rubbed his forehead. "Get Rocco, debrief with him. Winters, sit in. Keep your boy on point. You have whatever resources you need."

Parker stood back up, anxious energy making him bob and weave like a freakin' Whac-a-Mole. "Seriously, Boss Man—"

"What?" Jared growled.

"This is personal."

"Somehow, for the last decade of your life or however the hell long you've worked here, you've missed out on something basic. You got personal, we deal with personal. And, brother, you have never got personal. When shit pops up, as it's done now, we go in and fix it. Winters needed his girl. We got his girl. I needed a hand with Sugar. Even though she was kicking and screaming, we dragged her sweet ass home. Rocco, Caterina. Cash and Nic. Don't even make me mention Roman."

Parker shook his head. "This isn't like any of that." Except was it?

"Whatever it's like, it's the only outside-of-Titan personal connection you have. Whatever that woman is to you, you make her fuckin' day. That means you save her life, you kill some rogue attacker, you smoke out some terrorist fuck. You do a hacker thing. You get the job done. Read me?"

"Loud and clear."

Jared stormed out, and Winters grumbled in agreement. Parker, again, dropped to his chair, uncomfortable with everything that was about to happen and never more grateful for who he worked with and how good they were at it.

# CHAPTER THIRTY-ONE

Lexi crept down yet another alleyway and scooted into the mom-and-pop shop. Old Town Alexandria was filled with tourists, likely because it was warmer than it had been in weeks. The thick band of people gave her an added layer of protection, allowing her to blend in with random groups and grab onto their cell phones' hot spots whenever she needed quick access.

Hiding in plain sight, she wasn't in a faraway hole, as she'd just finished doing for the past couple of weeks. Staying close by wasn't her smartest move, but it was fueled by not wanting to be that far from Parker. From Black. One and the same. Even though she wouldn't let him help her. Dragging him into her nightmare terrified her. Just like Shadow. She still hadn't heard from him.

Lexi pushed through the door and waited in line, exhaustion making her mind cloud. Maybe she should've found a hotel room instead of an ice cream parlor…

"What'll it be?" the kid behind the counter asked.

She ordered quickly and quietly, as though if she talked loudly, someone would know where she was. Lexi paid in cash for an orange sherbet with hot fudge, dropped the change into a jar, and took the already melting mess to the back of the shop where she could hide and map out her next move. She had no idea what that'd be. Maybe she should call Parker back and tell him she was done being belligerent.

God, she wanted to call him, but how much more of a mess would she create by doing so? Instead, she stabbed her spoon into the bowl of ice cream, hoping it could temporarily fix everything. A couple of spoonfuls in, she wasn't ready to admit it wasn't working, but she wasn't ready to stop.

A shadow curved over her table. Her stomach shrank as much as her body tingled. "You found me."

It wasn't her broker or whoever had grabbed her at Union Station. Nope. Like her blood could sense how tall, dark, and handsome Parker was, it rushed and burned in her veins. She turned to see it was most certainly tall, dark, and maybe deadly, judging by the fire in his smoldering gaze. His muscles seemed relaxed, but given their lack of restraint in Union Station, she was sure that didn't matter. Parker and Black were definitely an impressive combination. But he shouldn't be there. He might be all muscles and brains, but he didn't deserve to have a threat in his life just for knowing her.

"You should go away." She took another bite of ice cream and hoped-slash-prayed that he would wake her from a nightmare then take her to bed.

"You should have gotten enough to share." His smile was as intoxicating as it was teasing. "Orange sherbet and chocolate, just like sausage and banana peppers. You have unique taste."

Spoon between her lips, she shivered from the tone of his words, not the chill of the ice cream. Her ordering choices weren't normal. Matt had never noticed, or if he did, he was an ass about it. Parker acted as if it was merely Lexi-laced trivia he was storing away for later.

"I was just teasing." Parker's growly voice ran over her goose bumps that didn't come from the ice cream. "I hate that you question yourself with me."

"I don't."

"It's simple, Lex. That's what you like. Not a big deal. If anyone had a problem with that before, then you need to know it's no longer a problem for you. Get me?"

She nodded.

He sat down. "The other thing you need to know is me. Who I am. Saying I was a Marine, telling you I was Titan, I get it. I was vague. It didn't occur to me you needed to know."

"I don't."

"You do."

"Why?"

"Because you're trying to protect me?" He tilted his head. "Admirable if not suicidal, sweetheart."

She blushed. "I'm just… I don't know."

He scooted closer, took the spoon from her, and rested it on the edge of the bowl. From there, he repositioned her face to face his, then his hands rested on the table. "My name is Parker Black. I sometimes work as BlackDawn. My employer is Titan, and my training is from both the Marines and MIT."

"I know."

"But you don't know what that means. I will kill to protect you. I will hunt what follows you," he said through clenched teeth. "I will seek out *anything* that has its sights on you, and I will destroy it. I'm not a muscle hound with a hard-on for electronics. I'm a mercenary for the good guys, an analyst of life-and-death situations, and I will, *I swear to Christ*, maim, harm, and kill anything that wants what I care about."

Her jaw hung open.

"You are my top priority." He closed his eyes for a second. "Understand what I've told you isn't to scare you. It's to make you feel safe. Get it?"

She nodded.

He picked up the spoon as if the speech he'd just given was nothing, then he took a huge spoonful of ice cream and fudge. He made a face but grinned. "Not for me. But you like what you like. Nothing's wrong with that."

He handed the spoon back, and God, she had to bite her teeth together to keep from uttering stupid words that were far, far too soon but felt like what was in her head that second. Things like *I love you.*

"Any thoughts?" The deep gravel of those words made her drunk, reminding her of what he could do to her body.

Her pulse flew, and her lips parted as if she would murmur how she felt. But instead, she whispered, "I really like you. You're an amazing guy."

Never in a million years did she think Parker had it in him to blush, but his chuckle was accompanied by a hint of color on his cheeks. "I won't complain about that."

Buttery warmness lit in her chest. She stole her eyes back, scooped up more ice cream, and decided the safest course of action was to keep at her original plan—focus on the ice cream—because she'd just said almost what she'd texted him at Union Station.

Parker must've read her uncertainty as she became self-conscious. His boots tangled under the table, locking around the legs of her chair, then he pulled her toward him. She was completely aware that their proximity was nearing the point of touching. Every time they did that, things got out of control.

His well-defined arms crossed over his chest. No less hot than he was at his house, Meredith's apartment, and Union Station. "Eyes to me."

She obeyed and focused on his black-as-night hair that was tousled just right, because if her eyes dropped to his blue-blue eyes, she'd be done. No way to protect him from the trouble she'd caused, no way to protect her heart any longer.

He scooted her chair even closer to his. The sugary air felt warmer. His full lips dipped down into a frown. "You need to know that I'm crazy about you too. But I'm also done with the secrets and skirting the truth."

The last part sounded... unhappy. With her. There was an intensity in his eyes that she couldn't understand. "Are you angry with me?"

"Not angry." He bent his head closer, letting their foreheads kiss. They stayed there forever until he inched back. Their breaths mingled, their gazes locked. "Many things, but never angry with you."

"Tell me."

He inched back with a tight smile. "Let's start with my short list. I'm frustrated. Annoyed. And pissed."

"*What?*" Her lips parted, trying to keep up with the roller coaster of emotions her mind was subjecting her to. "At me?"

"You asked." A quiet laugh fell from him. "And yeah, sweetheart. At you."

She swallowed, stuttering for a comeback. "Those are all the same thing."

He bent close to her ear, making fireworks explode on her skin. Deep below her belly tightened with want.

"Then let me break it down for you."

Maybe she shouldn't have asked for an explanation.

"Okay."

"First." His lips brushed her earlobe, and she moaned. "I'm frustrated that you're in trouble, and I don't know how deep."

The last part was drawn out and worked her senses like a masseuse. She inhaled, her eyes rolling into her head. "But—"

Parker shook his head, toying with her hair. "Next. I'm annoyed, Lexi, that we've been partners on pretty much every damn thing, and you didn't flag for serious help on this play. I had to get some bullshit semi-informed request from Shadow that didn't give me anywhere near the intelligence I needed."

Her heart palpitated when Parker let his lips brush her neck. "I—"

His finger reached her lips, pressing and quieting her rebuttal. All she wanted to do was run her tongue along it.

"Parker, please." But please what, she had no idea. They were in public, and she squirmed in her seat, nearly panting from his teases.

"And, finally, I'm pissed. *Pissed.* So upset I can feel my blood boiling in my skin. I'm giving you whatever I've got—talent, resources, knowledge—and I can still see in your eyes that you're assistance avoidant. I can't keep you safe if you won't let me, and I can't handle how much I need to take care of you."

"I didn't know you were Black," she said against his finger, unable to ignore the electrical currents telling her to kiss whatever part of him she could.

"But now you do. And I know Silver like I know no one else in the world. I know how you think, what you do, how you solve problems, and how goddamn smart you are."

"Oh," she whispered.

"And you being that sexy girl I've watched who let me protect her from that piece-of-shit guy? Combine all of that? *I like you too,* Lexi. Like crazy."

She held her breath, not responding. She was barely staying conscious from all the tummy swirls and mind racing he did to her with simple words. "I…"

"Now the choice is yours. Are you going to let me in? Or am I going to walk away, and when I never hear from you again, then I'll know they got you?"

She shuddered as a wave of panic rolled over her. “No one’s going to get me.”

His head tilted, showing he didn’t believe her. “I found you in less than a day.”

“You’re good.” She gave him a smile, but it was weak.

His mouth quirked. “You’re better in many things, and I still found you.”

“I’m better?”

He nodded. “Some things you are, but not when it comes to keeping you alive. Understand?”

“Starting to.”

“Alright, better than nothing.” Parker stood, took her hand, and tugged her out of the chair. “Let’s roll.”

# CHAPTER THIRTY-TWO

Hand in hand, Lexi let Parker snake them through the mess of chairs and scattered tables to the front of the shop. After a long, sweeping glance into the darkening street, he apparently didn't find anything that worried him and pulled them into the crowd.

Three things popped into Lexi's mind. First, she would've taken a lot longer to search the area for potential threats—though she didn't exactly know what she was looking for. Second, she didn't know where they were going. And third, Parker still had his hand on hers. Warmth radiated from his strength, and she couldn't hide her smile. She had her motorcycle helmet in one hand and squeezed his with the other, unable to act as if she wasn't love-sick, and he squeezed back. Her heart soared.

They stopped in front of his sleek gray-almost-black R1. They had superbikes in common, but his beast was a jet. She'd known from years of watching Parker and chatting with BlackDawn that he had more than a couple badass rides. But between this one and his Ducati, Lexi was about to fangirl.

"Did I ever tell you how sick this is?"

He didn't say a word but gave her a smile that was all power-and-sex, just like his bike, then nodded expectantly. The realization that she was about to hop on behind him with her arms wrapped tight… hell, her knees went to jelly.

But she had her Gixxer to worry about and had lost it once before. It was a freedom she didn't want to lose track of so quickly. "Mine's around the corner. Tell me where to meet you."

Parker towered over her, his hand still holding hers for a heartbeat before he dropped it. "Already found it. Already moved it. That was easier to find than you."

"Ha, um." She swallowed, more excited than she could have ever imagined. "Okay then."

He took her helmet, pressed it to her chest, then grabbed the handles, threw a leg over the bike, and readied for her, all while looking sexier than sin on a hot day. "Ready?"

Cotton-mouth silent with a dry throat, she nodded and acquiesced, doing as she was told and ignoring the deep need twirling low in her belly. She climbed on the back of the vibrating bike.

"Let's move." With a flick of his hand, the engine growled. "Hang on."

Slow and steady through traffic didn't require putting her hands on him. Then Parker dropped the gear, and she clung tight. Holy shit, he was trying to kill her with stomach-flipping butterflies. His rumbling laughter vibrated between their bodies, making her laugh too.

When she finally held on tight, he turned his head at a tourist-packed stop sign. "Better." Mischief crept into his voice, making her wonder what he had planned.

They sped off, firing her excitement, and wove through the streets until he hit the parkway. She took a breath as they eased onto the open road. This was her element. If it wasn't in front of a screen and keyboard, it was when the air rushed by. The curving lanes ran along the river. Trees hung overhead, making the darkening afternoon feel like night.

Finally they slowed in a quiet neighborhood and pulled into the driveway of a more-than-modest house. All the windows were dark, the shades drawn. The garage door lifted, and there was her bike. How the hell had that happened? And whose house was this?

Parker shifted. "You good?"

She slid off the bike, then he did as she unsnapped her helmet. Parker snagged her hand and tugged her past her bike as he hit the garage door to close. They went through one door, which opened into a small hallway, then stopped at another door. There he stopped for a security system. Like, an *impressive* security system complete with scanners, codes, and voice recognition. Seconds later, she was inside the belly of the house.

"Hungry?" He walked, and she followed, mouth agape.

"No…" A camera followed them down the hall. "Who's watching us?"

"No one right now. Motion activated."

"Oh." The colonial exterior didn't match the tech-laden interior. The place rocked. Everywhere she looked, something caught her eye.

Passing the living room, he grabbed two longnecks from the fridge and kept going. The living room was a shrine to an armed hacker nation. Her mouth dropped as she took in the operating station. The walls were lined with provisions, weapons, and lots of military-looking crap. She didn't know any other way to describe it. It was like a Doomsday cyber station.

"What is this place?"

He moved to the chair facing a wall of screens. "Safe house of sorts."

"You have a safe house here?"

"We have safe houses everywhere."

"We? Titan?" she asked.

He nodded.

Her eyes followed all the up-to-the-second technology. "And you're outfitted like this everywhere?"

"Not everywhere. Some places serve different purposes. I have work for both of us to do, and I didn't know what all we needed."

"So you brought… everything?"

He laughed. "Just about."

"Oh… my… God, this is fabulous." She ran her finger over the processor that had to be powering his work station. State of the freakin' art.

"Fingers off, sweetheart."

She pulled her hand back. "Sorry."

"Kidding." He smiled the kind of grin that could make a day on the run fade away.

She turned away, concerned that she'd look way too eager to touch any—and everything—in the room. "So…?"

"There's a strong possibility that Monarch was stolen by a terrorist organization interested in targeting the wives and families of servicemen overseas."

A wave of dizziness swept over her, and she dropped to the couch. "Excuse me?"

"There's not much to share, but until something's confirmed, I thought you should know."

"Oh, my God. I did this."

"No." He shook his head. "Evil people ruin good things."

"But…" She buried her head in her hands, groaning. "This isn't what was supposed to happen."

"Let me help work on it. We'll get it back before damage is done."

"What if we can't?"

"How many times have I asked you for help over the years? How many times did we fail?"

"Never." She jumped off the couch and walked into the middle of the room.

He prowled around the room, circling her tighter with each revolution, the circumference decreasing until he no longer circled the room. No, he stalked her body, pacing a tight circle around her.

"Parker," she whispered. "You're making me nervous."

He leaned close, brushing her hair off her shoulder. His soft, full lips tickled the top of her ear, and he spoke low. "That's the last thing I want to make you."

She gasped and flushed, exposed while completely dressed, barely stifling a moan that drifted through her lips. But he backed up the second before she begged him to strip her free of clothes, free of concerns. He could do whatever he wanted to her body—he was already doing it to her mind.

His eyes darkened, and her insides went mushy. Again. Same as she'd reacted in the ice cream shop and in his car, in the kitchen, just everywhere. Her lungs were full, her chest felt funny. Her breasts swelled, showing him just how badly she was in need of his touch. He grabbed her, his supporting arm pulling her tight and pressing her stomach to his. His free hand cupped her cheek, and she was done.

Softly his thumb curved over her skin before his palm pushed his fingers into her hair. "What do you like better, Silver or Lexi?"

She blinked, honesty bleeding through her mind. "I like sweetheart."

"You are *killing* me." His words sounded like an orgasm sliding off his tongue.

She arched toward him, and the tiniest groan burned her lips. The bit of space between them slowly evaporated. They were drawn together, eyes still open. Sparks swirled. His lips weren't on hers yet, and she could feel him deeply. She was desperate to relive their past private moments.

He was always so gentle with her. He parted her mouth with a soulful soft kiss that shattered her to pieces. Parker tasted like the hint of hot fudge, and he growled, promising that he wasn't nearly as sweet as he pretended to be. The stubble on his jawline rasped her skin, and Lexi wrapped her arms around his strong neck, running her searching hands into his thick hair.

"Christ," he murmured, backing her up fast until they hit the couch.

In one swoop, she was in his arms, on her back, with a very strong Parker Black pressing his hard weight and thick length against her. She moaned and licked his bottom lip. But it was the wrong thing to do because he stopped his onslaught and left her cold, wanting. Hell, begging for more of his mouth on hers.

"Parker…" Lips still close enough to flit across his, she wanted to catch their touch again. "Please don't stop."

"You have to know something, Lex. I'm not going to take you here, on some random couch in a safe house."

"Why not?" The desperation in her voice sounded close to pathetic, but she didn't care. His blue eyes neared black. She'd never seen a look more intense, more at war after kissing her.

"You want this?" he asked.

She nodded. Wanted. Needed. All the same.

"You've wanted this? Between us?"

Her eyes sank shut. Parker was calling her on her past, when she'd watched him when she shouldn't, when she'd closed her eyes to fantasize over a kiss she thought she'd never get. When her eyes opened, she couldn't lie to the man who seemed to know her in every conceivable way. "Yes."

"Then that's why."

"Okay." She couldn't hide the hurt falling from within her. Her body went limp, rejected and dejected.

"Don't be like that."

She blushed, embarrassed that her feelings were so evident. "Yeah, sure." She tried to roll out from under him, but he had her caged into the cushions.

"Lex, I want something better from you than a quick-and-dirty fuck, and you deserve that from me."

Heat hit her cheeks. She knew, yet again, that she was blushing while Parker was front row to her uncertainty. But then his hand took hers, tugging her upright. Words wouldn't come. She couldn't read his mind as he could so easily read hers.

"What—where are we going?"

He pushed her in front of him and wrapped his arms around her torso as he guided her forward with a hunger in his growl and his erection thick against her back. "You're convinced that since I'm not fucking you in the living room of a safe house, I don't want to hear you scream."

Her stomach flipped. "*What?*"

"I'm not letting you leave until this computes. You deserve the world, sweetheart. To be taken care of." He threw open a door and displayed a ginormous bed. "And we're not leaving this place until you know it."

# CHAPTER THIRTY-THREE

Nerves and butterflies swept through Lexi as she stood at the door of the bedroom. Parker held her from behind. He was both strong and gentle, her every temptation rolled into a massive package of a man ripped with muscles, a genius without shoving it into anyone's face. When he pressed her forward, she couldn't breathe.

"Changed your mind?" he asked against her neck.

Need pulsed between her legs as strong as the desire in her heart. "No."

"Thank fuck for that." His low rumble tickled her skin as he walked them to the foot of the bed. When her thighs touched the mattress, he slowly rotated her one hundred eighty degrees so that his arms still draped her, but they were face to face, stomach to stomach.

"Thank you for finding me."

He sighed, pressing his forehead to hers. "Just when I think I'm immune to the sweetness that comes out of your mouth. God, Lex. You do not have to thank me."

"Then I'm glad I'm here. Like this. With you."

If she thought about it, she'd only seen him twice since she and Matt broke up, and both times, something crazy hot had happened. She *shouldn't* have sex with him. This was only their second date or something, even though they'd known each other for years. No… more than a decade.

*Hear you scream...* she shivered as Parker's voice echoed in her ears, making arousal spark life into something that she hadn't felt in so long. Matt had never cared if she found hers, but Parker, God, he was different. Not just a man who wanted to screw, but a gentleman who wanted to give and give and give.

He shifted away and tore off his shirt. Her eyes went wide, hungrily drinking in the sight of his defined muscles. They had a smooth ripple, the taut skin pulled tight over the bulges of etched mass. Lexi pressed her palms to his pecs, and his eyes sank shut. He sighed in approval over something so simple. Matt had *never* made a sound like that, never appreciated her intent or touch. But this… this was far more than anything she'd ever experienced.

Needing to forget her past and concentrate on Parker, Lexi widened her fingers, spanning them across his chest, then dragged them down. The sparse smattering of dark chest hair and the rigid tips of his tight nipples teased her palms. His cut stomach had slight valleys and grooves, even in a relaxed state.

"Love your hands on me, Lex." His head lolled to the side.

His skin had goose bumps, a trail of explosions that followed her touch. The visceral reaction was stunning to watch. He wanted her. Like *really* wanted *her*… and didn't hide from it. His chest expanded with each of his breaths. His eyes remained closed until she placed her hand on the buckle of his belt then stroked the bulging length of his erection through his jeans.

Parker's eyes opened, and his head dropped down as he covered her hands with his. "I'm getting lost in you, but I think the plan was to make you know what you're worth."

The heaviness of his words coated her senses. Lexi pushed back onto the mattress, scooting toward the middle, and Parker took off her boots, one at a time. Each he tossed over his shoulder, his smile torturing her with whatever that devious mind had come up with.

"So all about me?" she whispered, breathy and bothered.

He crawled onto the mattress, kicking his shoes off as well. "Completely."

She moved to him, and they were both on their knees, eyes locked, in the center of the bed. Her fingers went to his belt again. "*I* haven't been able to do what *I* want in a long time. And what I'm dying for is this." The harsh leather belt was hers to manipulate, and she unbuckled it before running her hands over his denim-covered thickness.

His throat bobbed, and his eyelids were heavy. "Sweetheart…"

Sliding her hands back to his chest, she pushed Parker onto his back. He complied with a look of complete awe, and didn't that make her feel like his woman. She pulled at his jeans, unsnapping and dragging down the zipper to show dark boxer briefs. He lifted his hips, giving her the freedom to do what she wanted. Seconds later, Parker Black was completely naked, with his impressive, gorgeous erection reaching for attention.

"Damn you, Parker, you're the most handsome man I've ever seen."

He slowly stroked himself. "Got me naked. Wasn't my plan, so what do you want—"

She cut him off with her hands covering his. He quickly switched their fists so that the hot, silky flesh was directly under her touch, and his hands clamped tightly on top of hers.

"God, Lex." He worked his shaft with her hands. The tighter he squeezed, the thicker he felt in her fingers and the wetter she grew for him. She wanted the ache of an orgasm, but far more prevalent was a hunger, a curiosity asking if that bit of precum crowning the head of his cock tasted as good as her dreams.

Lexi bent, swiping her tongue over his very essence. It was more than she expected—completely virile and masculine—and she was drunk on just one quick lick.

"Fuck," he groaned, drawing out the word. His hips flexed slightly, as if it had been unintentional and he'd caught himself and held back.

Still with his tight hand over hers, he worked his length, and she opened her mouth, letting him fill her. Parker released her hand, and his palms threaded into her hair. She kept the same grip, the same rhythm that he had set, then she sucked him hard and licked him lightly. Every single gasp and groan that blurred from his lips urged her on.

He sounded gutted, ravaged. His hips pumped and his cock fucked her mouth while she all but tried to swallow him. Nothing like this had ever seemed fun, let alone erotic. But as she made his entire body react—limbs trembling, hands grabbing, and words lost in moans—she decided that she'd never held more power.

"Wait," he panted. "Lex. Lexi."

She ran her thumb over his crown when she bobbed up, then she slid down to the base of him, needing to feel him come. He gave her every permission to back away, to work him until he spurted on his own stomach, but God, that wasn't what she wanted.

"*Silver*, sweetheart." He groaned as his hips flexed up hard, and he came on her tongue, the hotness hitting her senses on several levels. "God. Damn."

His rigid body flexed, and his fingers pulled on her hair. She never let up, needing everything he gave her. It was an eternity of mind-altering arousal, and when his body went lax, she was in love with everything about him.

He was her friend.

Her co-worker.

A protector.

And her lover.

She wanted this again and again and again. She wanted to watch him, taste him. To feel him push inside her, to have him hold her close. To let her take him in her mouth again, where it wasn't just about him getting off—an experience her ex had used to debase her—but a connection that they both flat-out loved.

Parker laid there, looking at her in a way that made her swoon, with his heavy cock lying over his thigh and an appetite in his eyes. Even with all that, she knew he wouldn't have sex with her yet. But it wasn't just the location. Safe house or not, he didn't want to screw up a good thing. Her sense was that until her invisible scars faded, he wouldn't ride her deep.

All of those were assumptions, but she was going to take them as fact until maybe he realized aloud that he was in love with her also.

# CHAPTER THIRTY-FOUR

A calmness washed over Parker as Lexi curled next to his naked skin. Her mouth had been a complex heaven, with enough tease and taunt of promise and fulfillment that he might declare himself officially addicted. It was supposed to be all about her, but somehow he was the one naked. Not that he was complaining…

Even as she lay next to him, she faced away. That was her—close yet far. She was someone he knew—two someones he knew—but oddly enough, he was only starting to learn all about the real Lexi Dare. He turned on his side to hold her from behind and let his hand drift from her thigh to the hem of her tight cotton shirt. His fingers slipped on her flat stomach, dipping across her belly button then sliding around in circles. She let out a soft sigh and leaned back against his bare chest.

"Think we should lose this." He tugged on the cotton, helping her slip out of it without turning around.

Lexi leaned back against his chest, and his mouth pressed to the angle where her neck became her shoulder. She smelled like citrus, and he breathed her in as his hand cupped her breast, its tip hardening against his palm. Massaging its perfect weight, he let his tongue slide on her skin until she squirmed. Her hips writhed and her back arched just enough that he took that as his cue to slip under the lacy cup of her bra and worship the perked breast.

"God, Parker," she whispered.

He pushed up onto his elbow and, with his other hand, undid her bra. The thing fell away, and he tilted her back as he moved over her. Wide-eyed and pink-cheeked, Lexi watched him watch her. They stayed in their moment, him naked and nestled between her leather-clad legs, the length of his erection thickening all over again.

"You're gorgeous, sweetheart." Parker unsnapped her pants and peeled them off her, taking her panties and socks in one ravenous sweep.

There was complete trust on her face, and he'd never wanted a woman more. Hell, the *way* in which he wanted her was nothing like he'd experienced. It was possessive, protective… even branding, permanently imprinting her inside him. He wanted to know that the burning aggravation he felt for her was mirrored, that she was in deep for him that same way.

Parker dropped her clothes off the edge of the bed and held her slender ankle. Slowly, he kissed up her calf until he got to a sensitive spot behind her knee.

Lexi moaned and turned her head. "Wow…"

His tongue played in a circle as he grinned at her reaction.

"That's so not fair."

He laughed against that special spot then moved to the other knee—bending her leg to see if that same location had the same effect. As her hips moved and her lips moaned, he reached the conclusion that it did.

"Fair's no fun." He let his stubble scratch the inside of her thigh.

"Oh, right." Her hips wiggled again. "But torture is."

Tracing his fingertips along the same path, Parker spread her legs and put her on display, giving him all of her perfect, pink sweetness. "That wasn't torture, sweetheart. But I'm willing to give that a go too."

His lips hovered over her folds, making her thighs crush against him. She smelled like desire, and as his tongue licked her smooth skin, she sucked in a breath that he felt down to his toes.

"That's insane," she whispered hoarsely.

Parker touched her, teased her, danced his fingers over where his tongue had just been, and when she moved too much, he drew his hand away and clamped her hip in place at the same moment that lips found her clit.

Lexi moaned and moved, almost pushing herself onto him, and everything about him went into overdrive. His forearms pushed her thighs wide, and she walked her feet up the bed, bending her knees.

Her knees clamped down on his head, and she jumped back. "Sorry. Sorry."

Lost in the woman, it took him a second to realize that she was apologizing for… reacting to him. To what he did and how much she liked it. "No reason to say that." He flicked his tongue over the sensitive bundle of nerves.

"I know. I just…" Her body was tense, her mind not with him anymore.

Parker's deep-blue eyes darkened. "God, I should've killed that fucker for you."

"I'm screwing this up." Her forehead scrunched.

He rose up to kiss her stomach and leaned against her small frame. "I said it before. Now I'm going to promise it."

"What?"

His fingers moved between her legs, paying attention to her slick entrance. "I'm going to take care of you. I'm not between your legs because I'm killing time. I want it, and you deserve it." His thumb circled her clit. "Relax. Forget wherever your head went."

"Mmm," she whispered. "Okay." She moaned again. "Alright."

He chuckled as he kissed her side. "Good, because, sweetheart, I'm gonna eat you until you get it. I like your taste. Those sounds. The way you feel moving against my lips." He inched down, pushing between her legs again. "You want to clamp and claw on me, then fucking do it."

Parker slid his fingers into her tightness and covered her nub with his lips, lapping and loving on her. The more she moved, the harder he took her. He was relentless, and she was letting go. He fucked her with his tongue, his fingers. He held her open, teased her top to bottom.

"God, Parker. God." She gasped and thrashed as if she'd never neared orgasm before.

He wanted her to pulse on his tongue, shudder and shatter against his kiss, and he moaned into her body, telling her to come for him.

"Oh!" Her hands fisted the covers as she came. Her hips bucked, her back tried to arch off the mattress, but he held her in place, making Lexi ride her climax as long as he could.

Finally, her covers-knotted hands went limp, her body went soft, and he kissed her gently, eliciting the tiniest of shivers. The boneless woman before him was what he'd always wanted, and now that he'd finally had his taste, he didn't plan on letting go.

He pulled his frame over her and caged her face. Her ice-blue eyes radiated trust. Her fair skin was pink and flushed. He kissed her, tasting her as his tongue tangled with hers. They kissed forever, for days, until again he lost his mind, consumed by her.

Lexi held him, melding herself to his body, until finally she broke away, her eyes heavy-lidded. "I know what you said before, but please. This is me giving myself to you, erasing the past and wanting something different in my future."

Too drunk on everything about her, he had little resources to back away, to say no. He couldn't remember his reasoning for that logical decision he'd made. "Sweetheart…"

"Make love to me."

# CHAPTER THIRTY-FIVE

A part of Lexi's soul had never been bared, and she was handing it to Parker as though she was a virgin all over again. His features darkened, his deep-blue eyes firing with a need that mirrored the white lightning flowing in her veins. She wanted him to touch her, to love her, to smooth away all of her past and pave the way for a real love. A relationship that was fulfilling.

She gulped her nerves, refusing to apologize, but as the seconds ticked by, a slice of fear wrapped its ugly tendrils around her neck. "Parker?"

He dropped a kiss to her lips then moved to her ear. "It..." His weight pressed down, his tongue touching the bottom of her lobe. "Would be my honor."

Shivers cascaded down her shoulders, her spine, and she was consumed by the tension burning her. Parker rolled away, and a cold brush of air ran over her naked body. He grabbed his jeans off the floor, pulled a condom from his wallet, and rolled it over his hard length. The seconds it took for him to do that, Lexi drank in his physique. Parker was etched muscles, like a living, breathing Michelangelo.

He moved back to the bed and gathered her against his chest. Once again, they were on their knees, his full lips eating hers, his tongue driving her to the brilliant edge of madness. One of his hands threaded into her hair, and the other wrapped around her waist. Holding her, he sat against the backboard, her legs straddling him. His strong hands ran up and down her back. She was lost in the sensation. He wasn't rushing her, wasn't jumping at the green light to slam into what she offered.

Lexi lifted against him, pressing his sheathed head against her needy core. With her arms over his shoulders, his arms supporting her, and their gazes held, she inched down, embracing that amazing, intoxicating stretch as he invaded her muscles. Her eyes rolled, her head lolled, and Lexi's jaw hinged as she sank onto his shaft.

"Fuck, sweetheart," his hoarse voice ground out.

This was perfect. Of course he knew how not to push her, how to make her feel in control after not having any recently. Parker missed nothing when it came to her. He honestly couldn't be a better man. She swayed her hips and watched his eyes squeeze shut. Lexi tested herself on him, sliding up and down, back and forth, establishing a rhythm that made her want to die in his arms.

Parker flexed up, damn near impaling her soul, and it sparked a fire of reactions. Reading her mind as he always did, he owned the motions she had set. The speed, the sway, everything that she wanted, he took over as their mouths tangled and her breasts bounced against him. All of his strength surrounded her, and their fury blasted out of control. He growled into their kiss, pumped into her, holding her tight.

"Parker." Her heartbeat drummed as her climax built. She moaned and gasped and called his name against his ear. "Make me come again, please."

He moved them fast onto her back, and he hooked one of her knees, spreading her wide, opening her deep, and he pistoned inside her. There was immaculate pressure against her clit, perfect to reach that crazy spot, but it was the strain and focus and determination in his eyes that made her fall apart. She came again, crying his name, and as she finished that insane roll of orgasm, he dropped her leg and thrust hard and deep.

God help her, he was going to make it happen all over again. She was ultra-sensitive, and he changed to deep and slow, drawing out every inch of him until she begged for more. The low rumble of another earth-shattering climax started. His tense body bucked with hers. With delicious, bruising force, he growled his release, holding her tighter than any man had before.

The stars shined in her closed eyes. Tendrils of glowing aftermath raced through her system as they collapsed together. Their hearts beat where their temples and cheeks touched.

Minutes lingered on until he gently kissed her forehead and pulled away. "Damn. You are so… worth it."

And honestly, not because he'd said it but because he'd made her feel it, she agreed. "You too."

He kissed her again and pushed out of bed to ditch the condom. "Back in a sec."

She sighed and tried to melt into the bed, to drown in the down comforter, burying herself away from anything that would ever erase how she felt at that moment.

From far away, the familiar sound of her phone ringing brought her from her happy la la land. *Shadow?* Lexi snapped out of it and jumped up, tugging on her shirt and wrapping the blanket around her hips because there was no time to try to pull those tight leather pants back on. She found the phone in the pocket of her jacket and checked the screen. *Meredith.*

Not Shadow, and she was seriously beginning to worry about him, but talking to her sister was a rarity. No telling when she could get her again, so she hit OKAY and slid onto the couch in a loose-limbed haze. "Hey, Mere."

"Hey, yourself. So is the girl I know and love back?"

Lexi laughed quietly. "I hope so."

"Your bike is gone, your clothes are picked through, my makeup's missing, and my doorman has been babysitting Bacon. So you dumped the loser?"

"More or less."

"What's with that happy sing-song tinge in your voice?"

Meredith was always so good at reading her. "Just happier, I guess."

"Huh."

Lexi tugged the blanket high on her chest. "I have to run. I just wanted to say hi since I keep missing you."

"Sorry I wasn't there when you needed me."

"Don't worry about it. I had someone to lean on."

"You sound really good. Malcolm said that smile I hear might have to do with a man?"

She happy-sighed. "It does."

"Well, thank God for that. He better be a good one."

"He is. I know it seems so fast, but I've known him forever. I'm just totally, completely"—she stretched, loving how wonderfully sore her insides felt—"absolutely in l—" As she repositioned from her stretch, there was Parker. Standing. Listening. Watching her confess her deepest feelings to her closest confidant. "Mere, I have to go."

"Wow. Okay. Call me as soon as you can. I want—"

Lexi hung up, unable to read his face. "Hi."

He wore just his pants, which hung low on his hips, unbuttoned. "Hey."

The creases on his forehead said he'd heard every embarrassing word. She wanted to be mad at him—that conversation had been for her sister only. It was the first time in a long time she'd felt taken care of, and the words had rushed out. But he'd also said amazing, incredible things to her, so it wasn't news to him where her head was.

The sweet tension from before had shifted. He was concerned, and she felt stupid for wandering around in a sheet and forgetting that they were in a safe house with motion-activated cameras lining the common areas.

"I need to take a shower," Lexi said.

He nodded. "I've got some work to do."

"Sounds good." With her chin up and shoulders back, she walked past him in her ridiculous blanket wrap. With the cameras on them, his chest bare and pants unbuckled, she felt as if she was taking the walk of shame.

Her feet padded down the hall, part of the blanket dragging, when Parker called her name.

"Yes," she half-whispered, studying the floor.

Parker paused for a long time. "You're a very special person. I hope you know that."

Her cheeks burned. What had she expected? Just because she was clearly in love with the guy, and he was pretty into her, that didn't mean that saying—or even thinking—things about love was a good idea. It was enough to chase a guy away.

"I do. Thanks to you." Then she dragged herself to shower, where she could hide her fall from love-drunk heaven.

# CHAPTER THIRTY-SIX

Parker's ears burned. She loved him? She hadn't said that, but it had sounded like the lead up to that kind of confession. He hadn't meant to listen, but those few seconds had felt like eternity, and he couldn't walk away.

It'd been only a few weeks since she showed up on his doorstep, yet she loved him. Maybe that could classify the unexplainable reactions he'd had lately. A chest ache that wasn't heartburn. An urge to take on the world even if he didn't know what was wrong.

*Christ.*

He'd far past fallen for her. His visceral reactions were trained to jump at thoughts of her, and when she'd hustled by a few minutes ago, he'd felt like an asshole who should've said something intelligent. Instead it came out like a Hallmark not-so-fast greeting card.

The shower shut off, and wandering around the kitchen, he couldn't have been more aware that she was still naked nearby. For the second time in recent history, Parker found his fingers biting into a countertop. Problem was, this time he'd already been with her and knew how great her mouth felt on his dick, how she rode his cock with a finesse that made his mind explode, and how they were supposed to be in bed, drowning in goddamn orgasms.

His fingers flexed into the counter as his ears pricked. Bare feet padded down the hall, coming toward him. He took a deep breath and turned, jaw gaping at the temptation displayed before him.

"Hey." She wore a towel wrapped around her, squeezing her

breasts. Again with the towel-dried hair that hung around her face, and that was maybe one of his favorite looks on her. “I hung up on Meredith and jumped in the shower like I had something to hide.”

“You don’t.”

“That whole time, I was… embarrassed that you know what I think. But really, I’m done hiding. It didn’t do me any good with Matt, and I don’t want that to happen with you.” She shook her head, her cheeks pinking. “Not that you’d hurt me, not that you’ll propose to me. God, what I’m trying to say is—”

He grabbed her in his arms and kissed her quiet. “You don’t have to explain anything.”

“Are you sure?” She toyed with a strand of damp hair, spinning it around her finger.

“Positive.” Even though he wanted to hear the words again, wanted to see how his chest would have felt if she’d finished that conversation with Meredith. I absolutely, completely, *what*? Love? Sounded as though that was what she had almost said. Hell, he could finish her conversation for her because he absolutely, completely…

*Wanted her*? Check.

*Liked her?* Check again.

*More than that…?* Yeah, maybe so.

“Two years,” she said, biting her lip. “And only a few months of it was worth making a memory over.”

He dropped his head and ran a hand over the back of his neck. “Really, Lex. You don’t have to say anything.”

“I moved through the stages. I mentioned before… I didn’t have a family, and he filled the void. I felt nothing… like I do now. What I’m trying to figure out how to say… is…”

“Lex, we’re good if you don’t want to share.”

She pinched her eyes closed. “I haven’t had a man touch me *because I wanted him to* in a long time. And now that you did, I’m crazy scared that you think I’m confusing sex and anything else.”

He stepped back, hating and loving every word that’d fallen off her lips. “I’m not—”

“You *are* the guy for me. Code and numbers and MIT?

Black and Silver, partners for years. You are way more than Matt ever was. I want you to know that, no matter what you feel or say or think after hearing me talk on the phone. How I feel has nothing to do with the scars you can't see. Nothing." She closed her eyes and breathed deeply then leveled her icy blues on him. "I'm in love with you."

# CHAPTER THIRTY-SEVEN

Dawn's light bled through the safe house bedroom as a ringing cell phone tugged Parker from sleep. He took a deep breath and relaxed his body against hers, her blond hair in his face. After ending the night in bed, her words had weighed heavily on him, but she seemed comfortable with what she had said, what he hadn't said. So he'd fallen asleep holding beautiful. His lips quirked at that. Beautiful wasn't tangible. His analytical brain wanted to scream over how stupid that thought was. He was holding *her*. *She* was beautiful. But it was more than looks, and everything gathered in his arms *was* beautiful. The girl. The feelings. What she represented to him.

Didn't make sense. At all. But he didn't care.

"Hello?" Her sleep-drenched voice sounded like a dream. "Hello…? Wrong number." Lex dropped the phone back on the nightstand and crawled back into his arms. "Morning."

He bent over, lightly pressing a kiss to lips that had him mesmerized. "Morning, Lex."

"I like waking up next to you."

He brushed her hair with his fingers, nonchalantly toying with the strands and thinking that her sleepy grin was too damn sweet. "Another one of my favorite things I get to do with you."

That made her pretty features morph to almost embarrassed, and her fair skin blushed. With a quiet giggle and an almost shy cast of her eyes, she whispered, "You have a lot of favorites?"

Morning wood was quickly morphing into a not-to-be ignored hard-on, and he cursed quietly against her lips. "Wish safe houses stocked condoms. Actually, they might."

She quietly moaned as his hands found purchase under the baggy white shirt she'd found folded in a dresser. That was all she had on. His boxer briefs weren't doing him any favors as his length rubbed against her. Parker smoothed his hand down her stomach, between her legs, and found her wet with arousal. His stomach spun. His mind was just as turned on as his body, and she made the sexiest sound as his fingers strummed over her folds.

Kissing him in a drowsy, needing morning wake-up sex kind of way, her hands also drifted south, sliding over the rigid length of his shaft. Parker sucked in a breath as her thumb circled his crown.

"We could," she whispered, torturing him with her deft hand movements. "After I went dark, I, um, went to the doctor's, just to make sure and all. Doc checked everything from bruises to… um, testing. So… I'm okay."

"I've never not with a condom." Which didn't mean he couldn't with her…

Her hand stilled. "Right, sorry, I didn't mean—"

"Are you on birth control?" he asked.

"I get a shot, few times a year." She nodded, all cute, sweet, and nervous. Little things like birth control made her blush, but bold statements like *I love you* she was so damn confident about.

That feeling like a time bomb was going to blow in his chest, like he couldn't get close enough, deep enough, in her head enough.

"Parker…"

He slid down and kicked off his boxers then tugged off her shirt to bare her sinful body. With his heart in his throat, her phone rang again.

He held her hand. "Don't answer it."

She cringed. "What if it's Shadow?"

Shit, he had no argument against that, and he nodded.

"Hello?" Her eyebrows rose. Then she shook her head, pressed a button on the phone, and dropped it. "No one again."

"Wait a minute." He reached for the phone, his senses firing as much with worry as with arousal.

"It wasn't Shadow. It won't be Matt. Just you and me." She brushed her lips across his skin and let her hands roam until she had the weight of him in her hold. "I need this, us."

And thank heaven for that. He didn't just need her; he had to connect with her, to feel her in every way, because his exploding heart and emo-drunk mind were almost more than he could survive. He pulled her to him, needing to be inside her to alleviate the deep ache that threatened his sanity.

Lexi lifted her legs, hooking them over his thighs, and with that little gesture, the head of his cock was dangerously close to her center. Hot and wet, he throbbed to push inside her. His eyes sank shut as he inched in. Bliss. Fucking heaven. Her tight pussy on his bare cock was out of this world.

She sucked in a breath as he pushed deeper. On their sides, he kissed her, thrusting gently, waking her body up with his. Tangled in the sheets, they were hidden from the world, and the deeper he reached into her, the longer he wanted to stay there. There was no letting go of Lexi. He couldn't dream of this with another woman and didn't want it anyway.

Her mouth gaped, her breathing escalated. Their eyes locked, his dark blues to her icy ones, and just the same as last night, he fucked her in a way that made love, that made him reach past everything that made sense of his world. This wasn't about him giving a woman some gigantic climax, him getting his in the process and everything as it should be. It was just so them…so fucking catastrophic.

He flipped them, powering into her as they rolled. He didn't only want her today, tomorrow, whenever. He wanted her. Period.

Lexi met his every move, her fingernails tearing into his back. "God, yes."

Buried bare in her, her mouth open and moaning his name, her legs wrapped tight around his hips, he lost himself, living for the moment that she came. Her core clenched, her eyes pinched shut, cries and pleas fell from her lips, and everything she asked for, he gave. She came hard, rippling her most intimate muscles over his throbbing shaft, sinking her nails into him. Parker stilled and strained, releasing his climax as she spasmed with him.

He stared at the most important thing he'd ever held. His mind spun as he fell onto her, rolling them, still connected and locked in every way. "I love you too, sweetheart."

Her smile reached her eyes, which slipped shut as he kissed her. "We should wake up like this again and again."

"We should—" Her phone rang *again.* What the motherfuck? As he slid from her, he grabbed it. "Who has this number?"

"No one really. You, Shadow, my sister, um…"

"Matt."

She nodded. "Yeah."

Buzz kill. But that wasn't what bothered him. His senses itched, and as he pulled from Lexi, now that he was momentarily sated, his brain went into overdrive. "He's been calling and hanging up?"

She shook her head. "Unknown number."

The hour didn't sit right. Matt was a party guy, and it was seven fifteen in the morning. So either he hadn't gone to sleep yet or… it wasn't Matt.

"Get up. Get dressed."

"What? Why?"

"No idea. We're compromised. Let's go." He tugged her hand, dragging her from the warm sheets.

"Parker!"

"Someone's tracking you down. Pinging closer to your location every time you answer." His mind raced. "Have you talked to Shadow at all since he ran after the laptop guy?"

She shook her head, realization that they were being hunted clouding in her eyes. "I am *not* cut out for all this real-life BS." She sat upright. "But what about Shadow? What about him?"

Now wasn't the time to explain that Shadow's phone likely wasn't in his possession anymore, and if neither of them had heard from him through alternative methods, he also likely wasn't breathing. "Get dressed, Lex."

She tugged on her clothes as he did the same. For as talented of a hacker as she was, as much of the underground as she was aware of, she still couldn't see criminal activity. It wasn't in her training to sense, wasn't in her mind to search out. It should have been in his mind, but he was too stuck on the woman to see what was happening around them.

The doorbell rang.

"Fuckin' hell. Are you kidding me?" Guess they'd learned from trying to pick his lock last time. He ducked under the bed, running his hand around the frame until he found a Glock. He pulled the magazine, checked his count, and snapped it back in. "Let's go."

"Could just be Girl Scouts? Jehovah's Witness folks? Right?" But her face said she didn't buy it. Nervous energy radiated from her as she clung to his hand.

"It's seven in the morning."

Her worried face pinched. "Crap."

"Just in case, stick close and duck the windows." He held her against the wall then rounded a corner. All clear.

Parker held her again and snagged the keys for his bike as she grabbed her jacket. He followed, doing the same, and picked up their helmets. He opened a closet and snagged two Kevlar vests.

"We don't really need that, do we?"

"Better to be safe…" He pulled one over her head and cinched it tight then did the same for himself. If someone was at the front door, they couldn't see the garage, and they'd have to round the house to get to them. Parker and Lexi had a few seconds of head start if they rolled out on his R1.

"Helmet."

She took it and slipped it on.

"Now stay put. Just give me a second." He took her hand and pressed the Glock to her palm. "Anyone comes in here not me, just shoot."

She nodded, and he ran back into the house from the garage. Parker reached the room farthest from Lexi as the doorbell rang again. Just in case it was some pushy-ass cookie seller macking her entrepreneurial skills at the crack of morning, he peeked. Nope, just a guy in his twenties. Parker snapped a picture with his cell then ransacked the linen closet, finding a couple of cherry bombs amongst the stash of weapons and ammo. He took them and slipped into the front room again.

"Thanks for stopping by, asshole," he mumbled then slid the window open enough to toss lit cherry bombs outside for a loud, smoky, snap-crackle-pop distraction.

He beat feet back to Lexi as the cherry bombs detonated. Surely the mini-explosion turned the attention of the man at the door away from the ultra-silent garage. With the garage door opening, he pulled Lexi onto the motorcycle and waited for as long as he could.

"Duck, sweetheart." He switched the ignition, throttled down, and burned out of the garage, cutting off the driveway, heading down a sidewalk, and exiting onto the street from someone else's driveway.

A high-pitched squeal came from behind him, and his gut churned until he realized she wasn't screaming in terror. Lexi Dare had just enjoyed the hell out of their little escape. He'd laugh if he wasn't terrified of her getting shot in the back. Parker wove down side streets, swooping down a maze of two-ways. He was certain no one had eyes on them when he hit the interstate to head to the belly of the beast. Time to bring Lexi to Titan.

# CHAPTER THIRTY-EIGHT

Phiber climbed from the bush he'd ducked in then checked his surroundings to make sure no one had seen him dive like a coward. Only then did he pull the gun from his waistband and run to the garage. It had closed. While it looked like a harmless garage door, his fingers still had burn marks from when he'd tried to pick the lock at the last place Silver had been hiding.

Who was that woman? More importantly, why did she live like a commando? Maybe he hadn't given her enough credit. Then again, she had stupidly let him track her to this place.

Phiber circled the house, unable to see in anywhere. A window on the side of the second floor was cracked a few inches. While he might be able to get a ladder or something and crawl in, he was wary of entering that way. Maybe she had electrified windows.

His phone buzzed with a text message, and without looking, he knew who it was.

Taskmaster: *Complete?*

With a slightly bruised ego, Phiber scrolled up to see his previous message that he'd found Silver and it would be a sure thing this time. His fingers hovered before he responded.

Phiber: *Almost.*

All he needed was a plan, because they wouldn't send him another bank transfer until they had her. His greedy heart wanted that payday in a bad way.

Taskmaster: *New task at the incoming location. All you'll need to move forward will be in there. Consider it a thank you gift.*

Well, fuck him running. Maybe he wasn't as off today as he thought. A second later, a text buzzed through with an address. Phiber hopped back into his car and punched the location into his GPS. Less than a mile away. It took a few turns, and he found nothing but yellow-lined do-not-park curbs in a sea of driveways. At the fire lane, he threw his car in park anyway and jumped out. His phone buzzed again. Another address with one accompanying command. *Walk there.*

He got his bearings and headed down the suburban street until he found the address. The garage door was up, and a Mercedes sat inside. Holy shit. He pulled out his phone to ask if what he was thinking was what was happening, but the Taskmaster beat him to it.

Taskmaster: *Key in the ignition center console. Consider it a gift for the job done.*

Well, shit. He hadn't even finished yet, and maybe they didn't get that it was turning out to be harder than he expected, but what the fuck. A new ride ten times better than his current one? That he'd take. Phiber ran his hand over the frame from the trunk until he pulled the driver's door open and sat in leather-covered heaven. This ride was sick. Not really his style, but it was crazy high end and would sell quickly. But not before he checked out how this baby could burn rubber.

He ran his hands over the steering wheel and saw the keyless key waiting for him. All he had to do was press his foot to the brake and push the button that said IGNITION. He took a deep breath of new car smell as he rested his foot on the brake pedal.

The snap of the interior locks surprised him. "What the—"

The garage door began to close.

"Hey!" He reached for the unlock button and jabbed it several times, but nothing. His fingers pried at the locks, but they were small and barely peeping out of the door console. He couldn't get enough traction on the nub of plastic sticking out.

The car's engine ignited even though his foot hadn't moved, and he hadn't pressed it to start.

"Shit!" Phiber tried the windows and sun roof. Neither opened. Then he jumped to the other side of the car and tried that lock. No luck. Panic made him perspire.

He pressed the button above him that should connect him to an operator. But music blared in the car instead.

Then a robotic voice filled the speakers, repeating, "Three strikes, you're out."

The car's engine raced, and the scent of exhaust seeped inside. He put his foot on the brake and tried to shift into reverse, but the slap-stick gear shifter wouldn't budge.

"Fuck!" He slammed the steering wheel with his balled fists, then he grabbed his cell phone and called the Taskmaster. It rang until a robot-generated voicemail message told him to speak after the beep. "Let me go, you fuckers."

But nothing changed except the noise.

Phiber hung up and dialed 9-1-1. The phone clanged to a busy tone no matter how many times he redialed.

The engine still revved, the tachometer redlining. His fingertips bled from tearing at the doors and windows, all unbudging. The garage slowly filled with carbon monoxide, and a foggy, tired feeling ate at his mind.

He pulled his shirt over his mouth and nose, panicking, and leaned back to gain leverage. With his feet, he bashed at the windows to no avail. They didn't shatter. He coughed and hacked, growing weaker with every wheezy breath. What was this, bulletproof glass or some shit? With each kick to the unyielding glass, he grew more tired, coughing, until his fight was zapped.

Unable to do anything more, Phiber lay back, his mind swimming, his lungs burning. He couldn't keep his eyes open anymore…

Lexi leaned against Parker as they came to a stoplight. Riding like that after spending the night with him, every time he throttled, she felt it.

He turned his head and looked dead sexy. "We just have to make a quick stop."

They were dangerously close to her old house, but that also meant that they were very close to Parker's place. They hadn't had a chance to talk about what their next move was, but she thought his house, where she'd first known that she was falling for him, was the perfect location after their night together.

"Sounds good."

They rolled into his driveway as his garage door lifted. She swung off the bike and watched him do the same. Some men were born to ride motorcycles, fewer created to master that speed racer. As Parker removed his helmet and ran his fingers into his hair, with two days' stubble on his cheeks and his blue eyes aflame, she almost couldn't contain the need to kiss him.

*Oh, screw it.* She pushed onto her toes and placed her hands on his scratchy cheeks, pulling his face to hers, and she took the kiss she wanted.

A grin curled on his face, and he laughed quietly. "What was that for?"

"Just because."

"I think I could get used to this."

She giggled. "This?"

"Yeah, this. You and me, running around on an adrenaline-sex high."

Heat crawled up her neck. "Well, good. I'm glad."

He hooked his arm around her as they walked into his house. She hadn't had time to analyze his declaration of love in bed, but she was certain of one thing. A man who said "I love you" while having sex might not say it again. Except he was Parker. She trusted him. She *was* in love with him, and if he said he loved her too, then maybe he really did.

"What's that look?" he asked as they shed their jackets.

She shrugged, not ready to bare every single thought that moved through her mind. "I just haven't had a moment since this morning to think about, I don't know… us. And kissing you for the hell of it, just like a random, for-no-reason kiss, that was awesome. Just kind of makes everything feel real when the last few days, really the last few weeks of my life, have been absurd."

"Good." He crossed his arms. "So we'll hang here for a while. I have a couple of things to do, phone calls to make. You okay if I jump in the shower for a minute?"

"Yeah, yeah, sure. No problem."

"Okay. You've been here before, you know the lay of the land. Anything you want is yours. Got it?"

Everything she wanted was standing before her. Even though she'd had him that morning and last night, it was as if he'd tapped a hunger she couldn't stymie.

He snagged her close, laid his lips on hers, and made her senses explode before he set her free. "Alright, there's an untraceable tablet on the coffee table, and the remote's gotta be somewhere close to that. Be back in a few."

She padded to his living room and sat on the couch. Everything was very Parker. Straight lines and hard edges, as if he'd found a black-and-white rule book for how a room should be decorated to look like a man's place. But honestly, he'd nailed it. Thick, rich furniture, all of it dark. The walls were deep blues, the hardwood floor seemed more manly than elegant, and half a dozen techy magazines were tossed in a pile—well, there were military ones too. Ones named Tactical this, and Strategic that…

She sat down to Google Titan. The site immediately popped on the screen, and she paged through until she came to an executive staff bio page. Parker Black. What she read blew her mind. His career. His history. Where he'd been. What he'd done. And that was only what was public. She tried to hack past all of the safeguards in place but couldn't. No reason to do it really, except that was how she passed the time. But it was locked down, impenetrable. Primarily, she assumed, because Parker—or rather BlackDawn—had run point on the site. The man knew what he was doing, she couldn't fault him for that.

But after what she had read, if she'd been impressed before, she had a newfound respect for him. The guy just kept amazing her. Down the hall, she heard the shower running. Odd how that casual and intimate act made her swoon inside. A man showering, leaving her to roam his domain, was simple enough, yet it wasn't—especially given everything she continued to learn about him.

She could spend the next twenty minutes staring toward the bathroom, imagining how he looked showering, or she could search for breakfast. Or for ice cream. That cured all ills. What were the chances that Mister Muscles had ice cream? She opened the freezer and smiled when she found a pint of vanilla. *Not bad, BlackDawn.*

Then she went in search of a bowl and maybe some toppings. Nothing said life on the run like dessert for breakfast. After opening cabinet after cabinet, taking in the stock of boxed, non-perishable, open-and-eat foods like granola bars, rice pouches, and instant potatoes, she realized that he had nothing perishable or confectionary-focused, so she moved to the fridge. Nothing but condiments, protein shakes, and beer. This place really was a bachelor's pad.

With another quick search of the drawers, she found a spoon—

"There's fudge in the pantry."

Lexi jumped and spun. "Parker! You scared the—"

But as she took him in, tight T-shirt stretched and stuck across his semi-wet chest, jeans that hung low but were somehow molded to his hips and thighs, she lost her words. His hair was damp and the light scent of soap surrounded him, making her mouth water.

"I didn't mean to sneak up. Thought you heard me."

For a second time, her eyes raked down him. Sweet Jesus. "No problem."

"Breakfast of champions?" He nodded at the vanilla ice cream. "Gonna eat it or…?"

Right. She was standing there like a moron, likely with her tongue hanging out. "You're kinda soaked."

"I rushed—I didn't want to step away too long."

"Did you get your work stuff done?"

"Yeah, about that…" His face grew grim. "It's not orange sherbet, but did you want fudge or not?"

"Don't even tell me you have a sweet tooth." Big, lean, follows all the rules, stays inside the lines Parker stashed chocolate? Almost too funny to believe.

He smiled. "Maybe."

She wagged her finger at him. "You totally played like you

didn't at the ice cream parlor."

"Orange and chocolate?" He made a face but grabbed a jar of fudge out of the pantry she hadn't searched. "Not my thing."

"Want some vanilla instead?"

Parker shook his head, popped the cap, and stuck the jar in the microwave while she doled out her ice cream. When the microwave beeped, he grabbed the jar with a cloth and dumped enough chocolate onto her ice cream that she almost proposed to the man. Swishy warmness lit in her chest when she focused on him.

He licked his thumb. "Good stuff." Then took another thumb of fudge and pressed it to her lips. "Careful, it's still hot."

Apparently, she had died and gone to heaven.

"Thanks," she mumbled, licking off the last bit of chocolate. For as much as he was focusing on her mouth, something else was hiding in his eyes. "What's the matter?"

"Sit. Eat." He pushed out her chair then took his, flipping it around to straddle it.

Her stomach dropped as she did the same into her chair. "Really, I'd rather you just told me." The spoon hung limp in her hand, and all of the vanilla ice cream was quickly turning to sludge. She stirred the bowl into a creamy chocolate river. "It's about Shadow, isn't it?" Because what else was there that Parker would know about right now?

He nodded. "Sweetheart…"

She stole her eyes back, scooped up the ice cream soup, and decided the safest course of action was to keep at her original plan: gorge on sugar.

"Lex, I'm really sorry."

Sorry… like *sorry?* That couldn't be right. That sounded a whole lot like condolences. She smashed and splashed her spoon into the bowl. An overwhelming sadness broke through her. All the time she'd spent with Shadow over the years, all of his advice. The father figure she'd always leaned on. He'd taught her, guided her, pushed her to become what she was today. He'd tried to protect her from Matt and, in his own way, pushed her toward Parker. Tears pricked at her eyes, and a lump sliced into her throat.

"Maybe you're wrong," she said quietly and bit her lip, letting the tears spill, knowing Parker wasn't.

His head shook ever so slightly. "There's no doubt."

A sudden wave of guilt smashed her down, turning her world, drowning her away from even Parker as he sat there watching her. "Because of me. Because he went after Monarch."

"That was stupid. That was on him."

"Don't say that," she snapped.

Parker tossed up his hands. "Wrong thing to say. Sorry."

Letting the spoon clatter to the table, she curled into a ball on the kitchen chair. The chair opposite her scraped on the floor as he pushed up and lifted her, sobbing, into his arms. He shushed against her ear, murmuring for her to get it all out. Her insides were broken. Dull pain radiated from every joint, in every bone. Even her blood hurt as it pumped through her heart. Everything inside her was heartbroken.

He collapsed on the couch with her bawling into his chest. "You're going to be okay."

She shook her head, eyes swollen. "How can you say that? The only man who I could even think of as a dad is dead because he tried to help me. He's dead because of me!" Deep sobs stole her breath. Her mind stopped thinking forward, instead replaying their last moments over and over. "I'm an awful person."

"Hardly." He stroked her hair. "But I promise I'll make this right. Okay?"

"What happened?" She sniffled, letting the tears slow even though devastation had its stranglehold on her. "Was he hurt? In pain?"

"Details aren't important, and truthfully, I don't know yet."

Oh, God. He was. Shadow had died painfully because of her. "No… you have to tell me when you know. You have to. Promise?" She wiped at rogue tears. "I wish I could fix all this."

"That's why you have me. I'm a fixer. We'll make it work, and I'll take the hurt away."

Shadow was dead, and people were after Monarch. How did she not know this would happen? She wanted to escape, just push away and run. Even as she squirmed, Parker didn't let her go.

"You can't control things like this, Lex. You do what you can to protect yourself, your work as you best see fit, then you move forward. Every situation has a risk, some higher than others. Shadow knew there was a risk, he tried to mitigate it, but he also kept too much information to himself. He didn't ask for real help when he needed—"

"Monarch was mine."

"Just because you create a program doesn't mean it's your fault when someone tries to take it. Strictly speaking, in terms of risk analysis, Shadow knew too much and shared too little. He was playing with matches and gasoline. If he knew what I think he knew, then he should've put the auction on hold and done the right thing. He had to have seen this coming."

If she thought her stomach had dropped before, she was wrong. "What don't I know? What did you just learn?"

"ARO has Monarch. They've infiltrated a foot army into the States."

She'd armed a terrorist organization with dangerous information? "I think I'm going to be sick."

But she didn't run for the bathroom. She went limp, completely caught off guard by the intense panic and disgust that swirled in her bile.

"But there's a saving grace."

"What?"

Parker smiled carefully. "They haven't run it yet. No one knows why; they're working on that. My guess is, since they're tracking you so hard, they're too fucking dumb to figure it out." Delicately, he moved her to the couch. "I'm going to get you some water or something. Just sit still."

Nodding, she drifted alone in a world of darkness. "I created… something awful." Which she really, truly loved. Monarch was a gorgeous program. She'd worked those lines of code as if they were clay forming a sculpture. The end result had been breathtaking. Until it wasn't.

"No, sweetheart. Just like guns for protection aren't bad, but in the wrong hands, bad things happen."

"Yeah." She sniffled. "True."

"I think you're brilliant, and you were robbed. What you made was terrific, and in the right hands, it could help people, could ensure the safety of millions of families..."

"But it ended with the bad guys." She shook her spinning head.

"You can't do this to yourself. I won't let you."

She scoffed. "You're going to fix this too, huh? Just go back to work and take out a terror organization like magic?" Though she had seen him do some crazy shit, and that was just what he'd needed help on occasionally.

"Yes." Parker's face grew solemn as though he was selling his soul. "That's exactly what I'm going to do."

# CHAPTER THIRTY-NINE

They rode in silence in Parker's Range Rover as Lexi remained lost in her thoughts, still dealing with the sadness of losing Shadow in such a violent way. She wouldn't get over it for a long time. Maybe never. Because as she sat there, trying to hide from the world with the help of Parker's tinted windows and the Rover's seat warmers, she was painfully aware that sadness hurt. It ached in a way that made her head pound, her jaw lock, her limbs limp, and her stomach sick.

As they coasted down Interstate 95, Parker took her hand. When his long fingers gripped her balled fist, warmth bled from her heart, trying to fight away the darkness and threatening a chokehold. They drove the remainder of the way, still in silence, with him holding her hand. They pulled up to a nondescript building and slowed down the steep driveway to an underground parking garage. Along the way, Parker swiped a badge and entered codes. Twice.

They pulled into a parking spot, and all she could think was the office building had a custom parking garage. The ceiling was high, the spaces were wide, and she could see why. The trucks and cars in there were larger than life. She saw a couple military-looking vehicles and a few other cars that looked like throwaways. *Normal* cars that would blend into a crowd, and she was certain they were for just that. Over the years, she'd met a few friends of Matt's. Parker and his buddies, she had noticed, didn't blend into the crowd—even if they were driving something nondescript.

"This is where you work, huh?"

"Yup." He opened his door. "In we go."

Lexi's nerves kicked up, and she quickly got out also.

He took her hand again. "Look, whatever happens in there, whatever we learn and do, it's going to be overwhelming, but it'll also be fine."

"Okay."

"You might even see some familiar faces."

Groaning, she bit her lip. Even though she'd had a chance to shower before they left his house, she was still in the same clothes she'd been in for the past day, and she didn't want his co-workers thinking whatever people thought when they saw her looking like a two-day-old walk of shame.

He acted as though he sensed her unease. "You've met most of the guys before, right?"

She nodded as if that would make things better. "In passing."

"So that was them *relaxed*." They approached a door, and Parker pushed his face to it, letting the retina scanner identify him. "But here, they're more intense."

They were pretty damn intense to begin with. "Sweet."

"But it won't be a problem."

He guided her through more security hoops, and with each passing layer of safekeeping, she became more and more certain that they were walking into some kind of spy headquarters. Finally they came up an elevator, walked through solid, masculine-looking doors that were more utilitarian than for showing off, and passed a simple but strong block letter sign that read Titan Group.

She felt eyes watching her from somewhere, and her sixth sense kicked into overdrive. Power and danger hung in the air and permeated the walls, and with each passing step, she understood Parker Black and BlackDawn better than ever. "Titan must be way more than I've comprehended."

"Titan is—" He squeezed her close. "The most effective, efficient private security force in the world."

Private security *force*. "Badass."

"Generally." His smile reached his eyes. "Titan jumps in when the best of the best need a hand."

"Oh." Her lips rounded and stayed that way as he guided her to a door. "Fancy."

He laughed. "Here we go."

Pushing the door open, he led her into what had to be the nerve center. It was *sick.* She'd never been surrounded by so much state-of-the-art technology. It was enough to make that safe house look like computer day at a dollar store.

"Holy crap." Her eyes went wide, and curiosity exploded within her, dulling the hurt she'd been suffocated by for hours. Right now, all she wanted to do was fan-girl Parker's office. "This shiz is crazy."

"Decent setup, right?"

"I've never seen anything like it before. Ever."

He dropped into a chair, letting her wander and stare around the room. Besides the equipment, there were flat screens with what looked like live feed thermal imaging, live feeds into offices, foreign-looking cities and streets, and empty meeting rooms that looked to be no more than desert-sand camouflaged tents. Watching him on his home turf was incredible. Smart was sexy, and with his genius put to good use, that made her both impressed and proud.

"If I've never told you before, you, BlackDawn, are really talented."

"Thanks." He looked pleased, but his brow was creased, and worry painted his eyes.

Going back to his keyboard, he looked as though he was pulling data and reading quickly. Not that she wanted to look over his shoulder, that'd be rude—whatever, it was about her. Screw protocol and manners.

"Tell me what the problem is," she said.

"I'm just tapping in, trying to catch up. But—" He rubbed his hands over his face, more stress showing as he turned away. "It looks like a play's in action. The ARO is in over their heads, trying to run the Monarch patch. Intel reads they probably expected to be unable to execute your program, which is why they're after you. But it's actually good news, confirmation they can't run it."

She could see on his body that he had more he hadn't shared. "Might as well tell me everything, Parker. It can't be worse than what I already know."

His head dropped.

"It's worse?"

His head waffled from side to side. "Yeah."

"Please tell me. I have to know, or I'll go nuts trying to figure it out."

He stared forever at her before nudging his chin toward a chair. "Sit."

She grabbed the rolling chair and slid it closer. "Tell me. Is it about Shadow?"

"Intelligence reports indicate his death was… not an easy one."

She choked on the bile that sloshed into the back of her throat as nausea hit her. "Excuse me?"

"You don't want the details, but he went down fighting. Because the program hasn't been executed yet, I'd say he took his secrets to the grave. Chalk him up as a hero."

The room spun, and without thinking, she crumbled in half. Everywhere she looked, technology blinked and whirred at her. This world, these things that she loved creating, had fucked her. They were just a big middle finger pointed straight at her.

"I need to get out of here." She stood, rushing for the door, needing an escape.

"Lex—"

"Go away, please."

"You can't run around in here. There's no place to go."

"Then take me out of here! I don't want to see any of this!" She spun around, pointing at servers and mainframes and wires and everything she'd found comfort in her entire life.

Parker pulled her tight, stroking her hair, her back. "Take a breath, it'll be okay."

"He was in pain. He died because of me," she sobbed into his chest. "And I hate myself for that."

"No, sweetheart. He died protecting the only girl he ever called family."

She sucked a breath, tears streaming down her face. "He *was* my family. I have nothing. No one. I've never been so alone and hurting in my life."

He directed her chin up, forcing her eyes to his. "Not true. You have me." Then he wrapped her back into his arms and held her until the tears dried away.

# CHAPTER FORTY

Sometimes a girl just had to cry it out. So Lexi did. Then she ate a protein bar that Parker had stashed away—it was disgusting. She could feel strength recirculating in her bones, her attitude renewed. Somehow she was starting to understand Shadow's death and how he'd want her to live and laugh. Shadow had constantly pushed her to not be so serious. He'd want her to joke with Parker, which was what she'd been doing, slowly coming around.

She played on the internet while Parker took a few phone calls, updating whomever about what he knew or assumed, and he spent a lot of time listening, only to offer simple, confident, generally one-syllable answers.

*Yes. No. No. Yes.*

He rolled his chair back. "Hey, did you… want something to change into? I hadn't thought about that." He gestured with his hand. "You look great. I'm not saying that. It was just suggested that you might want to change."

She grinned, watching him squirm, but then squashed the amusement off her face. She glanced at her days-worn leather pants and tight T-shirt. "You think I need to change?" Inside, she laughed all over again at his expression of pure male panic. "Really?"

"No. Um, well, see—" He scowled at the phone he had on mute. "Like I said, someone thought you might want to change."

"So it came up in conversation that—" Her lips faltered, the corners dying to tug up in hysterics. "I needed different clothes?"

"No."

"Do these pants make my butt look flat?"

"What!" His brows shot up. "No."

"So it's the shirt. What, too tight?"

His eyes dropped to her chest, and she almost died laughing. "No, Lex." Then he could tell he'd been caught looking at her boobs. His gaze narrowed. "Are you fucking with me?"

"Maybe." But she fell apart in her chair, laughing with her head tossed back. It felt amazing to let go and just have fun.

Parker stood, grumbling but laughing, and bent over her to press his lips to hers. "Coloring outside the damn lines."

"What?"

"Nothing. Just something someone smart promised me I'd enjoy if I tried."

She kissed him back, forgetting even the laughter for a minute as everything heated. "Alright, get back to your important phone call about my clothes."

He smirked playfully, gave her another kiss, and said, "I'll have the last laugh. Have you met Sugar? She's pregnant, hormonal, and dead set on playing dress-up with you."

Lexi *had* met Sugar. The woman was actually the closest Lexi had ever come to seeing someone dress the way she did pre-Matt, minus the vampy-sexiness that Sugar rolled around with as though it were everyday casual wear. But they *did* share a common theme: leather pants and sexy boots. That was something she could totally work with.

Bring on the hormones—Lexi wasn't concerned in the least. "Have her call me."

Stomach grumbling, Parker wondered how long Lexi would be gone with Sugar. They seemed to hit it off. He wasn't sure why he'd had some initial nerves about siccing Sugar on Lex. Except the fact that he cared what Lexi thought about his friends, and he cared that Sugar had the easy ability to offend just about everyone on earth.

So… he was on edge and ready for dinner. Out of the corner of his eye, he saw two women strolling down a hall on the security feed. Parker pushed his chair over to get a better look.

They passed from the frame and were gone from sight until Lexi and Sugar walked into Titan's war room. They both had extra-large smoothies, and Parker was lust drunk over his girl as she toyed with the straw. Blood rushing in his ears, he needed in that room.

Sugar tossed a couple of magazines on the table and gave Lexi a hug before it looked as though she left her all alone. In that sinful outfit with her lips wrapped around that damn straw.

"What the fuck is wrong with me?" Feeling like a voyeur, he shook his head.

He couldn't rid himself of the image of Lexi kicked back in a skirt, crossing one dark-covered leg over the other, propping her boots on an opposite chair. She sipped her smoothie, her cheeks hollowing, as she paged through a magazine with a big-ass gun on the cover. Christ, he'd never seen anything sexier.

His phone rang, and the screen showed Sugar's name and face. Swiping to answer, he couldn't even manage hello for all of his distracted thoughts. "*That's* what you brought her as a change of clothes?"

Sugar laughed her ass off. "The girl's, like, five inches shorter than me, like a buck ten. We don't wear the same size. We went shopping."

"Where, Biker Bitches Depot?" But wherever that store was, he was getting a line of credit.

"Turns out we like the same stores."

"Imagine that. And you, what, suggested that skirt?" Or rather the scrap that was crawling up Lexi's legs every time she fidgeted. Really, he should thank Sugar. But hell, God only knew how many red-blooded, unattached men roamed this building—actually none, now that he thought about it. Some had cleared out for training, and some had just gone home. He was supposed to mine some more intel, yet he really wanted to stake claim on Lexi at that moment.

"No, boy genius." She laughed again. "The skirt was all her. My contribution would be the garters holding up that hose."

Holy. Fuck.

"You're welcome. I'm on my way out. Have her call if she needs anything."

"See ya, Sugar." Parker hung up the phone, grabbed a couple things, and headed to what was his.

# CHAPTER FORTY-ONE

After the tenth page of guns and knives and things that caused mass destruction, Lexi realized there were many things in the world that she didn't have experience with or even thought existed. Assault rifle upgrades? Who knew those bad boys needed modifications. And all these charts for velocity and accuracy? Guess it wasn't as easy as "point and shoot." Guns had specs like computers did, which logically made sense. But she'd never bothered thinking it over. She knew phishing, phreaking, spoofing, and spyware. Parker, it seemed, knew both.

Her mind slid back to him. She wondered what he'd found or where he was. Sugar had said she'd find him, but he was working. The door shot open, and Lexi jumped.

Parker.

That honey-warm feeling she now expected when she saw him rushed through her veins, making her legs and arms feel heavy. But it also reminded her that she had dressed for her, for him, to be noticed, and be her own person.

"Hi." She unfolded her legs from the chair she'd perched against.

"Hey." His eyes raked down her.

She'd taken time to brush her hair with a real brush, not just Parker's comb. They'd grabbed her new makeup, and she swore there was confidence in wearing new, sexy lingerie. Sugar had sworn it was true, and she'd been right. Though sliding back into a style Lexi loved had also been a boost.

His dark-blue eyes smoldered as he stalked to her, and her eyes dropped to his hands—a roll of duct tape? *Oh shit.* Her stomach dropped. What the hell was that all about?

The scratching crack of the tape being unrolled in his hands made her eyes go wide, but he quickly bypassed her. A breeze settled over her, and she watched in complete confusion, spinning in the chair. Parker took one piece of dark tape and secured it over the wall. Stretch, tear. He and another piece of tape moved across the room, where he did the same. One more time, Parker repeated the action then turned to her.

The heat burning between them was enough to singe her clothes, make them turn to dust and blow away. The thickness of his erection bulged in his pants, and the sight of him hungry for her, the realization that he'd just covered every camera in the room, consumed her.

Instantaneously, she was aroused. "Parker—"

He grabbed her hips and lifted her onto the table. His full lips took hers, her tongue hungrily seeking out his. With her thighs clenched to his hips, she moaned into his mouth, needing what only he could make her feel. The impossible. Loved without fear of abandonment.

His large hands cupped her legs, running high until his touch moved above the garter-supported stockings. "Fucking hell, you are the sexiest thing."

She refused to let him stop kissing her, and her mind wouldn't compose a response for her to speak. Instead, she reached for his zipper as he ran a hand over the tops of her legs.

"Damn."

Damn because she was soaking her panties? Damn because she'd found the silkiest things they sold? Didn't matter—the reaction was what she wanted. He slid the fabric aside, and she pressed herself against his fingers.

"Yes," she hissed. "Please."

Without a second's hesitation, Parker speared her with two fingers. She cried out, stifling herself with a bite to his shoulder. Their arms tangled, the masculine hair on his arm rubbing against her forearms as she unbuckled his pants. It was wild and rushed and absurd how they couldn't keep their hands to themselves in the middle of this… war room.

She freed him. His erection bobbed heavy, and Parker

wasted no time. One deep thrust, and she bit his shoulder again. Have mercy, this was incredible.

"Fuck, Lex," he growled.

"You're telling me. God." She wrapped her legs around him. Everything before had been sweet and deep, but this was a carnal drug addiction.

He powered into her, holding her to him, making her take every single insane inch of his pleasure.

Their breaths echoed in her ears. "So good."

He grunted in response. Lexi's climax built immediately. Her mind was already there, surprised and shocked by how brutally amazing this was.

"More." Seriously, she'd said it—hadn't thought it and didn't know how it was even possible.

Parker gripped her tight enough to crush her, and his rigid length pounded her until she was blinded with impending bliss. Her muscles banded tight and rippled. The orgasm sideswiped her to some other dimension, making the room fade. White light and all those sparkly, shiny fireworks ignited as forever spanned into a climax coma.

He seated himself deep inside her and strained his release. Her head lolled back, embracing that intimacy of his bare length coming inside her.

Parker took a deep breath, his head dropping on top of hers, his lips murmuring in her hair. Finally, he pulled away and slid her off the table. "I cannot get enough of you."

They both righted themselves, but she knew she looked like she'd just been fucked. God and every person in this building probably knew how loud she was, even muffled by Parker's shoulder, but screw it. She didn't care.

"Never going to look at this table the same way again."

She covered her mouth, trying not to laugh. "Oh, my God."

"I had every intention of taking you to dinner and updating you. Got a little side-tracked, but still seems like a good idea. You hungry?"

"Sure, yeah." She smoothed her skirt and could still feel him inside her. She needed to run to the ladies' room, but she also loved how he'd internally marked her. "Do you, um, need to remove the duct tape? Why was that there? I mean, I guess it makes sense, but…"

He guided her out of the room and laughed. "Trust no one. Plus, a couple years back, I busted Winters and Mia damn near getting it on against a motel room door. I got pictures and everything."

She smacked his chest. "That's awful."

He hooked an arm around her. "He's going to get me back one day, but today wasn't going to be it. Besides, their stuff was tame enough. They hadn't gotten through the door yet. I adore Mia, and Winters is my boy. All good fun."

"Well, if I'm the one he gets you back with, let me know—"

Parker pulled to a stop, scowling. "You really don't get it, do you?"

Her eyes went wide. "Well, um—" Was he talking about them? "I, uh…"

"If I could kill Matt, I would. Because Jesus, shit, he did a number on you."

Oh, yeah, her invisible scars. They were still there, but why was Parker scowling about them?

He grabbed her hand and practically dragged her back to office. There he sat her on a rolling chair and spun her around to see every screen, every piece of equipment that hummed and blinked for his attention. "This, Lexi, is what I know. I've told you, same as you've told me, how I feel. I've never done love. I don't do feelings because, until you, they didn't get in my way. I never noticed the warm fuzzies and whatever else. That's how my brain works."

"Yes," she whispered.

"I told you I loved you for shit's sake because I do. And you're all 'if *you're* the girl I get caught with'? Fuck me running, what the hell more do I have to do besides notify you how I feel and want to stick with you like I can't get enough? Because news flash, sweetheart: I can't."

"Parker—"

"I've said the words, done what feels like the right actions. But damn it, Lex, what more am I supposed to do? I am out of my element."

Her jaw hung open. "I didn't mean to hurt your feelings."

His hands ran into his hair. "Shit. I'm not hurt. Nor am I

concerned about you going anywhere. If that makes me a cocky motherfucker, fine. Call me cocky. But you need to realize what's in front of you."

"I see you. I do. I get it. I think. It's just, I don't know. I—"

"*You* are more amazing than even *you* know." His hands rubbed over his face. "And I have *no idea* how to do more than be by your side, saying the words that I thought were supposed to do the trick, holding your hand—I mean, tell me what you need, Lex. Then consider it done."

Unexpected tears streamed down her face. "I want you."

"You need to trust me."

"I trust *you*. It's me I don't."

"Then fix it, Lex."

She wiped her wet cheeks. "I'm trying."

"Good." He blew out a frustrated breath. "I can plan the crap out of a mission objective. Give me a little time, and this job is good as done."

"I'm a job?" she squeaked.

"It's the only way I know how to fix things."

Her eyes went wide. "What do I have to do?"

"Grab on." He extended his hand. "We'll find a way to figure it out."

# CHAPTER FORTY-TWO

Basketball played on Parker's flat screen as he lounged in the living room while sipping his beer with his woman in his arms. Lex played on her tablet and mindlessly petted Bacon, same as she had every night this week. Titan didn't have any teams on mission, and Jared had turned over all of Titan's intel on the ARO to the Defense Intelligence Agency. Life was good. Parker could be lazy and do nothing, and he enjoyed the daily routine he and Lexi had picked up.

She twisted to face him. "I've identified part of my problem."

"What are you working on?" he asked.

"No. I mean with me."

Muting the college hoops, even though his bracket was totally killing it, he thought it was interesting that she'd figured out an aspect of the trust-herself problem when he was no closer to the resolution. If he'd had one of those within his sights, he could at least mentally crunch the numbers and know statistically if it had a shot in hell at being successful. "Alright. Shoot."

His plan was to lie low, stay in bed, order delivery, make love, make her scream, walk the dog, and start over again. It might even be a solution. He wasn't saying it wasn't, but he had checked the computational value of just living as they were. Whatever, he was overthinking this. When she was ready to trust herself, she would.

She turned around again. Her back was on his stomach, her blond hair spread on his chest. Bacon was on the floor, snoring like a fat man, even if the girl had lost a few pounds. Lexi's arm hung off the sofa, casually petting her dog and sometimes rolling the poor thing over when she got too loud. The casualness of it all made him comfortable, made him feel complete, as though he shouldn't be anywhere but holding her and watching ball on TV.

"I don't belong anywhere," she said quietly. "I don't go home at the end of the night because I don't have anywhere to go."

One week. Seven dinners, seven nights in bed. Eight mornings of waking with her in his arms, and he had no intention of making the eighth night any different. Actually, he had no intention of changing the eighth, the eighteenth, or the eightieth night, and he was confident about her thinking that too. "You don't like staying here?"

She twisted to face him. "I love staying with you."

"So stay here." He shrugged.

"I can't just stay here. I need a place where I *live*."

"Seems like you're living now."

"You're a guy. You don't get it. I need a place that's mine. With my things. My stuff. I mean, everything at my old house, I'm sure he's sold it off or burned it or whatever. But I need more than just the stuff Sugar and I went shopping for."

"I like you being here, sweetheart, but I'm also not about to let you out of my sight when I'm not one hundred percent sure that no terrorist fuckers are going to try to grab you in the middle of the night."

"I'm a work thing!"

He laughed as she grumbled. "You're not a work thing, and you know it."

Lexi pressed her forehead to his chest as if she was burying her face. "I need a place of my own. It feels weird to just be here."

"Hmm." He stroked her back, basking in the quiet, trying to think of how to say what he needed to say without sounding like a bossy dick. Simple facts were what he could understand. He loved her. He wanted her in his house. He enjoyed waking up with her naked body pressed to his and died to be inside her every night.

"What does 'hmm' mean?" she asked, resting her chin on

his sternum.

"I hadn't thought about what we were doing; I was just living each day with you." He turned the muted television off and wrapped his arms around her. "So what do you want to do?"

"I don't know. I can't just sit and work from your office all day."

"You want to stay here and work?" Though watching her interact with the guys who'd come through his office had been… he didn't know the word for it. It'd been as it should be.

They all got on well, though a few had met her before. She worked hard, worked quiet. It was totally impressive to watch her think and watch her fingers fly over the keyboard. Hell, he could barely get shit done for watching *her* work. If he thought that leather rocker-chick look she had going on was hot, her brain gave him an instant hard-on. Because damn, she was brilliant.

She sighed. "I don't know."

"What's really the problem?"

"What if you get sick of me?"

"Back to you trusting you. Still not taking offense to it, sweetheart, but I am calling you on it." His cell phone buzzed on the table. The screen lit with his contact at the Defense Intelligence Agency. "Hang tight, I have to get this." With a swift move, he sat her up, answered the phone, and headed toward his office. "Hello?"

"Sorry to call so late," the familiar voice said. "But we have a confirmation and need direction on Flyaway."

Operation Flyaway was the working title of tracking down Monarch to ARO and seeing where it landed. He'd been itching for news on Monarch for days, but since they'd handed the job off, he hadn't heard a word. "Okay."

"Our eyes on the ground have seen the laptop. We're right about their intentions for micro-targeted, door-to-door attacks. But the computer was damaged, or something has corrupted it. They've kidnapped a few hackers and are forcing them to work. No one can pull it off, but with trial and error, they'll get it soon."

"Get the civilians out, blow the whole place up." That's what Titan would do anyway.

"We have different protocol, as you know."

Parker grumbled. Maybe they shouldn't have turned the Monarch problem over and just taken care of business on their own. "So what do you need?"

"A hacker who goes by the name SilverChaos. We have an opportunity to track the entire ARO network, but their system has to be infected with physical access."

"Bullshit, I can get in anywhere."

"There's no time to prove you wrong. They're decentralized, rarely hooking into network, always off the grid. They want SilverChaos, and we need physical access to rootkit the system and install malware that can harvest intel the rare times they hook in."

Damn it. Parker couldn't access what didn't have a connection. But Lexi couldn't do an in-person job. There were too many risks. "No. SilverChaos isn't possible."

"Any reason why not? The guy can name his price and any indemnification he wants for any outstanding issues."

"Outstanding warrants aren't the issue."

"Then get a price from the guy. We need to get him in there."

"The *woman* is under our protection, and we're not turning her over for you DIA dicks to run shop over."

"Come on, Parker. You're not putting one person above the safety and security of a nation?"

"Of course I'm not, asshole." Though that sounded exactly like what he was doing. Shit. "Give me another option. We'll work on it."

"We're up against a hard deadline. I don't have time to come up with another option. You can find anyone; our plan was for you to find SilverChaos."

"I call bullshit for having only one plan."

"You need to make this play happen. Run it by him—her. Whatever she wants. Done. Record cleared—"

"*That* is just one of the reasons I don't want to turn her over to you. You assume she's a criminal? No more than you and me, man. Plucking people out of nowhere—"

"Don't compare some hacker to intelligence work."

"She's elite."

"And I'm decorated. Get her in the goddamn office."

Parker rubbed a hand over his face, knowing that he'd walked into that one, but worse was knowing that if it hadn't been Lexi, he never would have balked.

"Parker, I'm one phone call away from contacting Jared Westin. No one wants to do that."

He cackled. "Call Jared. See if he doesn't defer to me, asshole. Let me be clear to you. If Silver does anything associated with this job, I call the shots and I run point. You got that? Because Jared *will* defer to me."

"Fuck me, tell me Silver's not actually Titan?"

"In every sense of the word. For all you care, Silver is Titan in every conceivable way you can imagine, then some you can't."

The man grumbled in Parker's ear before agreeing. "Call you back."

"Fine. Call, as long as you have more than one option." Parker hung up the phone, pocketed it, and turned to find Lexi staring at him.

"What do they want me to do?" she asked.

Damn it. "No idea. I didn't get that far because they didn't have another option for consideration." That, and no way was he involving her in anything like this. He could imagine the job—sending her to some Jihadist work site—and it didn't matter if it was in the States or overseas. It was a big, fat, hell no.

"I can help."

"They're going to ask for a lot more than help, Lex." Like her life. He wouldn't risk it, and he wouldn't let her consider it either. Parker shook his head, feeling anxiety grow in his chest. SilverChaos was the best option for the greater good. "No. Nope. No way. There's always another way. They shouldn't have approached me with a single option."

She pulled her cell from her back pocket. "I'll call Sugar. She'll call Jared, and I can talk to whoever that was."

"Lex."

"And then I'll get my way."

He rubbed his temple. "You have no idea what you're asking. I have no idea what they want, just a few assumptions. So to agree to that before we even know? I can't, and you won't."

"But I can."

"Why?" he near-shouted, frustration at the situation choking him.

"You know I'm the best solution. If I can keep people from being hurt, then I want to."

"Lex—"

"I created it, don't you get that? I have a responsibility to stop it."

"And I have a responsibility to you!" He threw out his arms. "I want you here. I need you here. In this house. Under this roof. I need you just as badly as I love you. Goddamn it, I don't want to run the numbers on this op's risk. I don't want to crunch data as to whether or not you will make it out alive. *Alive!* Don't you get that?"

She blinked, not saying a word.

His insides raged. Not at her. Just at the world, just because she was right. "I can't look at statistical computations and make any justification for what should be done, what's worth the risk. It eats me alive, but I can't choose them over you. You. Are. Mine. And I can't say I want you to help because it'd be a lie."

Breathing like a mad man, he paced the room. She didn't budge, just watched him circle as his phone rang again.

"Shit," he growled. It would either be Boss Man or his point of contact at the DIA. Either way, he didn't want to take the call. But he grabbed the phone, his sense of honor warring with his sense of self. DIA POC. Shit again, but he answered. "Better be good news."

"Sorry—"

He flung the phone on the bed and stormed out.

# CHAPTER FORTY-THREE

The phone's screen ticked seconds away, and Lexi alternated looking at it and at the door Parker had just stormed through. She'd put him in this crappy position, torn between doing the right thing and what he wanted to do. Well, she could make life a lot easier for him. Holding her breath, she climbed onto the bed and held the cell as if this was a make-or-break moment. And it was, on several levels. She was choosing to protect Parker from her, but at the same time, going against his wishes. She was also protecting the world from what she'd created. She couldn't live with herself if she didn't try.

Gingerly, she held the phone to her ear. This conversation could change the course of her life. Parker could walk away from her or, as he'd made clear, she might die.

Crap. No good solution.

Lexi took a deep breath and whispered, "Hello?"

"Hello? Who is this?"

Her insides trembled. "This is Silver."

There was a long pause, making her wonder if she had done the wrong thing.

"Hello?" she tried again.

Finally, a string of low curses. "It's ten fifty-seven on a Wednesday night. He's flipping out, and you're on the phone."

"Yes."

"You're Parker Black's woman?"

She nodded. "Yes." Though pulling a move like this might mean she would no longer be Parker's. "Can you tell me what's going on? Or at least why you need me?"

"Goddamn it. Hang on." There was noise in the background,

as if whoever it was was talking to someone else. Seconds ticked by. “I can’t share, Silver. It’s classified.”

“But it’s about me? I want to help, just talk to me.”

“Shit. Let me think. We’ll call back.”

“No. Wait. Tell me enough, what’s not classified.” Because if he got off the phone and started talking about her as Parker’s woman, not Silver the hacker, she didn’t trust that anyone would make an unbiased decision. “I can make this happen. I have to help. I—need to. But I can’t hurt him, and he won’t put me in a dangerous position. Just give me enough that I can tell you what to do with me, then you do what you need to.”

He cursed and mumbled, “Don’t hang up.”

She heard Parker stomping around the house. Soon as he realized she was on the phone with whoever this guy was, the conversation would end fast. “Hurry.”

But he was already gone. She waited, watching the digital alarm clock. One minute, then two ticked by.

“Ma’am?”

“Yes?” she said, watching the door for Parker.

“We’ll tell you what we can.” He spent the next two minutes vaguely talking about the program she had designed, who had it, where they had it, and why it appeared they were stuck. The laptop wasn’t far, likely in a stronghold on the east coast, where their so-called expert hackers had tried and failed to repair the improperly functioning code. Shadow had been tortured, and someone had made an attempt to find her twice. But the ARO hadn’t outsourced well in either their code-breaking or kidnapping talent.

The man then took a deep breath and rushed through the details that the Arab Resistance Organization was known for executing those who’d served their purpose or who had failed. No wonder Parker’s risk analysis aversion was so intense. All of the information scared the bejesus out of her.

Eventually the ARO’s trial and error would fix their Monarch problems, then lots of people would die. She had no choice but to get involved. But she was so far out of her comfort zone that she couldn’t see where her next move started. No way could she do this alone.

“I have an idea,” she said shakily. “Call back in thirty

minutes." Even though presenting Parker with the idea would bring a certain yes or no within a matter of seconds.

"Yes, ma'am." Then the line went silent.

Alright then. She steeled her nerves and went in search of the noisemaker who kept stealing her heart. She found him in the living room, pulling books that had already been perfectly lined up on shelves and slamming them back into place.

"Hey." She picked up a thick programming interface book and handed it to him.

"Hey." He slammed the hardback into a precise spot.

She grabbed another, this one on risk analysis of military security. "Don't be a baby."

His smoldering blue eyes narrowed. "Knowing the statistical outcome of any op that you might die in doesn't—"

"I have an idea." She pushed the book at him. "We could work together on this."

"No interest." He rearranged two books on reverse engineering of foreign state algorithms.

Not to be distracted by the scope of variety of his reading collection, she stepped in front of the shelf. "I'm going to help. You might as well be by my side while I do it. Just like I've been by your side every time you sent me an SOS for a set of hands."

"Not comparable. Virtual versus flesh and blood. *Your* flesh and blood."

"We go where they say, we do what we do. In person. Together."

"Shit, Lex, come on. It doesn't work that way."

"I think it could work a lot more in the way I want than you're giving me credit for."

He snatched more books and lined them up straight. "Only way I want you involved is if you're in a secure room a thousand miles away. Since it doesn't work like that—"

"Since it doesn't work like that, you're willing to let people die instead?"

"Fuck!" He threw a book across the room. "Goddamn it. No. Is that what you want to hear? No, I can't let that happen. But what do you want from me?"

"For you to be by my side. They, this ARO, keeps trying to

take me, right? Every time they try to abduct me, *we* are together. So *we* get taken." His eyes narrowed, and she knew he was thinking it over. Lexi leaned against his chest. "If I have to do this, Parker, hold my hand and make it safe. Please."

His body deflated even as he held her tight, breathing deeply against her neck. "I don't know how to risk someone I'd die if I lost."

She pressed her chin to his chest and gazed up. "Don't bother running numbers if you don't go with me." Her lungs ached as she readied to plead for what they had to do. "But if you do go with me, I'll tell you with one hundred percent accuracy what your programs can't. We will make it through because I want my life here with you too. I've wanted it for far too long, and nothing will stop me from loving you. If our problem was that I couldn't find it in me to trust myself, then it's fixed. I trust my gut on this. It's what we need to do."

He squeezed her tight but didn't agree.

"Don't make me break out the Semper Fi on you." Not that she would throw his honor in his face—she knew his eventual answer would be the right one—but hurrying up his conclusion and decision, yeah, that she had to do.

Parker's eyes closed, and he grumbled as though he was in pain before he took a breath. "If we're going to do this, Titan's on point. I'll call Boss Man."

# CHAPTER FORTY-FOUR

Sandwich shops always drove Parker crazy. They smelled yeasty like baking bread, and he hated to watch his food go down a conveyor belt. It all came down to control, reminding him that he'd rather be in his teched-out lair at Titan or the war room, with the ability to see the plays coming and make adjustments. Today wasn't like that. It was just him and Lexi with their asses hanging in the wind, waiting and baiting some terrorist motherfucker to whisk them away.

This setup was his nightmare, even though Titan and military associates had eyes on him. They could almost take over a third-world country with the amount of military know-how that was sitting in that sandwich shop, and still Parker wanted to bundle up his petite, leather-clad biker chick and head home.

"Don't you think this is a little obvious?" Lex said, playing on her phone. Whatever game she was into, she was winning, moving up a level, buying tokens and credits and whatever else under her handle, on the phone that they'd tracked her with before.

"Yeah, obvious is our goal." Simple plan. He repeated it again and again. Force the ARO to make a grab, embed themselves in their hideout, infiltrate their network, and shut down Monarch. With much more aggression, he jammed buttons on his phone as well.

"*Too* obvious, I mean."

Lexi's eyes kept darting to the back corner, where Nicola, Beth, and Sugar, all playing the part of innocent moms-to-be, sat watching the points of entry. Pregnancy hadn't slowed any of them down, though they had removed themselves from direct action involvement. Still, they were a force to be reckoned with, and he was glad he had those ladies behind him.

He finished his sandwich and balled up the wrapper, catching Winters at the farthest table by the back hall. He was on his second box of Dots and shooting the shit with the new guys. Everyone in the shop, with the exception of Parker's table, was relaxed while he and Lex were sitting ducks, waiting to be hunted.

His skin prickled. For as much as Lexi had been briefed about what would likely happen when they grabbed her, she couldn't understand the fear she was about to feel. She had been told, had seen videos, had listened to audios… the woman was the most intelligent person he'd ever worked with, but there was something to be said for when shit actually went down. No amount of brain power could squash basic human reaction. He slammed down his phone and took a stabilizing breath.

"We've got something," Winters murmured into a box of Dots.

"Roger that," Sugar confirmed, holding up a onesie. "He's searching for someone. Dark pants, green jacket. Full beard."

The man crossed Parker's line of sight.

A sick trickle of concern made his blood run cold. "Last chance, sweetheart. Pull the plug on this. Now."

She shook her head. "Nope."

He wanted to drag her outside as much as he admired her strength.

The bearded man stopped at their table, eyes bouncing between them. Discreetly, he showed the butt of a gun. "SilverChaos," he said to Lexi in his heavy accent. The words were as serious as the threat in his dark eyes. "Your assistance is needed. Come quietly."

Lexi's face went pale, and Parker would've died to make how she felt go away. Instead he grabbed her hand.

"Get up, go out the door." The man discreetly nudged the weapon inches from her head. "We need to talk about a business proposition. Five minutes, and this will all be done." He leaned closer.

From an outside perspective, they were chatting with an old, albeit intense, friend. But Parker's chest clamored at the point-blank range Lexi was in.

"Or do you want to kill your boyfriend?" he asked.

"No," she quipped.

"Easy there." Parker nodded to her. "If you have business with her, sit down and talk."

His eyes narrowed on Lexi. "Get up and walk out the door."

All Parker had to do was make sure they took him with her. "She's not going anywhere without me, jackass."

"Last chance."

"I'll go if he can come too." Lexi's eyes darted between the ARO asshole and him. "Please."

The man stared hard as seconds ticked by. Parker's certainty that this would work began to wane.

"Please," Lexi whispered, her voice shaking.

With the gun still trained on her, the man nodded, relenting. "Both of you, up."

Relief at the small victory flooded him. He didn't want to go to plan B if Lexi was taken alone. They both stood, grabbing their phones.

"Leave them," the man snapped.

Lexi whimpered. She was playing a part, following a script. So she was only acting scared… Parker repeated it over and over, except the fear coating her voice sounded so real.

"Okay." She met his eyes, left her phone, and turned to their abductor.

The man roughly guided them toward the exit, passing Winters, who gave him a discreet nod. Titan had eyes everywhere. Even if they stayed far back, they had satellite coverage as well. Parker would keep his mic and earpiece for as long as possible. They just had to get Lexi to a computer where she could work from within their system, manipulate Monarch to appear to work, install untraceable malware, and do it without suspicion. Sure. Easy. Why not. Shit… it was literally one of the most complicated pieces of code to ever have been created. His stomach dropped, and he held her hand tighter than was needed, holding on to what was most precious.

Like out of a cliché movie, a windowless industrial-looking

van raced up, and they were pushed inside the back door. Their abductor jumped in behind them, joining the four occupants already inside. Two were in the back, where the seats had been ripped out, and two up front in the driver and passenger seats. The van filled with Arabic, a huge advantage for them, since Parker had a solid working knowledge of the language. But even if he hadn't, the heated discussion was easy to decipher.

*Why are there two?*

*What do we do with the other one?*

For the moment, Parker wasn't concerned with staying alive. Everything from their clothes to the way they bickered said no one there was a decision-maker. That was the guy he had a real concern about.

"Where are you taking us?" Lexi's gaze bounced around the van. "You said talk. You wanted to talk about business!"

Black hoods were roughly pulled over their heads. A boot stomped on their handhold.

"Ow," Lexi cried.

"Careful with her, asshole." Head covered, Parker slammed his head forward, butting the jerk who had hurt her. His swift attack hit with nearly complete accuracy, and he felt the man's nose crack.

Another round of Arabic rang out, and one of the men weakly pistol-whipped the back of Parker's head. It might have been a pathetic blow, but it still hurt like a bitch. Goddamn terrorist prick. They exploded in Arabic again.

*Don't hurt him. He might be an incentive to make her work.*

He ignored the pain and listened to their bickering, as well as the bloody sniffles of the man with a now-cracked nose. He also listened for all things Lexi. For tears or worried breaths. For fear or pain. His senses were on hyper-alert when it came to her, and God help any man who hurt her, because Parker wouldn't give two fucks for tearing him apart.

Except right this second, he couldn't protect her. So maybe God help him.

# CHAPTER FORTY-FIVE

It felt like they'd hit a highway, and Lexi's heart hammered, adrenaline spiking. It was one thing to talk a big game and say she could help infiltrate a terror cell. Sure, jeez, no problem. But with a bag over her head, men yelling in a language she couldn't understand, and Parker *already* scuffling with them, this was the very definition of a bad idea.

The bag over her head was opaque and stunk like the bad breath of a thousand abducted victims. It smelled like tears and fear, vomit and blood. While she'd been prepared to be blindfolded, nerves made her stomach slosh.

The wicked words floating around her head were indistinguishable. She didn't understand anything they said, but they were furious at Parker to the point that she was scared they'd kill him.

They had to stick together and stay silent for them both to make it out alive. The drive felt mostly like interstates. They were speeding by hundreds of cars full of people who had no idea she was in there. But many intelligence operatives did, so she should feel some sort of relief. Parker had a tracking beacon on, and she had a tiny microphone sewn into the hem of her shirt. All she had to say was the job was done, and Titan would descend.

There was the sound of a scuffle and a grunt. Lexi cringed at what sounded like Parker absorbing a kick to the gut. Her heart slammed in her throat for every minute of their long drive.

"Please don't hurt him," she whispered.

No one said a word. Not even Parker told her it'd be alright, and that lack of communication made her anxiety grow.

Finally the van slowed, and she toppled over the floor when they made a sharp right turn. Pushing herself upright, one of the men pushed her back down again, catching her off guard.

"God! Ow." She shirked back.

A presumably blindfolded Parker attacked whoever was next to him, and they returned the hit. Her gut twisted. She needed to stay quiet if for no other reason than every time she made a noise, he lashed out at someone, and they hit back.

"I said don't touch her," he growled. "You want someone to push, you push me."

The van door slid open, and a man grabbed her arm and yanked her onto the ground. She kept the cry of pain to herself as her knees and palms were scratched on asphalt.

Her pusher hocked and spat, the grossness landing close enough to her that it hit the ground with a disgusting smack. "Stupid American slut."

Well, not so stupid that they could figure out Monarch. But she bit her tongue and wouldn't go near the slut part. They didn't like women, right? Second-class citizens?

She rolled away from the sound-of-spit landing zone and tried to get to her feet. Her ears burned for Parker. It sounded as if he had men on both sides, forcing him to walk with them. She was pulled and pushed toward where she assumed Parker was. Their shoulders bumped, and the brief contact was instant relief. She reached for his hand, but no—his were angled behind his back.

"You okay?" he asked calmly.

"Yes." A hand slammed between her shoulder blades. She lost her footing and went down, her hands scraping again. "Ow, damn it!" Her palms burned, maybe bled. She wanted to wipe them or look for gravel in the cuts.

"Son of a bitch."

Parker's struggles reached her ears, as though he was trying to take out the lot of them. Part of the act he'd been assigned was belligerent, antagonistic, overprotective boyfriend. Unplanned, untrained, and reactive. Honestly, she had no idea how much was an act and how much was him trying to kill armed men while blindfolded and handcuffed.

"I'm fine," she whispered. For her part, she had been told to act scared and untrained, like a hacker who needed her boyfriend. It was easy to play.

The ARO men pushed her and Parker forward across what felt like a parking lot. Everything around them was silent, abandoned. Like they were the only people on earth.

"Step," the man with broken English ordered.

She stepped high twice before she reached what she was supposed to step onto. An elevated floor. The chilly air smelled like metal. Another round of words she didn't understand came fast, and she was tugged away from Parker.

"No! Wait!"

But all she got was a push. Still stuck with the nauseating bag over her head, she lost her balance and stumbled, barely catching herself. A hand yanked her up, pulling her arm and making her scream. In the background, far away but echoing in the dark vastness, she heard Parker yelling for her to stay strong.

She couldn't. She was going to vomit, joining the others who already had in this awful, airless bag. Her legs were weighted, each step closer to wherever erased all of her confidence in her decision, her patriotic duty, her desire to be brave like she thought Parker was. Tears sprang and slipped down her cheeks. This was the worst idea she'd ever had, and it proved, without a doubt, she had no good judgment. He'd tried to warn her, begged her to stand down, but Lexi had been bullheaded and pushed this.

Parker was right. He was right about everything, and she wondered if he already knew what the risk analysis said. He denied it, but could he not? What was the chance she'd make it out alive if they stayed near the sandwich shop? If they took her hours away? If the ARO separated them? She thought of Parker and could almost guarantee that he was running all the computations of her survival, even without the luxury of his war room. She knew he stood by her decision to likely get herself killed all because she'd thrown words like honor and duty in his face.

God, she was an awful person.

Maybe they wouldn't kill her. She was blindfolded, and according to TV shows and movies, that was a good thing. If she couldn't see them, then it wouldn't be a problem to let her live. Even though Titan and whoever else was supposed to sweep in if things got too bad before she completed her assignment.

They came to an abrupt stop, and the bag was ripped off, grabbing her hair with it. "Shit!"

But no one cared. They simply tossed the bag on the floor, and two men were walking away. Oh no—their faces weren't hidden, and they didn't look concerned. Prime time TV 101 said that her likelihood of dying just skyrocketed.

Lexi sucked down the desire to puke or pass out and glanced around at where they'd left her. It was the middle of an open area with industrial ceilings, a metal door on the far side surrounded by pallet-made walls. The space was maybe twenty yards by twenty, and there was a desk and computer in the middle.

A man she hadn't seen before walked from the shadows. He circled her, assessing and judging. His intense scrutiny wasn't about her as a woman but a hacker. She could sense her people, and this guy was a wannabe-elite hacker, a man with no scruples. He was evil. It flowed in the air as he breathed. His eyes were as intelligent as they were dead. He had no morals, no compass, no thought for humanity. He was as emotionless as she'd ever seen a person. It was completely terrifying.

"SilverChaos." The man towered over her, just a little shorter than Parker, and he was pissed. In a major way. All because he couldn't figure out Monarch.

Her objective was the ARO network as much as it was pretending to fix Monarch. She needed to infect their system while she worked, creating a dormant program. Whenever the laptop connected to the internet, the malware would silently, automatically come to life and trace how large the Arab Resistance network was, both on US soil and abroad. The demon program would hunt and harvest the ARO's contacts, correspondences, uploads, and downloads. Every keystroke, every one click. Everything.

"It was hard for me to believe a slight woman like you, dressed like sin, was smart enough to be SilverChaos."

*Bam!* A gunshot echoed through the air. She jumped,

turning toward the noise. Terror ran through her. Parker had been shot? God. Wait. No. In her briefings, they'd said that the abductors might trick her, make her think they'd harmed Parker to get to her react. Or they might have actually harmed him, in which case there was nothing to be done.

Bile burned her throat. Now she was the one running the probability statistics, even though she had no idea what the confidence intervals or variable manipulation factors would be to correlate survival. A small sliver of what Parker had to have been feeling began to overwhelm her.

*Bam!* As the second shot rang, she cried out. She needed Parker to explain that the shots were simple tricks, that everything would be alright. Her lips trembled, her teeth chattered. With blurry eyes, she squeezed them shut to get rid of the tears and end the nightmare, but neither happened.

"I go by Taskmaster. You will do as I say." His lightly accented English was articulate.

"Please, I don't—"

He inclined his head. "I've been impressed with you. I will give you that. But I'm done with your games. The ARO revolution is in place, and you hold the key." Carefully, he reached behind him and unsheathed a long, serrated blade. "Your mentor did not go easy."

Eyes wide, she moaned at the thought of Shadow under the knife's blade. "No."

He nodded then tilted his head toward the desk. "You don't need all of your fingers to work. We will go one at a time if that is what it takes."

Tears flooded her eyes. "Please—"

"Or you will sit down and repair the Monarch files."

She sniffled. "Don't kill me."

"I'll kill you if you don't work, but not before I get what I need."

She moaned with fear. "I'll do it, and you'll let me go?"

"You're not in a position to negotiate."

"What can I do to"—her hands shook—"survive?"

"You're a resource. Prove your talent is worth keeping." A flat, uncaring smile moved on his lips, but he'd just given the reason he might not shoot her dead the second he thought she was done.

All she had to do was make sure he knew she was game. Careful to use the simple words she'd been taught by military psyche-war people, she nervously continued the conversation. "Keep me alive, and I'll do whatever you need."

His eyes assessed her again.

"Please," she whispered, wiping away tears.

"Sit. Work." He spun the knife in his hand. "We can discuss other options after you have completed your task."

Numbly she walked to the computer and booted it up, tears still quietly streaming down her face. She wondered if the gunshots were a tactic or if Parker was really dead.

# CHAPTER FORTY-SIX

Two gun shots in the old warehouse, and Parker was going to murder everyone that he didn't recognize as a friendly. The men guarding him cackled after the shots were fired, knowing it had gotten to him. Damn it, his mind was stronger than these petty maneuvers, which were not unexpected. But the mind games got to him more than they should. One of his guards paced closer, delighting in what had obviously made Parker react, and chuckled as if the inevitable had just happened.

"I'm gonna kill you first, fucker," Parker snarled with his hands still taped behind his back. "Then you next."

Both men laughed, and Parker seethed. They'd gone through a maze of hallways with his eyes covered before arriving there, where they took off his hood. The room held little that he could use as a weapon when the time came. A few chains hanging overhead. The table, a chair. Metal barrels marked as chemicals. His mind ran over every object, assessing how they could be used, even if right now, he wasn't in a position to do much but wait.

Another man walked into the room. His dress varied from the men who'd taken him. Motherfuckin' terrorist middle management.

"Ah," he said in a light accent, "I see we have SilverChaos's boyfriend. Unexpected, but a useful incentive if need be."

"You hurt her, so help me God, I will tear you apart."

"See?" He grinned like death. "We all do things in the name of our god. You want to kill me." He made a face as though he found humor in it. "And I want to kill you."

"I will."

"You might try." The man clapped. "She was hard to pin down, but I assume that has something to do with you."

"Eat a dick, asshole."

"Stupid American. All muscles, no brain."

How many minutes had gone by? If the ARO had put her on a computer already, they were almost golden. He needed to drag this out for another fifteen? Maybe? Then she would have done what she needed to to infect their system in a way that this dumbfuck never saw coming.

"You don't like a smart woman, do you?" Parker goaded.

"Smart and useful are different." A snide, self-important sneer crossed his face.

"Sucks to be outmaneuvered by a female, right? Is that what bothers you most? Or that your attempts to get her before were amateur?"

"You aren't worth my time."

Parker turned to the two men at the door. "Your boss was one-upped by a woman. God—Allah—whoever you fucks pray and kill for is laughing." The guy smacked Parker across his face, making him laugh. "No wonder a woman outsmarted you. You even hit like a girl."

That time, his captor roared back and punched him in the gut.

Parker laughed harder, arms still taped behind his back. "Pansy ass."

"Kill him."

Parker caught the man's eye. "Another thing you can't do yourself."

With a maddening look, the man charged. Parker dropped to the ground, pulling his legs up and sliding his duct tape-tied hands from behind him in the split second it took to fall. Wrists now in front of him, Parker wrapped them around the captor's neck, locking him inches from his own face. Parker slammed his head forward, rendering the other man stunned, then pinched his neck with his forearms, suffocating the leader as the other men ran forward, guns drawn.

"Don't shoot your boss." Parker released the stranglehold on his neck, keeping him alive and worthy of a terrorist-human shield.

The man gasped and sputtered in Parker's face. They backed into a hall as the guy fumbled for his side, trying for something, likely a weapon. As they rounded a corner where Parker had sufficient cover, he slammed the leader's head back against the wall then dropped the unconscious body. A serrated knife clattered to the floor.

After grabbing the blade, Parker ran down the hall, needing a place to hide and ditch his tape cuffs. Door after door was locked. Foreign voices echoed as people looked for him. When they found their leader, alive or dead, their rage wasn't good news for him, but it was potentially detrimental to Lexi.

Needing to find her quickly, he tried one more door and ducked into a dark bathroom. For the next forty-five seconds, Parker held the blade between his knees and sawed like all hell through the tape, nicking and scratching, slicing and tearing apart both skin and restraints. Finally he ripped his hands apart and palmed the knife.

The searching voices had quieted, and that was fine. As long as they stayed away from his woman, they could search all they wanted because now he was hunting them.

# CHAPTER FORTY-SEVEN

Lexi typed as fast as her mind could process and juggle both of her tasks. A ringing cell phone startled her, but she kept going. The man answered, snapped in foreign-tongued surprise, then her guards split. One with a full beard came at her while the other ran out.

"Hey!" She jumped from her chair. "I'm working. I swear!"

He pushed her back into the chair and pulled cable ties from a pocket. He grabbed her kicking feet and tied them to the chair legs as she fought. Next, he yanked off his belt.

"Hey, no!" Her eyes went wide. Her ops briefing had very quickly run through the types of attacks on women that could be expected, but this made no sense. Not now. Not when she was doing what they wanted. "I'm working. I promise. See!" She pointed at the screen. "See! Don't touch me!"

She batted his hands, but he didn't grab her how she expected. He wrapped the belt around her torso and buckled it behind her back, securing her to the chair.

"I was working." What had changed?

Her lone guard didn't say a word but used his foot to push her closer to the table and computer. Was something wrong with Parker? Was Titan there? Her mind raced, and her hands slowed. The man yelled at her, slamming his hand on the table and pulling her from her thoughts.

"Okay, I'm working." She picked up her speed, letting her fingers dance on the keyboard until finally she stared at the masterpiece before her. The malware was ready. It looked right. It read like it would do what she wanted, what the DIA had asked of her.

Another slam on the table, and the man yelled unknown orders in her face again. She pressed Enter without looking at the keyboard, just staring at his face.

"The job is complete," she said flatly, praying her hidden microphone announced to the world that she needed a rescue.

Her gaze dropped to the screen as the man stood down. Nothing changed on the laptop's screen, but it was working. An error message would have popped up if not. Her heart warmed that at least she was able to accomplish that. In addition to the malware, it looked as if the Monarch exploit program had been completed, but in reality, all the data would be siphoned and manipulated with any search the ARO tried. It switched like-named cities in different states and reversed specific numbers on street addresses with identical names on the file. If the Taskmaster did little more than a cursory check, her work would look correct.

Lexi turned to the man and nodded. "Done. I want to see my friend."

The man nodded as if he understood and stepped forward, but instead of releasing her, the black bag came out. Lexi gulped in surprise as he tugged it on and tied her hands to the chair. Fear erupted even though this was on her list of possible things that could happen. The DIA had told her so many things, so many possible situations and reactions that her mind couldn't process them until they happened.

Titan had to have heard her proclamation that the job was done. They should arrive in minutes. Right? That was the plan. But seconds felt like decades.

Her captor's phone rang again, and after another conversation she didn't understand, he also ran away.

The warehouse echoed with noises, voices, and sounds of heavy movement. What had been a dozen ARO sounded like twice that. Doors slammed far away, and muffled shouts boomed. Where was her rescue team—but more importantly, where was Parker? There was just no way he'd been shot. It had to have been a diversionary tactic. Her heart wouldn't make it if she'd lost him.

A door slammed against a wall. "Lexi!"

Her heart exploded at the sound of Parker's voice. His boots flew across the room to her. Seconds later, the bag was ripped off.

He sawed at the ties on her feet and wrists. "They hurt you?"

"No."

He unbuckled the belt, untied her limbs, and grabbed her with one hand. "Did it work?"

"Yes."

"Atta girl." An explosion ripped through part of the building, and he smiled as he palmed the knife. "Sounds like backup arrived."

Backup was a bomb? Okay…

Another sound boomed. He took off, dragging her with him. They made it to the wall and ducked behind pallet boxes. He pulled a gun from the back of his pants. "Here. Same thing—point and shoot. Aim, trigger, that's it. Got it?"

"Yeah."

He tucked the open knife into his boot and removed another gun that was tucked at the front of his waist. Jesus, when had Rambo found time to gear up?

"Come on, sweetheart. We need to make it to rendezvous." Parker placed her behind him.

Well, alright then. It wasn't the first time she'd held a gun with him in a sketchy situation, and hopefully it wouldn't be too often of an occurrence.

"These fuckers swarmed like ants. Must be a compound somewhere on site. Good thing is, not all of them are armed."

"Oh, great." Only some of them were armed and trying to shoot them.

Parker guided her into a hallway, and she wondered how massive the warehouse was, how long it would take Titan to find them, and how many terrorists constituted a swarm? Taking another turn down a maze of industrial hallways, they ran where the lights were low and noise ricocheted all around. She couldn't get a read on where it came from.

"Shit, turn around. Let's go." Parker spun them in another direction.

A loud foreign yell stunned her in place.

"Goddamn it." Parker spun, pulling her behind him.

A whole team of not-Titan was moving in on them. Parker pushed her down, firing at them as they moved toward him en masse. Four bodies dropped before he threw down the gun, and two men were left charging the hall—as Parker charged right back.

She was frozen, watching the man she loved about to die for her. Parker grabbed the knife from his boot and threw it, hitting the upper chest of an attacker with bull's-eye precision. Her mouth gaped as she watched the man gurgle and go down. But the other man dove for Parker as her man jumped up. In one fluid motion, Parker swung on a pipe to reach a chain then dropped down on his attacker, chain still in hand, and wrapped his neck in metal. A quick pull left the ARO man dead.

Too much was happening around them, and she couldn't keep up. Parker spun toward her as she heard the noise that had caught his attention. His arm reached out, pointing past her, as he sprinted. "Lex, shoot!"

She rotated. An ARO man was gunning for her. Her heart stilled, her breaths stopped, but she raised the gun and pulled the trigger. Point. Shoot.

When she realized her eyes were shut, she opened them. *Holy crap.* The man was bleeding on the ground. Parker swooped in, grabbing the weapon from her hand and lifting her in one strong motion. He ran them down the hall, jumping over the dead man like a bloody body wasn't a big deal. Her ears rang from the blasting shot, and her hands trembled from the violent kickback. But her mind was most affected. She'd just killed a man. Just *killed* a man…

They rounded a corner, and he tucked her close, pressing her head to his chest, as his hands ran over her body as though he was searching for an injury. "You okay?"

She shook her head, tears she couldn't classify brimming and stinging her eyes. "No."

"You will be. Swear to God."

He took her hand, and they moved faster than she thought she could run through a bevy of hallways. She had no idea how he knew where he was going. As they went around yet another corner, men in tactical gear moved low and fast their way.

*Titan.* The good guys. Whoever was there to lend a helping

hand.

"About damn time," Parker growled.

There was some kind of hand gesture. Someone came over, and from him, Parker took two weapons. The tactical guys motioned what she could only assume, with a thumbs-up and directionals, was an all-clear.

Parker nodded. "Time to take you home." With a possessiveness she almost couldn't comprehend, he walked her quickly out into the cold black night, where the edge of the sky showed a sliver of light, a smoky yellow ray of hope.

"Dawn," he mumbled as if all was well and they hadn't just run for their lives.

A vehicle rushed toward them. Parker picked up the pace, covering her from behind as if he was living, breathing Kevlar, and the vehicle's door flew open. She didn't have an option to jump in because Parker lofted her in, tumbling inside as well. When she got her bearings and sat up, they were speeding away. A quick look at the driver made her mind spin.

"Hey ya, hacker girl." Sugar laughed. "Like I was going to be sidelined on this one. Even if it is just middle-of-the-night carpool duty."

# CHAPTER FORTY-EIGHT

Lexi woke at the sound of the garage opening. Parker casually walked into his house and tossed his keys on the end table, shrugging out of his jacket. She was exhausted. The time on the cable box said it was close to five in the morning, almost twenty-four hours since he'd hauled her to safety.

"Scoot over." He plopped down on the other end of the couch then hauled her onto his chest so that she faced him.

"All in a day's work, huh?" she asked sleepily.

"Something like that." He rubbed her back lazily, letting her melt back to sleep.

"You're my hero."

His body moved as he shook his head. "Pretty sure you're the one who infiltrated a terror cell."

After they returned to Virginia, she went to Parker's, where Colby Winters's wife, Mia, had been waiting for her. Sugar and Parker went to Titan. Mia was beyond nice, even though she always had been when Lexi had met her in passing, but this was different. This was Mia working, helping, because Parker had quietly made arrangements for someone for Lexi to talk to.

Mia was non-judgmental, and they talked for hours, telling stories about the guys, about Mia finding a place in their crazy bunch before most of them had settled down. She made Lexi feel welcome, unlike a guest in their world but a person who was… not to be abandoned. Not a loner. Not to be made fun of. Nothing like that. Mia seemed to speak as though she spoke on behalf of every person Lexi had met or had known through the Matt-Parker connection. The whole gab session had felt less like therapy and more like a relief. She was unbelievably at peace considering the last day.

Lexi *had* a family, even if they weren't blood. It started with Parker, and apparently by default, she had inherited a large network of over-the-top people who seemed to really like her.

"Where's your head after today?" he asked, laying his forehead on hers and breathing in.

"Nowhere but here."

"Good."

"Right?" She snuggled against him. "I've always been alone, and it turns out now that I'm not."

He nodded. "Turns out." Then he pressed his lips to the top of her head. "This is my favorite time of day. Glad I'm spending it with you."

"It's, like, ass crack o'clock."

"It's the hour that feels the longest. When the night's always the darkest. You just have to make it to the next day."

"Yeah." She yawned. "Just have to make it through to dawn."

"Kinda my motto in life…"

His words played in her head, something itching for a connection despite the sleepy-fuzzies in her mind. Oh… "BlackDawn?"

"Yeah, nothing too complicated, I guess."

"SilverChaos was simple. Life was chaotic growing up in a dozen shitty foster homes. It was meant to be a play on a silver lining. Like 'Oh, I have a talent that can help with the hell of life.'"

"I get it."

She sighed. "That's sweet, and for some reason, I feel like you really do. But it's nothing a person can get unless you live with no place to call home and no parents."

He squeezed her tightly. "I was a foster baby too, Lex. No roots. No family. Nothing except for a drive to forget it all."

Her wide eyes soaked him in. "Really?" Not that it really mattered, but it kind of did.

"Yup. I don't think I bounced around as much as you, but each time a foster home caught me phreaking a phone line or trying whatever was in *Phrak* that month, they'd pull the plug on me, ship me off again."

"I'm kinda geeking out on you, Parker. Thought maybe you were too cool. Though you make up for it with all those muscles and militarism." She laughed and listened to him rumbling the same.

He spun a lock of her hair on his finger. "The hacker who dresses like a rock star and rides a Gixxer is using me for my body."

"I love you, Parker," she whispered.

"Love you too, sweetheart."

Then she closed her eyes and drifted away, at home with Parker's protective arms around her.

The familiar ring of Lexi's phone stole Parker from sleep. They were on the couch, and the late-morning light hung over the room. His wrists were sore from yesterday's scratches and cuts and where the tape had ripped the hair off his skin. He reached for the phone on the table, saw it was her sister, and nudged Lexi awake. "Meredith's calling."

"Oh." She sat up and answered it, all sleepy-sweet. "Hey, Mere."

"Lexi! Help me!"

The words blared loudly enough that Parker could hear, and they sent a cold rush down his spine. He took the phone before Lexi could offer a word. "Meredith?"

"The key from under the mat. He's here. He won't go. Help me."

"Who?" Parker's cloudy mind pushed to wake up, thinking about the little he knew about Lexi's foster sister.

"Matt."

"That motherfucker." He sat up, placing Lexi by his side. "Where are you?"

"In my closet."

Parker seethed. *In her closet?* "Why?"

"He's raging in the kitchen."

"He's drunk?"

"Yeah."

Fuck that dude. Whatever had happened in that guy's life to make him pull this shit… "Hang on." He switched lines, dialed 9-1-1, and merged the calls. When the operator answered, he urged Meredith, "Go on, Meredith." While he listened, he pulled his boots back on and grabbed his keys and sidearm.

Lexi's eyes were wide. "What's going on?"

"Your ex better hope the cops get there before I do."

She popped off the couch. "I'm going with."

"No."

But she ignored him, rushing off to grab whatever. Parker relented with a sigh, knowing he didn't have time to fight a battle he wouldn't win.

Lexi reappeared moments later, dressed and ready to go. "Ready."

He nodded, and she took off for his Rover as though he might change his mind. Which he might. The 911 operator gave updates on when the patrol unit would be there, and it made Parker's gut hurt that he would get there first. They screeched down the road, crossing the familiar path to her sister's apartment building. He threw the SUV into park on the curb, and Lexi was out the door before he could tell her stop. Jogging to catch up, he chided her to keep behind him, and thankfully she agreed. They waved at Malcolm, who shook his head.

"I knew that boy was gonna be trouble when he stumbled by."

"Sorry," Lexi said as they ran for an opening elevator. "Cops are coming. Send them up."

The ascent took forever, but finally they were on the right floor.

Parker continued to listen on the phone as they approached her apartment. "I'm coming in, Meredith."

"Sir," the 911 operator snapped, "please do *not* enter—"

He twisted the handle, cracking the door open, then he looked at Lexi. "Stay in the hall until the cops get here. Okay?"

"No—"

"Damn it, Lex."

"Parker," Meredith cut in. "He's banging so hard, the door's going to break."

Lexi's eyes searched the front door as if she could see through it. "I'm going inside too."

"No—"

"Can you hear me?" Meredith whispered. "He stopped. Everything's quiet."

"Tell her we're coming." Lexi pushed against the door.

Shit. She was going to do whatever she wanted anyway. "Stay behind me, Lex."

"Okay."

"I'm walking in." But as he said the words, he could tell the phone call had ended. Damn. He slipped the phone into his pocket and withdrew his sidearm. He heard Matt storming back down a hallway that fed blindly into the kitchen. "Get your sister, get out. Wait for the cops."

"Okay."

Parker stole toward the kitchen, and Lexi went in the opposite direction. His eyes swept for Matt. Parker had only been in the apartment once before, to meet her sister and scoop up Bacon, but it was oddly laid out. There were alcoves that worried him. He rounded the corner, and damn it, Matt wasn't there.

# CHAPTER FORTY-NINE

"It's me," Lexi said, tapping on the walk-in closet door. "Mere, open up."

The closet door pulled wide, and her sister tentatively peeked out.

"Come on—"

"*Peaches.*"

Everything in the room turned sideways at the sound of Matt's drunk voice. Lexi stared at Meredith's wide eyes, but she snapped to. The ladies jumped into the closet, trying to slam the door.

Matt snatched it before it latched. Lexi tried to shut him out while Meredith shouted for him to go away. Somewhere nearby, Parker surely had to hear what was going on. Matt's arm snaked into the open space, past Lexi, and hooked onto Meredith. His fingers bit into her hair, and he pulled her through the slice of open door, forcing Lexi to let go in surprise.

"No!"

With a shove, he threw Meredith down. Her sister stumbled face first as Parker burst into the room.

"Help!" Lexi called as Matt's fist connected with her temple. The world exploded. She lost her bearings and fell back, fighting against the spinning stars and tink of metal hangers falling on her.

Matt pushed her into the closet and slammed the door, making more hangers clink and clamor around them. Her ex hovered over her, his hand extended as though he wanted to help her up. "I didn't mean to do that, Lex."

She scooted back until she hit the wall, watching him twist the lock on the door. "Are you insane?"

"Open up!" Parker slammed a fist on the door. "Swear to Christ, Matt, if I come in, you're not walking out."

Matt swayed on his feet. "You're all the time causin' me to do shit that I wouldn't do unless you push me, peaches."

"You broke into Mere's!"

"I used the key." He shrugged, drunk and disinterested. "We needed to talk. It's time for you to come home."

"I don't want to be with you! I've *never* wanted to be with you. This"—she bounced her finger between them—"isn't how you have a relationship. You need help, Matt. For a lot of things."

"Oh, fuck you, goddamn overreacting bitch."

She threw out her arms. "You have me trapped in my sister's closet."

"Back up, Lex," Parker shouted through the door. "You good?"

Well, not if he was going to shoot through the damn thing. "Yeah!"

Matt's face contorted. "Don't talk to him—"

The door exploded as Parker plowed through, knocking Matt over. Parker drilled his fists into Matt, then Parker grabbed Lexi and pushed her out of the closet.

Matt staggered up. "Dick."

Parker pinned her with a look. "Girls. Hall. Now." Then he pivoted.

"Let's go, Lex."

As Meredith dragged her out the door, Lexi turned, taking a last glance back. Parker had the barrel of a gun under her ex's chin. *Oh shit.*

"If it isn't Prince Charming," Matt stupidly said with the bad-news end of a Glock shoved under his jaw. "Who'd you come here for: Lex or Mere? Moved from one sister to the next? Classy, bro. Class-ss-y."

"Dude, you are so far gone, you're not worth the damn bullet."

"Aw, fuck you," Matt slurred, blood running out of his nose and the corner of his mouth.

Parker pulled back from the kill shot but didn't relax enough to take his aim off Matt. "We're going to come to an understanding before the cops get here. This is your one chance to fix your life before you ruin it any more than you've done."

"Nah." Matt threw his shoulders back and stumbled into hanging clothes. "Mere's gonna tell Lexi it's time to come home. She's done with you, cocksucker."

The angry pulse of his blood thumped in his ears. "I could explain that you lost her, that you should rot for ever having touched her like you did." Parker shook his head, molars gnashing. "But I'm going to do you one worse."

Matt cackled, wiping his bloody mouth with the back of his hand. "Yeah, try me."

"You've *never* had her. She's been mine for *years*, and you didn't know. Might not be in a way you'll ever get, but I do. And that"—he pushed Matt—"is why she's the best thing that ever happened to me. So thank you, you motherfucking asshole, for screwing up the way you did. Because she loves me." Parker pushed him again.

Matt made a feeble attempt to push back, and Parker nailed him with his free hand, landing a solid left hook, and dropped the bastard.

"Summerland County police, stand down."

About damn time. Two uniformed officers were in Parker's peripheral vision.

"Sir, put the weapon down," an officer said.

Matt staggered up, fortified by the presence of cops.

"No problem." Parker laid the gun by his foot and kicked it back. "But real quick. One more thing." His fist flew, knocking Matt back onto his ass. Parker put his hands in the air. "Alright, now I'm done."

"Back up."

Parker did as he was told.

Matt moved, and both cops clamored, "Stay down. Sir, stay down."

But the uniforms' attention was on Parker's Glock. Parker turned to leave and saw Meredith peeking into the bedroom as he came out of the closet.

"Thank you," she said as her sister rushed by.

"Sure thing." He grabbed Lexi as she jumped into his arms. "Sweetheart, you okay?"

"Yes." Her lips planted on his.

"Ladies, sir, living room," the older officer said. "We'll need to talk."

The other officer had Matt in handcuffs and on his feet, pushing him past them.

"Fuck you, stupid bitches."

The cop shook him. "Shut up, man."

With Lexi still in his arms, Parker growled at Matt, "Never come near them again."

"Sir!" the older cop snapped at him.

"Right, right." He nodded. "Living room, let's go." Parker set Lexi down, and they followed Meredith.

There was a brief struggle at the apartment door as Matt decided to resist, but the younger cop yanked his arms back and left with Matt cussing.

The older uniform watched until the door shut then shook his head. "Alright, whose apartment is this?"

The next few minutes were a recounting of everything from Matt using the key under the mat to Parker knocking in the closet door. The ladies bounced back and forth as they told their opinions and explained how the events had unfolded.

With his lips pressed into a firm line, the officer stared at his small notebook then flipped it closed. "You'd like to press charges?"

Both women answered in unison, "Yes."

"And…" Lexi pushed her shoulders back and raised her chin as though she were readying for a fight. "I kept a diary of things I want him in trouble for as well. I have pictures too."

Parker cringed inwardly that she'd ever had to do that, but it didn't surprise him that she'd kept details. He put his arms around Lexi and dropped his chin on the top of her head. "Whatever you want to do, we'll get it done."

The officer nodded. "A lot goes unprosecuted because of a lack of documentation. That will help."

Relief spread on Lexi's face.

As Meredith fell into conversation with the officer, Parker gathered Lexi in his arms, pressed his mouth to her ear, and promised her the world, ending simply with, "I love you."

"Oh, hey," Meredith said. "Since you're here, you should grab what's left of Lex's things to take home."

Lexi's face turned bright pink. "His home isn't my home, Mere!"

He laughed. That again. Except she was kind of right. He looked around at Meredith's place, full of not-overly-girly touches that made the place look as though a woman was invested in everything within the walls. Lex deserved that—they deserved that and more.

"Yeah, we'll grab the box, and whatever you have over at your old place while Matt's otherwise detained, then we'll figure it out." He dropped a kiss on the top of Lexi's head. "Lex thinks she's going to scare me away with a box of clothes and digging her roots into my house."

Meredith's protective, sisterly gaze narrowed. "Is she?"

"Not a chance. Where's the box?" The girls chatted away as he formed his plan about housing. Lexi would either freak out or love it. And even if she freaked, she'd love it five minutes later, so all would be good.

# CHAPTER FIFTY

Boss Man grumbled from across the table as Cash and Roman tossed the football back and forth. Nicola, Sugar, and Beth sprinted, field stripping and reassembling AR-15s, timing themselves to see who was better. It was very, very competitive, and pretty damn entertaining to see their pregnant bellies pushed against the table as they raced. Winters was asleep on the floor with Thelma the bulldog lying across his legs and Bacon snoring on his chest. But Lexi's eyes were locked on the main flat screen, almost unmoving for the last thirty minutes.

Their group was chained to the war room, waiting to see if the malware Lexi had activated worked. They'd had a ping from the DIA that it was moving through the ARO system but then nothing. So they were waiting and watching.

Parker's chest felt tight. A lot was riding on whether it worked or not. Even if it didn't, they had broken up a terrorist cell hiding in plain sight in the middle of Pennsylvania Dutch country. Which, obviously, was a great thing. But if the malware did work, they'd gain access to worldwide information on the ARO. That was a big deal. It could save a hundred times the number of lives, civilian and soldier alike.

"Think fast!" Roman snapped the ball at the girls.

Nicola jumped up and snagged it, having a sense that the football was incoming. Call it a brotherly-sisterly vibe. Whatever it was, she moved fast. "Like you'd catch me off guard." She tossed it back.

Roman threw to Cash, who tossed it back to Nic. She snagged it, spun her pregnant belly around, and lofted it back at her husband.

"Easy there, princess." Jared paced. "You're liable to pull something with moves like that."

"Oh." She doubled over. "Damn."

"Haha, very funny."

"No—ow, damn it." Nicola's eyes latched onto Cash, who jumped over a chair before Parker could wonder if she wasn't faking it.

"Nic?" Concern painted her husband's voice.

"No, God." She shook her head, waving him off. "I moved too fast. Baby must've—shit." She doubled over. "I need to sit."

"Nothing's wrong. You're okay." Cash held her shoulders, easing his not-quite-at-her-due-date wife into a chair. He nodded at Roman, who sprung wheels and sped out the door, no doubt to get a vehicle ready. The room was oddly quiet as worry hung heavy between them.

Beth pressed her phone to her ear, likely calling their shared doctor. Those two shared everything. She whispered into the cell, eyeballing her best friend. After a minute, she hung up. "Cash?"

He raised an eyebrow. "Yeah?"

"Doc says head in."

Without a word, he swept Nicola into his arms and headed across the room. Beth ran in front, getting the door as they went. It all happened so fast, Parker couldn't register the magnitude of something going wrong.

Winters was up and leaning against the wall. Sugar had her hand over her swollen stomach. Parker's eyes landed on Lexi. There was something innate about knowing she was his family. They might not be at that place in life—maybe their future would never be about babies and things like that. He didn't know, hadn't talked to her about it. But what he did know was he wanted to have that conversation. Wanted to figure out what they wanted, more than playing house, and he'd thrown together ideas that constituted one hell of a plan. Tonight, assuming they weren't visiting a happy newborn in the arms of its parents, Parker would show Lex what he'd spent the recent days planning.

"We've got something," Jared said, turning back from the door and focusing on the main screen.

It had lit up. The green outline of Middle Eastern nations was suddenly aglow with yellow flicks of light. Lexi's malware streamed data to the DIA before their eyes. Parker took a deep breath for her, so proud, so relieved that this was something she'd gone after, risking her life, and it had worked in a huge way.

"Holy crap, hacker girl." Sugar dropped into a chair, watching the screen as if it were fireworks.

Jared clapped Lexi on the back. "Nice job, Lex."

With Boss Man moving around the room, Thelma rolled over and groaned. Bacon did the same, copying what could only be called her canine best friend. Sugar and Lexi took those two dogs everywhere together, and both were losing a little bit of weight.

Titan had seen what they'd all come to see, and the show was over, even though Lexi still stared at the screen between smiles and saying thanks to the congratulations.

Winters, perched on the side of the table, slapped Parker's back. "Lex, don't hog this guy too much this week. He's withering away. Needs to work out."

Parker wrapped his arms around his girl as Winters walked out backward, waving and grabbing his phone, likely to call Mia and update her on Nicola. Jared and Sugar followed, leaving Parker and Lexi to stare at the screen, now completely lit up in hostile zones.

"I'm really proud of you, sweetheart."

She spun in the chair. "It's unreal. Though I feel kinda bad being this excited when Nic and Cash just took off—"

"They'll be fine." Right? Because they had to be. Statistically speaking, she was far enough along and healthy enough that everything would be fine. Except he didn't know what was actually causing her pain. Was that labor? If not, what was it? Didn't matter. They would be fine.

"You're worried too."

He bunched up his shoulders. "Weird seeing Nic in pain. That girl can take a beating." Parker pressed his chin to the top of her head. "It's really gorgeous."

She sighed and looked up. “But it’s over. Time to go home.”

“About that.” Screw waiting to share what he’d been planning. He spun her in the rolling chair. “Give me a few minutes. Okay?”

Tilting her head, she gave him an inquisitive look. “Alright. I’ll sit and watch.”

“Good.” He kissed her forehead and hustled to his office. He pulled out all the papers he wanted and lit up all the screens he needed. All in all, not a hugely impressive display. Certainly not a damn light show covering terrorist hot zones in the Middle East, but he was still totally stoked.

Parker looked like a kid on Christmas morning when he bounded into the war room, snagged her hand, and almost carried her back to his office.

“What’s going on?” She laughed and squirmed as his lips stayed on the back of her neck.

“This is my idea.” His arm swept wide over his office. “We need a house. One that you won’t call just mine. You want a place for our worlds to collide. So… here.”

She blinked, and her mind stumbled to make sense of the empty green spaces labeled by number, plus the drawings and designs for what looked like architectural plans. She numbly moved forward, jaw hanging open, in complete shock at the display he had assembled for her.

“You want something that’s just us, Lex. Here are some options, but there are a million more. You point and choose, and I’ll make it happen.”

“You’re going to build me a house?” Holy crap, she couldn’t breathe. It wasn’t just the enormity of the gesture; it was the thought behind him building her a home. He was offering her the world just by offering her the very thing she needed in so many ways. A foundation. Literally. Figuratively. Lexi launched herself into his arms. “Oh, my God! I love you more than I can think.”

Which made him laugh, she guessed because he had a good idea of how much her mind could process. “Good idea?”

“The best.” She smothered him in kisses, letting his thoughtfulness reach down into her soul.

"I want to spend the rest of my life with you, Lex. Figure we need a good home to start that journey."

# CHAPTER FIFTY-ONE

The club beat filled the tightly packed area. Bouncing green-and-blue strobe lights spun in the abandoned-for-the-night airplane hangar, and the outpouring of grief—in only a way this community would—floated away as people danced into the night. The tribute to Shadow was legendary, and the acknowledgment of SilverChaos as Lexi made Parker's heart squeeze. Everyone seemed to know her face already, and now that they connected the girl in the corners of these parties to the genius behind SilverChaos, it made tonight all the more special.

With every turn, someone said, "Hey, Silver… nice job, Silver…"

He couldn't see a blush on her cheeks but knew the color was there. She wasn't after the attention, but she was also done hiding who she was. Anonymity hadn't protected her, so she embraced the more public role of being Silver—though she had turned down every reporter's interview and every opportunity for publicity. Seemed the news bureaus couldn't get enough of a leather-clad rock star lookalike who rode a GSX-R and risked her life to save the families of soldiers. He didn't blame reporters for trying. She was, without question, the most interesting, complex, intelligent, beautiful woman walking the planet.

Parker and Lexi posted against a wall, each with a beer in hand, and he watched her survey the crowd. "You did a really good thing for Shadow, you know that, Lex?"

Anyone who had ever used him as a broker was there, Parker was sure of it. The talent in the room was epic, and the whole event had been pulled together with just a few strokes of a keyboard.

"I think he'd appreciate it." She took his bottle and put both of theirs on the cement floor, then she wrapped her hands around his neck and swayed with the music. "Think he'd appreciate it even more that you're here with me."

His mouth brushed against hers. "Maybe."

"And the money, he'd be stoked about that—though not in his name. He'd kill me for pulling that move." She laughed and let her lips drift against him.

Lexi had taken the proceeds from her last auction and established a fund that encouraged and gave resources to tech-sharp kids stuck in the foster system. She had also promised that a significant portion of her future earnings would be used to continue funding it, all in Shadow's name.

Smart. Sexy. *And* generous. Parker couldn't ask for more. As they swayed to the music, he pushed them into the crowd, letting the sea of bodies swallow them. Lexi pressed hard against him as they lost themselves to the beat. Songs shifted, the beat changed, and they danced as time slipped by. But as much as he loved her on his arm, surrounded by people who nearly adored her for what she'd done for their community, Parker wanted her alone. Now.

He cupped her ass, and his hands moved up her back. Her breasts pressed into him, and when she leaned against his chest, smoothing her hands between them, her fingernails scratching his stomach, he was done.

"You're begging for trouble, sweetheart." He let his tongue touch the tip of her earlobe, and she jumped, hotter and harder than she'd been dancing a second ago.

"A lot of talk for a guy who's not doing anything about it."

He cursed under his breath and took her mouth hard, not caring that they were in a room of people. None paid any attention, or even if they did, Parker didn't care. She was reckless, stroking down his stomach, rubbing herself against his hardening erection.

He snagged her. "Come on."

She let him guide her from behind, his hands roaming on her waist, her back against his chest and nestling his now-throbbing erection. Soon as they broke through the crowd, Lexi turned around, locking her grip behind his neck, and let him lead her back, back, back in the dark until they hit a wall.

"I just need you." She gasped as he pushed up her tight shirt. "Tonight, I don't need all this. The people. The hellos. I want you."

"You've got me."

"I *want* you."

"Sweetheart, I know exactly what you want." He ducked his lips to her neck, and whatever she had to say morphed into a low growl, making her press forward. "I want to take you somewhere else."

"Parker, if you don't take me *now*, I might kill you."

He squeezed her ass through the skirt and rubbed her body against his cock. "You can try, but I'll probably enjoy it." Pressing his lips to hers, he breathed her in. Even in the chaotic night, she smelled like citrus and tasted like sugar.

"Not fair."

"Come on, let's go." He laughed, and she gave him a look that she might combust but willingly followed. They moved from the hot air in the hangar into the outside coolness. Walking under a sky marbling with the first light of day, he took the long way to the other airport hangar.

"But before we get to where we're going—" He pulled her in front of him. "I need you to tell me where we are. You and me."

She giggled. "An airport."

"No, Lex. You and me."

"We're together, forever. That's where."

His palms cupped her face, and he pressed a kiss to her lips. "Good." He traced his hands down her neck, down her arms until their fingers intertwined. He took both of her hands in one of his, and with the other, he pulled a black-diamond ring from his pocket. "Because you're my best friend, because we built a house that we turned into a home… God, because you're the smartest person I've ever met. The most fun. The sweetest. The sexiest." Parker dropped to one knee. "Because you're my world, sweetheart, will you be my wife?"

A slip of sunrise painted a halo behind Lexi as her lips

parted. She sucked in a surprised breath. "Oh, God. Of course, yes."

He slipped the unconventional ring on her finger and stood to lift her in the air. She bent her head and kissed him, still murmuring her agreement. Parker's cheeks hurt from smiling, and as he set her down, he thought about how to word what came next.

"And I don't want to wait," she said. "Like, I could marry you tomorrow."

Turned out he didn't have to figure out his wording. Holding her hand, he guided her a few hundred feet then pulled open the hangar door and let Lexi step in. "I thought maybe you'd say yes."

She giggled. "I'm a sure bet."

As they rounded a corner, he took in the partially lit hangar, complete with a flight crew and fueled jet. "Go to Vegas with me? Right now?"

"Are you kidding me? Hell yes!" Laughter bubbled from her throat as her smile reached her icy blue eyes. "This is insane."

They approached the G6. Parker hugged her close, waving to the captain as he brought her to the stairs. "We're a go."

"Excellent. Congratulations." The captain nodded. "We're ready now."

Lexi's eyes bugged. "You *planned* to take me to Vegas?"

Parker already had a reservation waiting for them at a little chapel there. He couldn't keep the grin off his face. "I've been planning to take you to the altar since the day you told me you loved me."

"What?" Her blush painted her cheeks. "I was so embarrassed!"

"You stormed up and laid it on the line. There was no question you would be my wife."

She squeaked as he carried her the last few steps into the cabin. "Wow, I love you."

"Me too, sweetheart."

As the captain said his spiel, Parker ran them to the bed in the back, where he tore off her clothes and shed his. Their bodies clung together, their hearts hammering as they always seemed to do.

He held his world in his arms. Not only had he made her a home and given her a family, but she gave him all the same. That connection was something he'd never known he wanted or needed, and now there was nothing more clear than his need to know her as Mrs. Lexi Black.

# EPILOGUE

*Ten years later…*

Lexi's phone rang, and she jumped to silence it before it woke the baby. But it was the school, so she had to answer it. She *almost* could say verbatim what the call was about, but there was always a chance that there was a real emergency.

"Mrs. Black?" the yippy voice of the kid's principal sounded.

She rolled her lips into her mouth. "Yes."

"We have a problem. Again."

This time, Lexi accidentally let loose a small laugh. No matter how often the school called, she couldn't be mad at her kids. Yeah, they'd be reprimanded, and they'd never know that she thought most of their… *antics* were genius. But that was how they rolled, she guessed. "Okay."

"Addy had show-and-tell today."

"Yes, I know. She brought in that Molly Talks-A-Lot toy."

"Yes, well, apparently Molly Talks-A-Lot has a potty mouth."

"Oh no…"

"Oh, yes. When Molly Talks was brought in front of the entire kindergarten class, Molly didn't say 'Touch your toes' or 'Count to ten.' *Molly* said, 'You are a silly snail,' 'Toots smell like poots,' *and* 'Mrs. Snyder is in time out,' which, to five-year-olds, is hysterical."

Lexi squeezed her eyes shut too. Hardly a potty mouth *and*

kind of hysterical to adults too. "I'm sorry. I'll have a talk with the boys."

"Yes, *again*, please."

The call disconnected. Lexi scrolled through her phone until she found Parker's name. He answered on the first ring.

"Hey, so guess who called me today?"

He groaned. "Again? The boys?"

"Yup."

"What'd they do?"

"Hacked Molly Talks-A-Lot."

Parker burst out laughing. "God, they're good."

Maybe it was the age for mischief. Last week, Sugar had had to tell her girls not to booby trap the neighbors, Nicola and Beth had to have a talk about projectile devices having a time and place, none that were in the cafeteria, and both Mia and Caterina had practice unarming various toys.

"You didn't help?" She smiled, rocking the baby and brushing the dark locks on the little guy's head.

"Hack Addy's doll? No."

Lexi whispered, trying to keep the baby asleep, "You're the one with genius genes. I'm going to blame you."

"Oh, sweetheart. Blame me all you want. They're the ones who found that article in the *New York Times* about your—"

"Shhhh." The wiggling bundle sleepily blinked. "Okay, fine. We're both to blame."

"If making genius babies with you is trouble, then life is good."

Lexi looked over the nursery that had slept four babies, then her eyes drifted out the window and over the lush green land. "Life's better than good."

They'd given each other a family and so much more than just love and acceptance. Everything was possible for her because of him, even if her husband made her feel as though she was the reason the world kept spinning.

Lexi closed her eyes after telling Parker that she loved him, and she rocked their baby back to sleep. Carefully, she placed him in the crib and walked down the hall, passing an anniversary present Parker had given her. It was a black-and-white sketch of their family with brilliant bursts of color all over the portrait. All he'd said when he gave it to her was, "Thank you for letting me color outside the lines."

THE END

# ACKNOWLEDGMENTS

Sometimes, when life's the hardest, when the hurdles seem almost insurmountable, that is when true colors show. This book would not be possible without the hard work of so many people.

Thank you to my family. Your support has never wavered and your unconditional love is more than I could ever have dreamed of. Simply put, I love you. Courtney, you're an expert I can call upon for research, but you're my sister and best friend more than anything. Mom and Dad, thank you for giving me that inner fight that it took to make this book happen.

Tackle hugs for Team Titan. Your book pimping skills are phenomenal, but your love and support for *everyone*, not just me, but each other, sets the bar for how people should act. With love, grace, and an uplifting spirit. I truly can say you make me laugh and smile each day. I hope you love Parker and Lexi as much as I do. This book was a labor of love with so many of you in mind.

Sara Shone, welcome to the team. There are so many reasons why this book is possible, but you are a major factor. Thank you for your dedication, your intelligence, and your beauty, both inside and out.

Julia Sutherland, there are days that I thank God you have come into my life. There was a reason we met, and I didn't know the extent and the purpose, but I can't imagine life without you.

JB Salsbury and Claudia Connor, there are days that I knew all would come together for Lexi and Parker because you believed in this story as much as I felt it. Thank you for the line by line work you did on Black Dawn. Sharon Kay and Racquel

Reck, you have been a valuable resource that I appreciate more than you'll ever know.

Finally, thank you to Parker and Lexi. Yeah, I know. They're *not real*, but for so many reasons they are to me. I love this story mostly because of how they triumphed in the end. Love should never hurt.

# ABOUT THE AUTHOR

Cristin Harber is a New York Times and USA Today best-selling romance author. She writes sexy, steamy romantic suspense and military romance. Fans voted her onto Amazon's Top Picks for Debut Romance Authors in 2013, and her debut Titan series was both a #1 romantic suspense and #1 military romance bestseller.

Join the newsletter! Text TITAN to 66866 to sign up for exclusive emails.

**The Titan Series:**
Book 1: Winters Heat
Book 1.5: Sweet Girl
Book 2: Garrison's Creed
Book 3: Westin's Chase
Book 4: Gambled
Book 5: Chased
Book 6: Savage Secrets
Book 7: Hart Attack
Book 8: Black Dawn

**The Delta Series:**
Book 1: Delta: Retribution
Book 2: Delta: Revenge

**The Only Series:**
Book 1: Only for Him
Book 2: Only for Her
Book 3: Only for Us
Book 4: Only Forever

Each Titan and Delta book can be read as a standalone (except for Sweet Girl), but readers will likely best enjoy the series in order. The Only series must be read in order.

8/15

CPSIA information can be obtained at www.ICGtesting.com
Printed in the USA
LVOW04s2202040815

448799LV00018BA/1243/P